Death on the Silk Road

Russell R. Miller

BeachHouse Books
Chesterfield Missouri USA

Copyright

Graphics Credits:

Cover design by Dr. Bud Banis assembled from Royalty Free stock photo of a Isolated Dagger with Splatter of Red Blood Stains ©anyka, 2011 ID: 71395379 licensed from Pixmac.com, a CIA map of Kazakhstan Courtesy of University of Texas Libraries, The University of Texas at Austin, and photographs throughout from the Author's private collection.

ISBN 978-1-59630-074-3 BeachHouse Books Edition, November, 2011

Miller, Russell R., 1928-
Death on the Silk Road / Russell R. Miller.

.

ISBN 978-1-59630-074-3 (regular print : alk. paper)
1. Retired executives--Fiction. 2. International Executive Service Corps--Fiction. 3. Americans-- Kazakhstan --Fiction. 4. Kazakhstan --Fiction. I. Title.
Library of Congress PCCN reference number 2011939424

BeachHouse Books

PO Box 7151

Chesterfield, MO 63006

(636) 394-4950

ALSO BY RUSSELL MILLER

A Spy with a Clean Face

Journey to a Closed City

Doing Business in Newly Privatized Markets

Selling to Newly Emerging Markets

Some Recent Reviews:

"Russ Miller • Not the Retiring Type" Iowa Alumni Magazine

"[Miller] weaves the threads of the disrupted Ukrainian business environment with his own uncertainty in his first significant retirement activity. The story captures the mood of that not-too-distant past, so familiar to visitors to former Soviet countries.This autobiography is also an armchair traveler's window into a backward environment that still exists in corners of Russia and its former empire. Further, the story is very typical of the experiences of consultants from developed countries engaging with the Third World, whether on two-week or two-year assignments. Armchair Interviews

"Miller tells it like it is in Eastern Europe--Terrific! What a great book!"--Travel Helper.com

"The dawn of a new internationally co-dependent economy" --travelsage.com

"This book is interesting reading to anyone, retired or still employed, who is interested in volunteering his or her time and talents to "doing good" around the world."--- IESC.org

"We have to build up a picture. It's like a jigsaw, but with key sections missing, and pieces from other jigsaws mixed in."

Sir John Sawers—head of the U. K.'s foreign spy agency MI6

To the Family

Elsie

Cheron, Mike, and Paul

Mark, Margaret, and Cindy

Timothy and Melinda

Introduction

Music to read by:

The Silk Road by Kitaro: 1985 Canyon Records

The Silk Road Suite: London Symphony Orchestra 1996 Domo Records

Jazz Impressions of Eurasia: Dave Brubeck Sbme Special Markets Label

Music to Spy By: Music from the International Spy Museum Recording

For a thousand years, the Silk Route spun the thinnest of links between China and the Mediterranean. Since the time of Marco Polo, the trade route between China and Western Europe has been a source of commerce, conflict, and corruption. The road travels through some of the most hostile environments imaginable, including the Taklimakan Desert, which is sometimes referred to by the local inhabitants as the *Land of Death.* It is here that temperatures climb with the sun, only to plummet after dusk. Sandstorms are common, made even more dangerous by the velocity of the prevailing winds. Formidable mountain ranges surround the area. To the south are the Himalayas, which provide a barrier to the Indian subcontinent and to the west are the Tianshan and Pamir ranges that provide barriers that complicate passage to China.

The Silk Road would have never been developed as a route for the caravans if it were not for the great value of the goods traded along the way. While silk from China was undoubtedly the most significant, the route was also used as a means of conveying rare and precious metals such as gold, iron, lead and zinc; as well as rubies, jade, ivory, glass, and exotic animals and plants destined for the royal courts of Western Europe.

Religion supplied another important and highly varied commodity that traveled the route through the centuries. During different periods in diverse areas, residents became Buddhists, Christians, and Muslims. Each belief had its distinct effect that later provided an added element of potential conflict between the surrounding cultures.

Very few merchants traveled the entire length of the road. Most covered only part of the route selling their wares, and then returning home with the proceeds. As a result, goods changed hands many times, moving slowly from Asia, through Central Asia to connecting seaports, before ultimately arriving in the trading capitals of Europe.

The road, and its surrounding areas, in addition to providing a critical chain for international trade, also became the source of considerable conflict between the major powers wishing to control strategic areas along the way. "The Great Game" is a term relating to the early strategic rivalry between the British Empire and Russia for supremacy over Central Asia. The conflict initially centered on the English control of India and their prevailing fear that the Tsar's later penetration into Afghanistan would serve as a staging area for a Russian invasion of India. The original clash between East and West, during the 1800s, served as a training ground for the early development of national intelligence agencies that competed clandestinely in what later became known as *The Tournament of Shadows*.

"A New Great Game" is currently playing out on a gigantic and deadly geopolitical chessboard between the United States, the United Kingdom, and supporting NATO countries against Russia and the Peoples Republic of China. The desired prize this time, instead of geographic areas and overland trade routes, centers more on regional petroleum products and their connecting pipelines, tanker routes, and associated oil driven consortiums.

In addition to the traditional combatants, new entries to the game include Turkey, with its cultural ties to Central Asia; Pakistan armed with nuclear weapons; Iran, the historical seat of the Persian Empire with rapidly developing nuclear weapons; and India, which has now become a recognized nuclear power. This devastating combination of oil wealth and atomic weaponry is forming a highly volatile and unpredictable contagion of conflict leading to new geostrategic calculations. Further complicating this already incendiary mixture is the relatively recent demise of the Soviet Union's control over the Central Asian republics, followed by its embarrassing withdrawal from Afghanistan. This, combined with the advent of the "war on terror," is reforming alliances among the newly independent republics with their vast wealth of oil and mineral resources.

The historical trade route is once again gaining importance, now supplemented by pipelines, railroads, and sea routes, which are providing further sources of conflict and corruption as the newly independent republics compete with each other for lucrative contracts and geopolitical influence. This is creating a developing mosaic of national interests, operating in an ancient area, with conflicting cultures. The Silk Road and the Central Asian Republics are again the focal point for foreign armies, with new and more deadly weapons actively supporting their competing intelligence agencies.

It is in this unpredictable and volatile environment that Death on the Silk Road takes place.

CENTRAL ASIA :: KAZAKHSTAN

CIA - The World Factbook -- Kazakhstan

1.

Istanbul

Dusk was fading into darkness, and the lights were beginning to better define the extended spans of the Bosporus Bridge. Charlie Connelly nursed his Bombay martini as he gazed thoughtfully through the darkened windows of the Istanbul Hilton's rooftop bar. It had been many years since he was last here, but the view remained magical. He still considered it extraordinary that he could watch the lights flickering across the bay in Asia while enjoying a martini in Europe.

He watched a ship steaming slowly through the darkening harbor, being careful to avoid the ferryboats criss-crossing its path. The port had become a center for arm shipments to the Middle East and Central Asia, competing for space with the petroleum-filled tankers destined for Europe and the United States.

As the ancient freighter approached the Golden Horn, it picked up steam expanding the foamy wake rising on its rusting hull. The ship's onboard lights soon faded in the distance. Charlie wondered about its destination, and tried to guess its cargo. He had always been fascinated with distant places. Back in an earlier life, as an international marketing executive for Apex Electronics, he traveled to many of them. Even so, going to a new location with unknown people never lost its appeal. Since retiring, he had managed to find some assignments with international development organizations as a consultant, which allowed him to continue traveling, while earning a few extra bucks on the side.

Earlier in the day, his trip from Ataturk Airport to the hotel was not as peaceful as his present view. Istanbul had turned into a modern city while retaining all the romance and most of the drawbacks related to its ancient origins. The narrow streets were jammed with vehicles competing ineffectively with bicycles and darting street vendors.

As his taxi had approached Taxsim Square, a short man with a tall fez, riding a three-wheeled bike, his skinny legs peddling like pistons, pulled a homemade cart loaded with a gigantic anvil, as he weaved his way through the stalled traffic. Suddenly, a short distance ahead, the man seemed to disappear in a cloud of smoke, immediately followed by a deafening explosion.

The cab's windows imploded, raining shards of glass over both driver and passenger. The cabbie veered crazily into a narrow side street, while falteringly exclaiming "suicide bomber—up ahead—police station." With worry beads wrapped tightly around his fist, and blood trickling down his cheek, he maneuvered his way through the military vehicles that appeared out of nowhere, and were now choking the route.

Welcome to Eurasia, Charlie thought trying to brush the shattered glass from his hair and clothes. Conflict and corruption were becoming the hallmarks of the area.

Turkey fielded the second largest army in NATO, backed by a population that was overwhelmingly Muslim, and it had become a critical ally to the United States in its War on Terror. Now a power struggle was developing between the country's Islamic rooted government, and its more secular military.

Earlier that morning, prosecutors had brought charges against a senior officer accused of plotting to overthrow the country's civilian leadership.

According to the *International Herald Tribune,* Charlie had picked up in the airport, the Turkish government believed dozens of other officers might have joined the General in a conspiracy to destabilize the country. They feared this could rapidly develop into a civil war. The entire city was in turmoil as a result, providing an excellent opportunity for terrorists to strike.

Gazing out of the window of the cocktail lounge, Charlie was beginning to regret his choice of Istanbul as a layover point on the way to Almati, but flights from the United States to Kazakhstan were infrequent and this provided the only reasonable place to break-up the tediously long flight. Now, because of the security crackdown, it appeared he would have to wake-up even earlier to arrive at the airport in time to clear the Aeroflot flight to Almaty.

"Meester Connelly?"

Startled, Charlie turned toward the inquiring voice.

"Yes. What is it?"

"I have been told to give you this valentine," the linen clad bar boy replied timidly, before abruptly turning and disappearing into the artificial darkness of the crowded cocktail lounge.

Irritated by the interruption, Charlie quickly opened the small sealed envelope. Inside was a number. A telephone number. A telephone number he recognized, but had not seen in a long time. A very long time in fact.

Glancing at his watch, he signaled for the check then shouldered his way through the growing crowd of questionable characters, and their expensive women, who frequent up-scale bars in late-night Istanbul. The night was going to be even briefer than he had expected.

Back In his room, Charlie threw a few items into an open bag before setting his travel alarm and laying down for a quick nap. With the time change, it was too early to call Washington. Falling into a fitful sleep, he wondered how they knew he was in Istanbul, but somehow they always seemed to know.

Three hours later the alarm jolted him awake. Swearing, he went into the bathroom and splashed cold water on his face. Afterwards, he dialed the number written in the envelope. He could hear the phone ringing, then stopping, replaced immediately by the once familiar whirring of the scrambler kicking in at Langley.

"Hello Charlie. Good of you to call."

"Well, well, Emmett Valentine, I thought you retired from the agency a long time ago."

"I had, but you know how it is my friend. Old fire horses still chomp at the bit when they hear the sound of the alarm."

"You aren't a horse Emmett. You are a very old man, and I didn't know there was any alarm sounding."

"And you Charlie were always far too literal. I intended it only as a metaphor, but a very appropriate one. You see, ever since the Agency got a new Director there have been alarms going on all over the place. Shortly after he took over, he feared there still wasn't enough attention paid to the Muslim world. Instead, he believed the agency continued to focus far too much attention on the Soviet Union. As a result, they were poorly prepared to combat the global militancy of Islamism.

"The Agency is not unlike an old man. It likes to concentrate on doing what it knows best. You know yesterday's battles and all that. Anyway, the Director pretty well finished clearing out the Russian House, and all of the old experts, and put them out to pasture. The Agency has been effectively gutted, and over 50% are new-hires"

Charlie was not surprised at what he was hearing. It was common knowledge that prior to 9/11, the CIA was still concentrating a good deal of attention on the Soviet Union and

Communist China, with only a minimum effort directed toward the Mideast. This left the intelligence agency poorly prepared for the global struggle with Islamism in a realm where ideology, ethnicity, and national interest would inevitably collide in a new form of asymmetrical warfare.

Even after bin Laden became active, the Agency relied on Israel's intelligence agency, the Mossad, for information on his whereabouts. When the CIA attempted to retaliate on its own for the USS Cole disaster, they sent a missile into a vacant aspirin factory, and later into an empty training camp in Afghanistan hours after bin Laden left.

"They cleared you out as well Emmett?" Charlie asked with some sympathy. "Did they get rid of you too?"

"No, no, my boy, I was already out to pasture. See how well the old horse metaphor continues to work," he chuckled.

"Anyway, the Director cleaned house, and began staffing-up with new people. At the same time, someone in Washington formed a committee--you know that is what we do best here--made up of some of the former spy chiefs. Their function was to evaluate the government's entire intelligence network--all 16 different agencies. It seems there was a rift developing between the head of the CIA and the Director of National Intelligence, and between the two of them and the people in the Pentagon.

"Apparently, the old hands believed the present structure was too dependent on intelligence leaders getting along personally. Eventually, the committee concluded that if personalities didn't mesh it could be dysfunctional—imagine that," Emmett added sarcastically. "

"What the hell does this have to do with you Emmett--and for that matter with me?

"Oh Charlie, you were always so impatient. You would never have made it here in Washington. You should realize that the bureaucratic battles in Foggy Bottom are fought more fiercely than any of our foreign conflicts. Wait until you hear what they did next."

While the old man talked, a far younger man entered the room and sat silently beside the desk. Emmett acknowledged his presence with a faint nod of recognition, and placed a finger to his lips before continuing his overseas conversation. The young man nodded in acknowledgement. He would never think of distracting Mr. Valentine. Listening intently, he marveled at his mentor's conciliatory tone. It was considerably different from the tutorial approach he employed in their conversations. However, his curiosity was aroused regarding the unidentified man on the other end of the line.

"You see Charlie," Emmett continued while searching his desk drawers for his pipe, "the Agency has had five different directors in the last six years so the recommendation to combine the agencies scared the hell out of everyone. No one knew which agency would ultimately be in control. Who would be in charge, and which organizations would disappear?

"At the same time," Emmett continued warming to his subject "while the people in the new administration want to focus their attention on the Islamic countries, the Russian Bear hasn't been so accommodating. Putin is resisting the idea of providing any cooperation on Iran, and instead is flexing his muscle by invading Georgia, while working to re-establish control over Ukraine. Now, he is helping the opposition in Kyrgyzstan who are threatening to kick us out of our airbase in Manas. We need that base to supply our troops in Afghanistan. Without it, it is almost impossible to move supplies and personnel overland. The way it stands now, Manas represents our new hub of the old Silk Road, and it is in danger of going away. I am sure that you would agree Charlie that things are not going smoothly.

"That is why, old friend, they brought this old warhorse out of retirement, and set him up in a basement office nobody knew existed. My role is to use some of my former cold warrior contacts to see what I can do clandestinely to counter our communist cousins. Once again, I am off the books, so the bean counters can't object to my expenses when they don't even know I exist".

This arrangement came as no shock to Charlie. He was aware, from his previous association with the Agency, that while it was not usual for an organization to operate hidden from the basic channels, it was not particularly uncommon either. He knew the CIA had occasionally concealed some of its more questionable activities from most of the Washington bureaucracy, and Congress as well—particularly Congress. In such situations, *black money* becomes the coin of the realm and deniability the watchword. If anyone knew how to operate effectively under such circumstances, it would be Emmett. He had operated several times before, sequestered away from the eyes of only a few people at the very top of the organization.

"In order to gain better control over its own organization," Emmett continued "and divert attention from the committee's recommendations, the Director announced the development of a new five-year strategic plan that would invest considerable resources in new technologies to combat cyber warfare attacks from overseas. Particularly after we found a foreign spy agency was able to breach our computer network by inserting a flash drive into a military laptop they somehow got their hands on.

"By the way, isn't that what you do Charlie? Aren't you going to Kazakhstan to set up a strategic plan for a lead and zinc mine?" Emmett inquired, getting back to the subject of his call.

"Yeah, you're right. I did work on strategic plans before I got on the international circuit, and it is what I will be doing for the Global Bank Corp in Kazakhstan--but how did you know that?"

Unfazed, Emmett ignored the question and continued. "To make the plan work the Director wants to make better use of spies that work undercover in roles where they have no public association with the U. S. government." Chuckling, he added almost to himself, "He keeps telling everyone that you have to plan the work then work the plan."

"I have heard that once or twice before, Emmett."

It was now becoming clear to Charlie what was happening. He had been involved with the Agency in an unofficial way several times in the past, and it had usually led to trouble. He did not want to get involved again. His children were grown, with families of their own. He and his wife Beth had settled into a life that fit their temperaments, and the times. He had enough excitement with his occasional assignments with the Global Bank Corp, and he wanted to keep it that way. He had promised himself that he would never again let the old man use him on his cockamamie missions. But, damn it, he couldn't help himself. He was curious why they contacted him now, and how the hell they knew where he was.

"Are you getting the picture Charlie? All I want is for you to keep in touch. You have my number. Nothing specific, but you are going to be in a new hot spot. At least one that is, let us say, warming-up.

"Kazakhstan is turning into a major oil supplier, and they have access to every mineral known to man. I have been told by some of the wizards here that, if they wished, the country is fully capable of exporting the entire *Periodic Table of Elements*--all at the same time. They have a very authoritarian leadership that could be toppled like the one that was just kicked-out of Kyrgyzstan. If that happens, Russia could regain control of that chip too. You can be my eyes and ears there—just like before."

Looking out of his window, Charlie could see a small chink of light beginning to penetrate the inky darkness of the swiftly fading Turkish night. He realized any chance for additional sleep was fading with the rapidly approaching dawn.

"No Emmett. Forget it!" he almost shouted in frustration. "You are a nice guy, and I wish you well, but I am going to do my job at the mine, and nothing else. That's enough for me. I don't want to get involved with you again. Ever!"

Charlie Connelly had sailed under Emmett Valentine's flag before, and he remembered it had invariably led him into very rough waters.

"I know Charlie. I know just how you feel. I only wanted to warn you there could be problems where you are going. You have my number. We will stay in touch."

The line went dead before there was any chance for a reply, or any opportunity to gain answers to the countless questions racing through Charlie's mind. Instead, he rose stiffly from the bed, angrily zipped his bag shut, and bolted out of his room; hoping he could find a cab at such an early hour.

2.

Washington

In a small dimly lit office, deep in the bowels of a mammoth shielded structure in Langley, Virginia Emmett Valentine flipped a sequence of switches before replacing the handset on the phone's oblong base. Satisfied with the results of his conversation, he turned and fiddled with the dials of an antiquated stereo receiver setting majestically on a narrow table in the sparsely furnished enclosure. He smiled to himself as the militant strains of the iconic "Ride of the Valkyries" leaped from two large speakers' bookending the glowing receiver.

The old man presented a commanding figure. He was impeccably clothed in a well tailored suit that, none the less, was beginning to hang more loosely on his still powerful frame; as if it were originally made for someone even larger—or perhaps younger than its present owner. A silk handkerchief carefully tucked in his breast pocket meticulously matched the regimental tie and the buttoned suit coat. His fastidious appearance was in mark contrast to the sweater and sport shirt culture that currently prevailed in the Agency's hallways.

Turning to the young man sitting across the desk Emmett asked, "so Roger what do you think?"

"Well Mr. Valentine," the young man replied nervously, clearing his throat before continuing, "I have always liked the Ring Cycle myself, but I never had that much time to listen to the full seventeen hours." He had heard that, at one time, the old man had gone by the cryptonym "maestro" and he now understood why, as the music swelled and ebbed in the background.

Momentarily taken aback by the reply of his young acolyte, Emmett quickly recovered. "No, no Roger, I was referring to the telephone conversation. What did you think of what you heard of the telephone conversation?"

Chagrined, and trying to make amends, the young man offered that he had not heard too much of what was said, but it seemed as if the man on the other end of the line was not too pleased with the direction the conversation was taking.

"I fear you are correct Roger, I have known Charlie for a long time and, while he is always reluctant, eventually he does as we ask."

The contrast between the two individuals sitting across from one another was striking. One was a reed-thin young man with a bland complexion, sitting nervously erect on a straight-back office chair. The other was a broad shouldered, still powerfully built elderly individual, with deep-set wrinkles lining his weather-beaten face, casually relaxing in an ancient leather recliner.

Roger had only come in to see if he could leave early that afternoon. Tomorrow was the big game between Princeton and Harvard. As a recent graduate, he felt it important to attend, and he planned to spend a full weekend with old friends. Now, it appeared he was in for a long afternoon of reminiscing; something the old man was increasingly prone to do.

"Who is he sir?" the young man inquired deferentially. "Is he a spook?"

"We really don't use that term very much Roger. We prefer to refer to them as agents in play, however in your context let us say he is a "graying ghost." Emmett smiled at the appropriateness of his witticism.

"Charlie Connelly is above all a good man-a very good man, and he has served us well. When we first met, he was head of an international marketing organization that required him to travel to many *funny* places, as he liked to refer to them. Mostly, they were newly emerging markets in South America, and Africa; then later in China as it awoke from the Maoist slumber. He was valuable to us because he always appeared to be exactly what he was—a businessman. We never had to create a legend because, everywhere he went, he carried his own with him. No one would suspect that he had any connections with the Agency—he was a "clean face" as we like to say. However, he was a little different from most of the executives, since he was willing to cooperate with us.

"At that time, the CIA was not very well regarded by many people. We had screwed-up in Cuba, and we may have deposed a dictator or two along the way. We did whatever was necessary, but it gave us a bad reputation in some quarters--including the administration at the time. "Later, of course," he added lost in thought, "George Tenet telling the then President that finding Saddam's WMDs would be a *slam-dunk* didn't help a lot either. But, what the hell, that's all water over the dam now."

Roger was not too sure about that. He still heard a lot of criticism of the Agency from his friends at college. He hadn't shared their opinion, and that was why, when he was recruited by his international economics professor, he agreed to come aboard. Nevertheless, he certainly wasn't going to voice his doubts now.

"Getting back to Charlie," Emmett recalled. "We first recruited him merely to provide us with basic information regarding the political and economic climate in some of the more difficult countries he visited. It was pretty much then as it is now, we could not afford to be fully staffed in some of the backwaters of the world, in order to concentrate our resources on the bigger fish. The problem was sometimes the little fish bit us in the ass and we couldn't do anything about it. Where we did have people, they sometimes would not have access, or understand the type of information Charlie had available. "

Roger fidgeted in his chair. He knew this was going to happen, but there was nothing he could do about it. He had to humor the old man if he was ever going to get ahead, anyway he was becoming more curious about the association with Charlie Connelly.

"As our relationship grew, we sometimes began to ask him to take a more active role. Nothing big you understand. Just deliver a message or two—sometimes carry some money to people who did not want to have any discernable connection to any part of the U.S. Government. We felt that we could trust him, and he was willing to do things if it did not interfere with his real work or in any way jeopardize his company's reputation. He was never willing to do that."

"Why did he agree to help, Mr. Valentine?"

The old man adjusted his position in the recliner. Sometimes that damn leg of his would begin to ache after sitting too long in one position. It was a little reminder he carried from the Cold War—not that he needed it for God's sake.

"For the most basic of reasons Roger. He loves his country. They say in our business that there are three Ls that dictate what a man does. Loot, lust, and maybe love, I have forgotten exactly. Whatever they are there is definitely love of country. That was a basic element of his generation, and it has not changed—with him at least. Maybe not so with everyone right now.

"Also, his regular business relationships provided him with a cloak of anonymity that we at the Agency sometimes find difficult or awkward to provide. You have to understand Roger--when you get in the field--the brash and colorful James Bond types do not populate the real world of intelligence. They would stand out like the proverbial sore thumb. The good ones live in a shadow world of obscurity. It is their second nature. Charlie fits that well."

As new as he was to the Agency, Roger knew enough to pay close attention to what he heard. Emmett Valentine had assumed the cloak of legend in the eyes of many, at least among those who knew of him at all. Never the less, in a time when the Agency was trying to clear the decks of its old hands carrying Cold War baggage, his return presented a living breathing conundrum to all of the water cooler strategists attempting to find a template for their own questionable careers.

The young man had heard stories about him from his trainers at the Farm. Apparently, the old man had been on board since the beginning. Even before the beginning, some said. During WWII, the Agency became known as the OSS, and it was under the leadership of Wild Bill Donavan and his men who were belatedly trying to quickly absorb a trade the Brits had been pursuing for over a century.

Emmett had never risen to the top, but managed to retain a position of influence as Directors and Deputy Directors came and went. He had retired twice before and then brought back into the fold when there was a need for a man who knew how to work in the shaadows, using the influential contacts throughout the world that he had spent years developing.

The music of Wagner filled the room, as the old man warmed to his task of educating his young assistant on the real world of espionage and intrigue.

Roger sat nervously, furtively glancing at his watch.

"The inactivity of retirement created a void in his life," Emmett offered as he continued his description of Charlie Connelly, "as it does for many people," he added offhandedly. He might even include himself in that category he thought, but made no mention. "Charlie missed the travel, and if the truth be known he missed the challenge and excitement of new people and new places. Anyway, he began to do some consulting for NGO organizations such as the UN and the World Bank on assignments to help publicly owned companies, in the newly independent states, convert their operations to a market driven economy.

"The Agency suddenly found there was a pressing need in Ukraine, for someone who could go there under nonofficial cover, an NOC as we call them. I had connections with an old friend who now heads up the Global Bank Corp in Vienna. He hired Charlie and sent him into Kiev. We contacted him there, laid out our need, and he reluctantly agreed to help us—one last time. It turned out to be more demanding than we originally thought. He got the job done, but had to kill a man and leave the country with one of our agents hidden away on a tour boat going down the Dnieper River to Odessa.

"We hadn't had any contact with him since, until we found ourselves shorthanded in Kazakhstan. I learned the GBC was running a privatization project for a mining operation there. After that, it was easy to convince my old friend at the Bank to send Charlie out to nose around a bit."

"He doesn't know that you arranged for him to be hired and sent there?"

"No—not yet, but I am sure he will—eventually."

The Valkyries had finished their ride, and the old man was getting tired.

"What was is that you wanted to see me about Roger?"

"Nothing pressing sir, it can wait till Monday. Is there anything you need over the weekend?" he asked going out the door.

Emmett still liked to be referred to as sir, even after so many years. "You might check on our man in Almati sometime. I haven't heard anything from him for quite awhile. First thing Monday morning will do."

Roger stopped abruptly and turned to face the old man. "The man is dead. A message from our embassy there was just deciphered this afternoon. I forgot to tell you. "

“What the hell happened to him?” Emmett shouted, overlooking for the moment that he wasn’t notified immediately.

“All we know is that they found him yesterday. The oil company reported it to the embassy, and they passed it on to us.”

“Was it an accident? Did he fall off a rig or some damn thing like that?” Emmett asked without conviction.

“Not a chance.” It was obvious the old man was furious that he was not informed immediately, but it was too late now. All he could do was continue. “The maid at his hotel in Atyrau found him when she went to clean his room. His neck had been sliced from ear to ear.” Roger shuddered just thinking about it. “Nothing was taken, not even his passport. He was murdered no doubt about it. Did you know him Mr. Valentine?”

“I certainly did. His name was Barry Durand, he worked for me once before. He was a geologist. Smart as hell, and dedicated. I thought he was the perfect person to put in the Tengiz oil fields. They are one of the largest in the world, and all of the major countries are trying to gain control. Now he is gone. Someone obviously realized that he worked for us, probably the Russians. It was not just murder Roger. It was a message.”

Emmett’s pipe had gone out some time ago. He paused, and vigorously emptied its dead contents in a nearby ashtray.

“It used to be that agents would never kill another agent, unless they had to,” he continued. It was important to him that the young man knew what the real world was like.

“But, things are changing. New people new protocol. Putin recently said in a press conference in Ukraine that the secret services live by their own laws, and those laws are well known to all secret service co-workers, but I guess that doesn’t apply to other agents—just theirs,” Emmett added sadly.

“I’m very sorry he is gone”, Roger offered as he edged out the door, leaving Emmett alone with his thoughts.

Son of bitch, Emmett swore to himself. What a way for a good man to go. There must have been a fight, Barry was very strong, and would not let someone in his room he did not know.

There is always something terribly sad about the death of an agent. They usually died alone unheralded in some crazy place. No one will ever know what they have done to protect their country. The only recognition they get is a star, among the many, on the wall in the lobby at Langley.

Now he was even more short-handed than before in Kazakhstan. There was only that fellow working as the Commercial Attaché in the American Embassy in Almaty, and Charlie Connelly, of course. But, Christ, what could two people do in the ninth largest country in the world?

What can be done now he wondered? You just have to make do with what you have he guessed. That's why he was paid the big bucks, he thought to himself with a sardonic laugh.

But my God, was he ever as young as Roger--and as dumb he wondered. Probably, he concluded, but it was different then, no one knew any better. After all, the young man had finished at the top of his class at The Farm at Camp Peary, and that 's not easy. It's just that things were so much different now from when he started.

Emmett glanced at his watch. He had a few more things he wanted to do before leaving for the weekend. Anyway, there was nothing waiting for him at home, other than a small apartment in a resident hotel. It was not always like that, but since his wife died, there was no particular incentive in trading his small office for a lonely apartment. Here, at least, he had the world at his fingertips.

3.

After Roger left for the weekend, Emmett let out a deep sigh. He could barely remember when he was that age. Then some of the old memories began to flicker erratically across the movie screen of his mind. Parachuting into France, working with the underground, and then when his cover was broken, having to be smuggled-out in the hold of a stinking fishing boat.

He blinked his eyes tightly, and shook his head slightly, futilely attempting to prevent the next sequence of events that invariably followed. The recurring mental picture was of him and his Czech associates huddling together in a dank and dirty cellar in the center of Prague. He was attempting to radio Washington to inform them of the calamity that was rapidly and unexpectedly taking place. All the while, on the cobblestone streets above, Russian tanks rumbled menacingly through the city-center, destroying everything and everyone in their path. He could hear them yet.

The Agency had dispatched him there during the "Prague Spring" to set-up an underground cell to impede the Russians should they feel required to crackdown on the increasing liberalization of the local puppet Czech government. Now that the time had arrived, Washington ordered him out. He reluctantly abandoned his friends, and then was extricated to neutral Switzerland before the Russians knew he had been there. He was the only one of his undercover cell to survive, and always regretted what he had done. He vowed to never again abandon his people—and he never did.

Years before, men like Emmett had, perhaps unknowingly, but certainly willingly, denied themselves the advantages of nostalgia that psychologically supported many of their contemporaries. In doing so, they freely devoted their lives to the cult of intelligence in a monastic manner without benefit of a recognized creed or companionship afforded by membership in an established church. However, they did this with few regrets, and it was now far too late to look back.

To stem the tide of even more recollections, he unlocked the top drawer of his desk and removed a file with **Secret** stamped in block letters on the cover.

His pipe had gone out long ago, and he carefully refilled the bowl before opening the file. He knew he should stop smoking so much but what the hell, it hadn't killed him yet, and he had faced much worse than tobacco during his long career.

Inside the file was a recent internal report relating to Russia's strategic approach to its former Soviet Republics. It was disquieting to say the least, but held no great surprises for Emmett. Reading further, he found the report merely confirmed his previous suspicions. With the break-up of the Soviet Union, Russia struggled with its own economy that had been previously stimulated solely by the enforced productivity of its former satellites. Once these countries were no longer under Soviet control, it was critical for the Politburo to concentrate on its own economy. They privatized their local industries and began selling them off to a select group of oligarchs. These men took full advantage of the profit motive to run their former enterprises far more effectively than they ever did in their previous apparatchik role. One of the most improved sectors was the previously inefficiently run oil industry. Fortunately, at the same time, the global price of crude began to skyrocket enabling Russia to replenish its once empty treasury, and eventually become a more powerful player on the international scene.

Almost simultaneously, the United States had concentrated its efforts on the Mideast to the exclusion of its other less pressing, interests in the breakaway republics. Russia was more than willing to fill this void, all the while benefitting from the global financial crisis.

As he read, smoke billowed from his ancient Meerschaum, rapidly filling the small office with its noxious odor that to Emmett seemed highly aromatic.

Putin was now using the country's expanding financial resources to strengthen ties with Germany, France, Italy and Spain. As a result, these countries were becoming Russia's closest partners in Europe. At the same time, Russia was actively, and often clandestinely, acquiring industrial and energy assets in the Baltic's, Belarus, Ukraine, and Central Asia.

Emmett had read enough. It was the same old stuff, torn right out of their cold war playbook he remembered so well. Closing the file, he carefully returned the classified document to his desk, and carefully spun the lock.

What he read was upsetting, but he was still glad to be back. There really isn't a hell of a lot a retired spy can do to remain active. He can't go to work for another country. If he did that he would be sure to end up in some gutter with a bullet in his head, either from his outfit or some other. A few of them write books, but that was not the type of thing that appealed to a man like Emmett. He knew of a few old spies (he even hated to think that term) who were consulting for the private sector, but he knew too many secrets for the Agency to be comfortable with that. Overall, he thought it was good to be back, up to his neck in the same old crap.

The music had stopped some time ago. He searched through his collection of CDs and found what he was looking for. It was Yo Yo Ma's Silk Road Suite. He listened intently for several minutes before reaching for the phone. After first setting the scrambler, he entered a familiar number. A curt response from late-night Vienna quickly followed.

"Hello Emmett, how goes the battle?"

"Badly Vincent, sometimes I fear the dragon is devouring the knights."

Vincent St. Clair was now head of the Global Bank Corp in Vienna. He and Emmett had worked together years ago when they were both young; Vincent with the British MI6 and Emmett the CIA man in London and acting as liaison with the vastly more experienced English intelligence agency.

Many years later, at the continued urging of his wife, Vincent had agreed to hang-up his cloak and sheath his dagger. He then relied on the vast international knowledge and many contacts he had developed through the years to become an investment banker, quickly rising to the top of the international development efforts at the powerful GBC.

Through the passing years, the two men kept in close contact. They had much in common. Both had lived and thrived on a secret life that on the surface never existed and remained shrouded in shadows. In spite of their continued sacrifices, they both remained fascinated by the intricacies of the *black science* of foreign intrigue that was the hallmark of their profession.

They also loved their respective countries, but were still able to acknowledge their own nation's political shortcomings without becoming disillusioned and cynical. The two aging cold warriors had both lost their wives of many years. Without this connection, combined with the critical nature of their jobs, they gradually grew apart from their children. They now filled the resulting void by devoting their entire attention to the daily demands of their individual professions. Tied together by the bonds of friendship and shared experiences more tightly than any organizational allegiance could ever establish, they often relied on each other's assistance to accomplish what they might be unable to do under the constraints of a slow moving and traditional bureaucracy.

Normally, the CIA will use the State Department's foreign embassy staffs, or the Department of Commerce's trade missions, to establish cover for their agents. While convenient, this can often present problems since foreign government officials can more readily identify the agents and monitor their activities. In contrast, a representative of a nongovernmental development organization such as the Global Bank Corp is far less likely to draw a foreign government's attention.

Most recently, because of their close personal ties, Vincent was occasionally willing to ignore the usual NGO policy of avoiding any perceived association with national intelligence agencies. The two covertly worked together to provide a legend for some of the Agency's unofficial representatives. Earlier, this association was the basis for the assignment of Charlie Connelly in Ukraine, and it was now the reason the Global Bank Corp. employed him for the project in Kazakhstan.

"I take it," Vincent observed wryly "that your *Operation Silk Road* is not exactly progressing as you wished."

"*Not exactly* is an understatement. One of the problems working off the books for the CIA is that you have access to very limited resources. Congress is currently budgeting around $80 billion for intelligence, and I have limited resources. My most scarce resource is manpower. I have a new hire working for me straight out of the Ivy League. His only exposure to the Agency was during the recruit training program at Camp Peary.

I have two more people in Kyrgyzstan who are busy trying to keep their heads down while the revolt there is taking place. Besides Charlie, I had two more men in Kazakhstan. Now, damn it, we just heard that the one who was working undercover in the oil fields was found in his hotel room with his throat cut.

"I am sure that somehow his death will be eventually traced back to the Russians. Dear old Vladimir continues to see Central Asia as his god-given stomping grounds. Now he is in a better position to use his petroleum resources to buy his way back in control of the region. However, Russia's new intelligence organization seems unwilling to rely on just economic power.

"The FBI recently broke-up a ring of eleven Russian spies here in the U.S. They were apparently operating out of Moscow Center and were living under "deep cover" in a sleeper cell with tentacles reaching up and down our entire East Coast. It turned out that, along with obtaining research on nuclear "bunker buster" bombs, they also wanted to acquire information on the Administration's real policy toward Central Asia. It appears, they couldn't believe what they saw us doing in the area actually reflected our real policy."

Vincent interrupted, "I even read about that over here in the European press. It was big news. The Agency can't be too happy to learn that what the Russians are seeing on the surface is just too simple to be believed."

"On top of that," Emmett added slouching further in his chair, "after we generously sent their operatives back to Russia, Putin embarrassed us even more by awarding all of them the Russian Medal of Honor. Hell, one of them even got her own reality show."

"The one with the...ah...ah,"

"Yes, yes, that's the one," Emmett snapped. Her code name was *chesty* for obvious reasons.

Why the hell did you ever send them back?" Vincent inquired incredulously.

"Beats the hell out of me old friend," Emmett exclaimed waving his hand in the air. "It seems that we want to be loved rather than feared.

"Neither you nor I would have ever done that, but it's a totally new generation here. Unfortunately, our desire for friendship doesn't seem to be widely shared. We have the Russians trying to reassert control over Central Asia. The Chinese are relentless in their view of the area as part of their original domain, as well as an important source of necessary gas and mineral resources. Then, of course, the US and NATO continue to need the region as a supply route to reduce the exposure of their convoys coming over the Khyber Pass on their way to Afghanistan.

"Other than that, Vincent old chum, everything is progressing just seamlessly. Thanks so much for asking," Emmett added in a voice tinged with sarcasm.

"In our business, as you well know", Vincent reminded him "you learn early on that nothing is what it seems on the surface. Perhaps your country's strategy of benign neglect is not as incomprehensible as it appears to the Russians—and to you.

"Is Charlie traveling heavy?" Vincent asked changing the subject

"I hope to God you're right regarding our policy. On Charlie, I just don't know. Bringing a gun to a knife fight is the Chicago way, and Charlie lives in Chicago. So maybe he is, but I doubt it. If necessary, could you possibly get something to him Vincent?"

"No way! I can't compromise my own people that way. Did you ever think you may be getting a little too old for this type of thing?" Vincent chided his old friend,

"Constantly, but discarding any semblance of humility, you and I both know that I am the most knowledgeable cold warrior they have available. I used to eat and breathe fighting Russia. After we won, the others either died or became consultants, so I am the best they have. Now, I desperately need time to get more agents into the field, and I can't do that without being able to point to some tangible successes. That's why I am grateful to you, Vincent old boy, helping me get Charlie somewhere operable. He is competent, as you well know--this is not his first rodeo, and since he is on the GBC payroll, he is cheap. You can't beat that combination in my type of work. That's why I wanted to call to thank you for your help."

Vincent gave up trying to figure out Emmett's "rodeo" reference, probably some obscure American colloquialism. He wasn't completely sure what he had meant about the "Chicago way" either. Sometimes he thought that the Americans had a language all of their own, but decided it was far too late at night to pursue the subject any further.

"Glad to help old man. If you are successful, both the Agency and our bank will benefit. Actually, I really have nothing at risk. If Charlie screws up there is an adequate basis for plausible deniability to cover my old ass. You might have a small problem, but that comes with the territory. Of course, if that happens you can always cut him loose, and see if he can operate on his own. We have both had to do that before."

There was no response from Emmett, so Vincent closed the conversation with "Good night my friend, and have a good weekend."

The line went dead. Emmett's music had finished several minutes earlier. He replaced the receiver and turned off his stereo. Staring glumly around the office he finally decided there was no reasonable alternative but to go home. He called the Marine guard at the gate to order his car.

Before Emmett could make it to the door, a red light flashed on his desk, and his phone emitted a light hum indicating a scrambled overseas call was coming through. He returned to his desk quite quickly for a man his age.

"What?"what?" he asked briskly. "There is no one else? You are sure. Then I will have to," he told the caller sadly. "I don't even know his ex-wife. I am not sure she is even aware that her husband was with the Agency. They often don't know. However, she deserves to learn that he died a patriot. It's just that after all of these years I have never been very good at notifying someone their loved one has lost their life in the service of their country."

"Will I replace him? Yes, I already have someone in mind. I will get him there as soon as I can."

After talking to the CIA officer in Almaty, Emmett put down the receiver, and left his office for the weekend, more disconsolate than before.

4.

Almati

Charlie Connelly's head bobbed him awake for the hundredth time since leaving Istanbul. The Air Astana's aging Tupolev-204 was bouncing its way through another thermal draft from the Taklimakan Dessert far below. With only a few hours sleep the night before, he still was not able to doze on the plane. It didn't have anything to do with this particular aircraft, or this airline for that matter. With all of his travels, he never had been able to master the art of in-flight deep sleep, as many of his associates seemed to do so effortlessly.

What was that fellow's name—Gibson—Walter Gibson, that was it. Hell, old Walter could fall asleep as soon as the fasten seatbelt sign came on. Even before it came on, to the occasional anger of a flight attendant or two. He recalled their trip to Jakarta. It was like traveling alone. Charlie would shake him awake to eat, and he usually fell back to sleep before the attendants removed the trays. When they finally hit the ground, old Walter was ready to howl all night.

Last night's telephone call from Emmett Valentine was not particularly conducive to sleep either. Through the years, he had grown to respect him, even like him if the truth were known. But damn it, he resented the intrusion on his well ordered life. After the job in Ukraine, he had promised Beth he would never get involved with the old man again. His relationship with the Agency was almost like having an illicit affair that both parties agreed to keep hidden from everyone else, but were mutually committed to continue.

Their association originally began very casually, with just an introductory contact by some of the Agency people visiting his office at Apex Electronics. They only wanted an insight to unimportant things like the import restrictions in Peru, or the economic stability in Sri Lanka, or some other seemingly reasonable request regarding a tedious detail occurring in some far-off place from which he had recently returned. Then things began to snowball, and he soon found himself dealing directly with Emmett, or one of the other people in Washington who worked for him.

He had actually found his little errands flattering and was initially pleased to be asked—to be trusted as it were. But, gradually he found himself getting in over his head. He usually felt more like Maxwell Smart than James Bond. Even then, he had to concede, it made him feel important that he could develop the skills that were so alien to his normal area of competency. He learned how to check to see if he was being followed, elementary dead-drop routines, and brush-pass-offs. Later, he was informed how to use simple encryption, as well as ways to contact certain people in Washington, if he needed to, without anyone becoming suspicious. Even later, if it became necessary, he learned how to cover his identity and purpose without detection. It was almost like on the job training in some kind of crazy corporation with the Mad Hatter acting as CEO.

All these things, he had to admit, added a little spice to an otherwise bland diet, providing melodrama to a more sedentary life of a recent retiree. However, he fully realized he was at best a knowledgeable amateur in a world where there were none. At least not for long.

Now Emmett had contacted him again. The old man back on the job once more. What was it he said? Something about old fire horses chomping at the bit. Charlie chuckled. That was Emmett all right. Charlie suddenly wondered, did it possibly describe himself as well? No, of course not! Not even close, he decided.

What did it say on the old Marlboro packs, back in the days when he was a smoker? Something about how cigarettes could be injurious to your health. Well talking to Emmett could be just as injurious—even more than smoking. Or practically anything else he could think of.

Although, he guessed, the old man certainly would not have called if it didn't involve something serious, and if it was serious it could also be dangerous. When Emmett called it was always about something dark and grave, and he knew from past experience he could very likely be drawn into things that he did not fully understand; and then he would be unable to reverse or withdraw.

But what the hell, maybe he should go along with the old man one more time. He would not have called if he didn't need help. Charlie didn't like the way his thought process was taking him, and he began gazing around the cabin to force his mind in a different direction. Any direction would serve the purpose.

His traveling companions certainly constituted a mixed deck. He had watched them as they boarded the plane and found their seats. Many of them were Asian in appearance, mostly short and squat in ill-fitting suits. Charlie mentally classified them as bureaucratic mandarins of one government agency or the other. Before Kazakhstan became independent, the regime operated almost entirely under the direction of Russian apparatchiks. After independence, this was turned upside down with Russians taking a more subservient role, but still controlling the major operating levers of power.

Another group of men, Charlie guessed, were business managers with distinct Russian characteristics. They had a lighter complexion, square jaws, blond hair, and seemed to exude the confidence that comes from years of leadership.

There were also a few pale-skinned Europeans, or possibly American executives, traveling to establish or burnish a business relationship in resource-rich Kazakhstan.

Further back in the cabin, there was another group that caught his attention. They were middle-aged couples, huddled together, looking as though they were attempting to draw strength from one another.

The flight attendant had informed him earlier that these people were making the long trip in hopes of adopting a Kazakh child. With Russia's current freeze on adoption, the country had become the world's sixth largest source of available children. As a result, Kazakhstan was suddenly an important destination for American couples who previously never knew the country existed.

Bored with studying his fellow passengers, and still unable to sleep, Charlie's mind drifted back to his previous trip to the Central Asian Republics. Actually, it began with a brief late night arrival at the Almati airport. Once there, a driver hired by the United Nations Development Program in Bishkek, Kyrgyzstan met him. The new countries had just claimed their independence from the Soviet Union after generations of Russian control, and they were eager for assistance from the international development agencies to help them convert their economy to a free market system.

There was no airport in Kyrgyzstan that could accommodate international flights, and overland transportation was the only alternative. He had to carry several thousand dollars in expense money, concealed in a money belt, because credit cards were not yet accepted. The night was inky black-not a star in the sky. The driver was a stranger, and he knew the route had the reputation as the location for bandit families. He was damn glad to get to Bishkek safely.

Kyrgyzstan's transition to independence had been sudden, and many of the country's leaders still felt a strong affection for their Russian patrons. While many of the Soviet countries were angrily tearing down the statues of their former Russian leaders, Bishkek still prominently featured a huge statue of Felix Dzerzhinsky, founder of the KGB, in the center of their Gorky Park.

His interpreter had recently graduated from medical school, but had entered a local business college because he could not make a living as a doctor. The young man and his wife were paying their college expenses by smuggling and selling prescription drugs from India.

Charlie spent several weeks on the privatization project, working with the Kirgiz Government, before returning to Almati. He was able to get a brief look at the Kazakhstan capital before catching an Austrian Air flight back to his home in Chicago. He wondered if he would notice much of a change now that the country had more experience at self-governance, and independence.

The fasten seat belt sign began to flash. It was a welcome sight. The night had been short and the flight long. The service was satisfactory—as much as on any flight lately. However, the plane was old and the ventilation system was not up to its task. Charlie felt tired and clammy, and somewhat apprehensive about what lay ahead.

Kazakhstan is a strange country, and he was unsure of what he might find. He also felt unsure about his assignment—both official and unofficial. He was to prepare a strategic plan for the privatization of a mining operation.

He had never been in a mine before, and didn't know what it might entail. On the other hand, in his career he had worked for a communications company, a computer company, an aircraft company, and finally a consumer electronics organization, so perhaps a mining operation might not be too different. But then, the Valentine contact was adding another element of uncertainty. He had always adapted to what was required, but the last time he damn near got himself killed.

The ancient Tupolev smacked the tarmac, and then bounced, causing the fuselage to shudder. The brakes screamed in resistance as the treadless tires attempted to gain traction on the damp runway. Oxygen masks fell from their hidden receptacle, and some baggage toppled unceremoniously from the overhead bins. The approach was necessarily abbreviated because of the proximity to the Tien Shan mountain range surrounding Almaty, and the resulting hard landing was not accompanied by the usual applause that marks most countries where Charlie frequently traveled.

The flight attendants, in their drab uniforms, smiled for the first time during the trip, and unclipped their seat belts before policing the aisles. They commanded their temporary wards to remain in their seats until the plane came to a stop at the terminal. Like travelers the world over these passengers ignored the warning, and began to gather their bags; at least those that were not already littering the aisle.

Charlie rubbed his bruised knee while uncoiling his long legs before standing to revive his dormant circulation. Retrieving his carry-on, and checking for his wallet and passport, he joined the exiting travelers driven forward by Kazakh officials eager to get to the front of the customs line.

The attendants, whose smiles had now been replaced by glazed glares of officialdom, opened the exit doors and quickly stood aside to avoid the moving mass of deplaning passengers.

Gasping the cool fresh air, Charlie moved toward the terminal. The airport carried its mantel of history well. The building had provided a destination for the first flight of the first supersonic passenger jet, the Soviet Tu-144 that flew just ahead of the European Concorde. Inside, there were signs of a much-needed renovation, and idle construction workers were in the way of the passengers who were attempting to locate the incoming custom desks. There was also striking evidence of the recent revolt in neighboring Kyrgyzstan. Soldiers in ill-fitting uniforms and pie-plate hats closely scrutinized the new arrivals, while nervously clutching their leftover Russian Kalashnikovs.

The lines forming at immigration moved sluggishly forward, penguin fashion. No matter how many times he had gone through customs he always felt a level of nervousness.

Eventually a scowling face of a woman customs official confronted him. She stared at him with practiced bureaucratic contempt as he slid his entry documents over the soiled counter and under the cloudy glass partition.

Her hand shot out from the tattered sleeve of her gray uniform, and he wondered if he would ever see his passport again. It now became clear why the line moved so slowly, as the dour faced official inspected each page of his bulging passport. She then stared at him intently to verify that he was the same person in the faded photograph.

"It's an old picture," Charlie offered feebly.

"Get a new one before you come back again," she spat back.

"Next," she shouted, as Charlie quickly moved on.

Entering the baggage area, he was surprised to see a short man holding a large sign with GBC lettered in bright red. Below the Bank's name was the name *Konnely*. Assuming that must mean him, Charlie waved to get his attention. The grinning Kazakh sign bearer took his sleeve and led him rapidly through the gate. In passing, the attending guards studiously ignored them while the customs agents casually examined each piece of incoming luggage. The Bank's driver quickly deposited him in a large room with overstuffed chairs, supervised by a flag-draped portrait of "President for Life" Nursultan Nazarbayev staring down at the shabby room.

After exchanging his passport and baggage claim for a large cup of tea magically provided by the Bank's greeter. Charlie relaxed and waited. The room quickly began to fill up with a scattering of Kazakh officials and visiting businessmen. Each group kept to themselves, assuming an air of indifference, while nervously waiting for their luggage to appear. The small air conditioner wheezed valiantly as the room became engulfed in clouds of strong smelling cigarette smoke exhaled by the previously nicotine deprived passengers.

All eyes turned toward the doorway as two burly guards pushed a man into the room, and shoved him toward a chair by the exit. The prisoner struggled vainly until one of the guards cracked him across the face. The man staggered, and fell awkwardly into the chair with such force that it almost tipped over.

Charlie was relieved to see the driver reappear, carrying his bag and happily waving his passport. The little man motioned to follow him outside. Charlie pointed quizzically toward the cowering man in the corner. The driver's response was a shrug of the shoulders and a whispered "Uighur-- all thieves and crooks." The two of them walked, with their eyes averted, past the pitiful man attempting to wipe a bloody nose on his sleeve.

Outside, the driver carefully squeezed Charlie's bag into the small trunk of an indistinguishable car. The airport was on the northeastern edge of town, 12 kilometers from the city center. The driver maneuvered his vehicle expertly through the increasing traffic, speaking rapidly in an unknown language, while pointing to buildings that seemed to look like all the others.

Finally, the car came to a stop in front of the old Hotel Kazakhstan. As Charlie unfolded himself from the back and retrieved his bag, the driver searched his pockets for an envelope from the Global Bank Corp. He triumphantly handed it over with a broad smile. "Tomorrow—tomorrow," he sing-songed holding up nine fingers. His assignment satisfactorily completed, he climbed behind the wheel of his car and roared away with a cloud of noxious black exhaust.

Russian architects apparently knew no other form-factor than the rectangle. From Soviet city to Soviet city, the only difference in their buildings was the number of floors that were included. In the case of this hotel, however, they capped their efforts with a distinguishing golden crown that glistened in the afternoon sunlight. Charlie remembered he had stayed here when he returned from his consulting project in Bishkek.

Going through the lobby, he could notice a few significant changes of questionable taste that had taken place since then. The older conventional Soviet light fixtures were missing, recently replaced by modern brighter lights. The new management had attempted to introduce an artistic element by randomly scattering throughout the now bright lobby golden statues of buxom Kazakh girls carrying baskets of fruit and goblets of koumiss, the traditional national drink.

He noticed one dramatic change when he checked-in. The desk clerk was friendly and accommodating, unlike his predecessors who seemed to place a premium on hostility. He also noticed that the traditional floor-ladies no longer occupied their place of authority. They had been a fixture in Soviet hotels, keeping a jaundiced eye on the arrival and departures of the intruding guests.

Once in his room, he tried placing a call to his wife, only to be greeted by their recorder. After leaving a message that he was well and on schedule, he closed with his love. A shower and an unsuccessful attempt at a nap followed his unsuccessful call home.

Charlie decided to take a walk to unwind, attempting to recover from the time change and cramped quarters on the long flight. The sun was beginning to disappear, being gradually replaced by threatening clouds. He was struck, as he had been on the drive in from the airport, that Almaty was a city without a soul, or even a strong sense of identity. It was built originally on the site of a former Silk Road town that was later destroyed by marauding hordes of Mongols. It was now definitely Russian, with masses of box-like apartments and straight grid like streets. Towering in the background, Charlie could see a range of the Tien Shan Mountains. Their snow capped peaks managed to add a scenic element to an otherwise drab city.

Charlie studied the faces of the sons and daughters of Genghis Khan, liberally mixed among those with a more East

European appearance. It was late in the afternoon, and a dark cloak of melancholy seemed to hang heavily on the workers making their evening trudge home. They presented an interesting blend of nationalities, Kazakh, Russian, and their Ukrainian look-alikes, along with Uzbeks, Uighur's and Tatars.

Russia controlled Kazakhstan since the 1700s. Over the centuries, Russian soldiers and settlers poured into the country pushing the Kazakh nomads off their land, and relegating them to the status of second-class citizens.

The city's fabric was now a tantalizing mix of cosmopolitanism combined with the atmosphere of a gold rush boomtown. Even though the oil driven economy had improved considerably, the benefits did not appear to have trickled down to the average Kazakh, and were not reflected in the faces of the people he was passing. They appeared grim, and only a few seemed to be talking among themselves. Instead, they stared directly ahead, unsmiling and determined.

Charlie felt very much alone, as he had many times before walking in a strange city. Perhaps it was a reflection of his fatigue. He wondered what was ahead and what tomorrow would bring.

It started to drizzle, and he decided it was time to turn back. It grew colder and he tugged at the collar of his Burberry trench coat, attempting to protect himself from the frigid dampness. Soon the steady chilling rain coated the black city streets, leaving them looking even shabbier then before. He was glad to see the brightly polished door of his hotel coming into view.

He welcomed the warmth of the hotel room. Laying stretched out on the too short bed he tried to sleep, but it came grudgingly. He thought of home and his wife. They had been married forever and were comfortably accustomed to each other. Through the years together, it was commonplace, but never easy, for them to be apart for long periods. Early on, he had been a corporate nomad moving from company to company and city to city. Sometimes out of necessity, and other times to seize an opportunity while chasing the American dream. Wife and family followed with some difficulty, but always without complaint. In the end, they all seemed to benefit from the experience by making them individually independent, but collectively compatible.

Since he retired, life seemed to continue drawing them apart. After Beth learned off his association with the Agency, she had become more uneasy about his travels. Never the less, she kept her concerns to herself.

Now here he was in Kazakhstan, a place few people were even aware of, and of those that were, fewer still could spell. The fact that his location was so far from home only served to draw him closer to his family.

His last thought was of his wife before sleep finally overtook him.

Charlie stretched out to kill his ringing travel alarm, only to discover the source of his irritation was coming from the hotel phone on his nightstand. At first, he thought it might be his wife retuning his earlier call, until he heard the soft purr of the scrambler, quickly followed by the all too familiar voice of Emmett Valentine.

"Did I wake you Charlie?"

"Of course you did, what the hell is that music?"

"Is it too loud?" Emmett inquired solicitously, turning the dial slightly on his stereo receiver. It's Puccini—one of my favorites. Poor Madam Butterfly, Lieutenant Pinkerton took advantage of her, and after Cho-Cho San renounced her religion and her Asian culture, the callow officer leaves her alone and returns to his own country. How sad.

"Sometimes I think that is what the Agency often does to its agents," he mused, leaning back in his recliner and staring at the picture of the man he had just lost working in the Caspian oil fields. "But it can't be helped can it?" he added recovering quickly. "We are constantly at war with a ruthless enemy that wants to destroy our way of life. As soon as we think we have won one battle, a new enemy arises. However, that's what keeps the old juices flowing. Right Charlie?"

"God damn it Emmett, I just got to sleep," Charlie answered, furious at being awakened. "Why the hell are you calling in the middle of the night?

"I am afraid the time change slipped my mind. I'm terribly sorry," Emmet added without a great deal of sincerity, "but I thought it was important to warn you of the situation that seems to be developing there.

"It now appears that Central Asia is becoming a simmering cauldron of intrigue, with all the major powers trying to stir the pot. The Agency believes that spying on the U.S. from Russia, China and others is now at Cold War levels—perhaps even greater.

"My *Operation Silk Road* has suffered a severe blow. (Even as he voiced the cryptonym, it sounded to him like a glorified reference to a pitifully meager effort.)

"They recently found one of our men in Kazakhstan, in his hotel room, with his throat sliced from ear to ear. He had been working undercover over in the Caspian Basin trying to find out who the power players were. Who controls the oil fields is becoming extremely critical to us.

"Who did it?" Charlie asked, becoming more sympathetic with the old man and his middle of the night calls.

"We don't know. We may never know. It could have been the Russians or the Chinese--or God knows who else. Some of our people are trying to walk back the cat to see what could have gone wrong to blow his cover, but it's becoming obvious things are heating up in Central Asia, and I thought that you should be aware of it. We don't want you to end up the same way."

"I appreciate your interest Emmett, but my connection to you and your people is so nebulous I barely understand it myself. I leave tomorrow for the mine, and the place is so far up in the hills that practically no one can find it, much less have an interest in what we are going to be doing there."

Emmett closed with "Get a good night's sleep old friend."

Charlie tried as hard as he could to take Emmett's advice, but like many things connected to Emmett, it was so easy to say but so hard to do.

5

The driver was waiting at the hotel as promised. His impressive collection of gold teeth glistened in the harsh lobby lights. After grinning a greeting, he led Charlie to the waiting car, and tossed his bag casually on the back seat.

As they sped through the rough streets, Charlie thought about his late night conversation with Emmett. He was concerned about the death of their agent. Emmett had made his point. Any association with the Agency had an element of danger, particularly, when someone is dangling alone on a tenuous thread in a distant and remote country rife with conflicting interests.

He automatically turned to study the traffic behind him. It had become a habit since his association with Emmett Valentine. A bad habit—a foolish habit—a mark of paranoia, but a habit he was unable to break.

To hell with it he decided, and sat back trying to enjoy the ride. The rain had stopped in the night, and the morning broke brisk and bright. Charlie's mood eventually lifted with the clouds over the peaks of the *heavenly mountains* as the locals refer to the sheltering Tian Shans. The buildings they were passing, more rapidly than Charlie would have liked, looked less drab and the city appeared more serene.

As his driver sped along his route, they passed an imposing marble megalith facing the east side of the presidential palace on Ulitsa Furmanova that the driver haltingly identified as the Central State Museum. Amazing, he thought, what oil revenue can produce.

In stark contrast to the museum, the Global Bank Corp's Almaty office was located in an unassuming gray office building in the heart of the city. In the dimly lit lobby, he had to squint to read the directory and decipher the alphabet soup of international aid and development agencies spread throughout the five floors of the Russian-built structure. Scrolling down the English list that included the ADB, CICA, CSTO, EAEC, EBRD, ECO, FAO, he finally located the GBC neatly nestled alphabetically between FAO and the IBRD.

Two years earlier, President Nazarbayev riding a mounting wave of prosperity, decided to invest some of the country's burgeoning oil revenues in building a new capital city of Astana in the northern part of the country.

It appeared to him, from scanning the list that the majority of the NGOs had, so far, decided to keep their offices in the more socially desirable Almaty.

An "out of order sign" dangled by a dirty string on the elevator door. It looked as if it had been there since the building opened. Realizing he might be late, and forgetting his accumulated fatigue, Charlie vaulted the first flight of stairs, then more slowly puffed the remaining four to the top.

On the way, he could not avoid noticing that the walls were spider-webbed with cracks running crazily all the way from the bottom floor to the top. It looked as if a passing earthquake—earthquake hell---even a faint tremor could turn the old building into a pile of rubble. Russian buildings have the unenviable reputation for shoddy construction, beginning to deteriorate even before they are completed. This one appeared to conform to the established norm.

Reaching the top floor, a series of unmarked doors lined the dim hallway. One was slightly ajar at the opposite end of the corridor, and Charlie headed in that direction.

All eyes turned as he entered a large conference room. "Charlie Connelly," he offered casually, introducing himself to a group already seated around a gray metal conference table.

The two women, seated at the opposite end glanced at each other with approving looks.

Charlie was an impressive man, tall, well built, with slightly graying temples, and a firm square jaw. He carried himself with an air of authority acquired from many years of increasingly responsible management positions.

Not waiting for an invitation, he chose a chair closest to the door he had just entered. This positioned him facing a younger man at the opposite end who waved in acknowledgement to the new arrival.

"I told your driver to pick you up earlier, but he is always late," the young man offered apologetically. "I guess we are all here now," he continued. "I was just going to start the obligatory introductions," he added looking over his assembled listeners. It was really his first real opportunity to study them closely.

"We were only chatting until you arrived. I am Trevor Gunn, head of the Global Bank Corporation in Almaty," he began. "All of you were selected by our office in Vienna for your particular skills, and I have looked over your CVs. You look perfect for our job. Before I give a rundown on what we expect as a work product from you during the next three weeks, why don't each of you sound off with name, rank, and serial number," he suggested nodding to the man seated to his left.

"Henry Butts, Certified Public Accountant, from Devonshire, more recently London," the gray haired man provided cautiously—almost as if he expected an argument or rebuttal. "Worked on projects in Belarus and Lithuania for the World Bank," he added as an afterthought.

When Henry finished, the man to his left offered, "Andre Malott, Mining Engineer, and man of the world. Originally from Paris—more recently from Santiago, Chile. *Hola,* and *bonjour*".

Dave Dieter took the nod from Andre. "Process Engineer, Cairo, Illinois—USA, and yes people there really is a Cairo, Illinois. I can assure you it is far less interesting than the city on the Nile; although it was made famous by Mark Twain and Clark Gable who hunted geese there." His attempt at clarification only further confused the majority of his listeners. "We also have coal mines. That's where I worked before retiring," Dave added, his voice trailing off.

It was now Charlie's turn, and the attention at the table focused on the late arrival. "Charlie Connelly, former international peddler and world traveler. Strategic planner for this gig," he told them with a grin. "Former project experience with the UNDP in Kyrgyzstan, and with GBC in Ukraine." It seemed he was the only one of the consultants who had worked before with the Vienna based organization. "Home town Chicago," he added, waiting for the usual gesture mimicking a cocked pistol that was the typical response to the windy city, but it didn't come.

"And now......" Trevor Gunn motioned to the people seated together on his right.

"Sammie Wang," the Asian appearing man offered. "I am going to be your man Thursday on this project. I have been at the mine for the last three weeks coordinating with the local management trying to get them to organize the basic information you will need to make your recommendations and prepare a plan. I have asked for organization charts, head counts, production levels, and whatever other information I could think of that you might need. These may or may not be available when you arrive." he added with a broad grin to emphasize his uncertainty.

"Thank you Sammie. By the way, the reference is to a man Friday, not Thursday. At least in England that is. Sammie has worked for our office here in Almaty before, and has been of enormous help. He speaks Russian, Chinese, and passable English" he chuckled. "His wife is also secretary to the

American Ambassador's wife, and she has been of great help to this office.

"Now let me introduce our two lovely ladies who will be traveling with you to Tekeli and acting as interpreters with the Russian mine management after you arrive. They are also accomplished computer operators and translators. They will be invaluable when you need to convert your presentations into Russian, which you will need to do. As you may already be aware, Russian is the *lingua Franca* of Kazakhstan. Nadia, has worked for us before, and just returned from the Tenghiz oil fields -over in the Caspian Basin--where she worked as an interpreter for a Canadian exploration company"

The older looking of the two gave a slight flutter of her hand in recognition.

"Elaina," he continued "is also from Almaty, and has been working in our office here for the last three months."

"Now for the project," Trevor continued. "The Government of Kazakhstan commissioned the GBC to provide restructuring advice on how best to prepare their mining combinat for purchase--hopefully by outside investors. Or if that is not possible, to remain more profitably in government hands."

"The study objectives are:" Trevor began, flipping on a slide.

-- *Determine Tekeli Combinat Financial and Operational Viability*

-- *Assist the Restructuring Efforts Being Pursued by the Combinat*

-- *Provide Recommendations and Strategy for Financial and Operational Restructuring*

-- *Provide Technical Advice related to Mining and Mineral Processing*

"The operation is quite large," Trevor continued, "and includes two distinct mining operations, employs over a thousand people, and even includes its own brewery and railroad, in addition, of course to the operating shafts and concentrator. You will have to………"

While Trevor Gunn described the project, Charlie studied the people who he would be working with for the next three weeks. It was easy to do. The room was cramped and the conference table large, leaving little room for anyone to pass behind the seated attendees. The area was windowless with bright yellow walls. A single bank of neon fixtures, with one flickering tube, cast a jaundiced reflective glow on the tightly assembled occupants.

Henry Butts--that is certainly an insignificant name--Charlie thought, looking at the small bookish man with wiry gray hair. He noticed that Henry furtively observed what was transpiring around him through myopic eyes, partially aided by thick, metal rimmed, British Healthcare glasses. He wore his life studying balance sheets and P&L statements as he did his wrinkled gray suit.

"The mine itself has not been actively worked for several months," Trevor was saying. "The miners claim the vein has been worked-out. The mine management tells the government that this is not true and that the miners are afraid to go back underground."

"What are they afraid of?" Andre asked, becoming more attentive.

Andre Malott was the physical opposite of the accountant. He was a large powerful man, his thick white hair made him avuncular appearing. Cheerful and confident he gave the impression of being as much at home in the conference room as he undoubtedly was in the mineshafts. His rather large nose revealed a latticework of red veins that seemed to establish a crimson road map to his past failings.

"They believe it may be haunted," Trevor chuckled dismissively. He continued, "The concentrator capacity is under-utilized. That is why we brought in a process engineer.

Ore reserves may be limited. Working capital and investment funds are tight. Uncertainty about the future is.........."

The reference to the process engineer caused Charlie to focus attention once more on the man from Cairo, his fellow Illinoisan. Dave Dieter was a big man with deep wrinkles and a quick smile. He seemed to be a pleasant man, reminding Charlie of his old high school chemistry teacher. The man would probably be competent and easy to work with he decided.

The two mining experts were dressed casually in old sweaters and Khaki trousers; in contrast to the accountant's suit and tie, and Charlie's navy blue blazer and turtleneck. He was pleased with the two men, but the number cruncher was still a question. He would be living closely with these men during the next three weeks, in a remote area of a remote country. It would be necessary to depend on their ability to do what they were hired to do and still maintain, at least some level of civility, if not friendship.

"Tekeli is a typical company town." Trevor persisted. The mine is the sole support of the surrounding community. The entire area depends on it for support, as well as continuing its social infrastructure for schools and hospitals."

This situation was familiar to Charlie. He had worked before on a consulting project in an out-of the-way village in Ukraine. The Russians had isolated the town from the outside because of ICBMs concealed in the surrounding Carpathian Mountains, and secret military electronic factories hidden in the town itself. Under the Russians, no one was allowed to enter or leave. He was the first person from the "outside" most of the people had ever met, much less someone from their former enemy the United States. His assignment was to assist one of the former military electronic organizations to convert their product line from defense to consumer products.

The situation was similar to Tekeli. The factory couldn't support its former level of employment so people were not only losing their jobs, but their access to medical facilities and education as well. It was a hell of a situation with no good or immediate answer. As a result, he felt some sympathy for the plight of the miners.

While Trevor continued speaking, a young woman silently entered from a door behind him, expertly balancing a large tray with cups of tea and coffee, cream and sugar. She was tall, and blonde, amazingly well proportioned, wearing a sheer black blouse with a deep cut neckline, as well as an eye catching micro skirt that with four inches more material might have been almost long enough.

The men at the table, now completely oblivious to Trevor's prepared remarks, followed the woman's every move as she bent to serve them. Finishing, she slipped out of the door as quietly as she had entered, leaving the two women and the Kazakh assistant unserved. She apparently did not consider her associates to be as deserving of her attentions as her boss and his guests.

"Let me emphasize that it is absolutely critical," Trevor Gunn continued "to finish this project on time. The Government demands that they receive their information within the designated time frame, or they will take action without it. There can be no margin for error."

Charlie understood the importance of maintaining the schedule. Apparently, the other consultants did as well, and they had refocused their attention on the speaker.

Briefly at least.

The coffee server re-entered the room less silently than before. As the men watched appreciatively, she stooped and whispered something to Trevor who grimaced slightly before continuing his theme "The company is now insolvent, it's ..."

Charlie looked at the two women interpreters who would be traveling with the group to Tekeli. One-- Nadia he thought was her name--was a redhead, with very pale skin, and the older of the two. She sat ramrod straight, almost militarily so, taking in everything while also seeming to study her new associates. She was painfully plain, peering through glasses, and her complexion appeared faintly pockmarked by some former disease. The Soviet Union was notorious for not providing any type of immunization that might add to the expense of caring for their massive populations.

Her associate, on the other hand—a brunette, was strikingly good-looking, with olive skin and a faint hint of almond eyes. She would have been the one chosen as high school homecoming queen he decided if Soviet high schools had such a thing.

They were both conservatively dressed. Slacks and boots. Boots can be very attractive on a woman, Charlie decided. The two interpreters apparently didn't share the same fashion sense as the director's assistant. Probably a good idea if you are cloistered with a group of men at a remote mining operation in the mountains.

Once more emphasizing the necessity of finishing their study on time, Trevor closed the meeting by warning the visitors that Kazakhstan is famous for its poor communication systems, and they might wish to call home before leaving.

As they all filed out, Trevor motioned to Charlie. "Can I see you in my office for a few minutes Mr. Connelly?"

Once inside, Trevor removed his tweed jacket and draped it casually on the back of his chair. Extending his hand, he began the conversation with, "my boss, Vincent St. Clair, told me about you. He was very pleased with your conduct on our project in Ukraine. According to him, it was a very sensitive situation there, and you completed the assignment on time without ruffling any feathers."

If he only knew, Charlie thought. He never wanted to get caught in a situation like that again.

"Since you have previous experience with us," Trevor continued, sitting back in his upholstered swivel chair, "I will look to you to coordinate our efforts at Tekeli. Things are getting very dodgy in this country. There are a lot of conflicting elements at play just now. Oil company against oil company. Russians versus the west; and the Chinese are always trying to gain control over their neighbors.

"So far, President Nazarbayev has managed to keep a tight lid on the bloody pot. More recently, however, the Kazakh Government is beginning to turn the screws on the western companies like Chevron, Exxon Mobil, and the Italian company Eni, pressuring them to renegotiate their joint venture deals with the state-owned companies."

The names of the local Kazakh companies rolled expertly off Trevor's tongue, but were unintelligible to Charlie.

" Wow," he interrupted, "How did you ever learn how to pronounce those names?"

"Well, like you Yanks love to say--it ain't easy," Trevor replied in his droll British way. "If the companies refuse to renegotiate it could open up the country to even more investment by Russia. Or, for that matter, by our neighbor China who is desperate to get control of more oil to fuel their industrial machine.

A telephone rang on Trevor's desk. He appeared oblivious to the sound, and continued talking until it finally stopped, or perhaps his secretary answered it.

"In addition, our friends in the Peoples Republic need vast quantities of mineral resources to support their expansion. Right now, they are consuming 40% of the entire world's supply of lead, and would love to get their hands on some of Kazakhs mines such as the one at Tekeli.

"We sometimes feel, here in Almaty, as if we are dancing on the top of a volcano. You can't get off, and if you stop dancing you burn. Not literally of course." he added unconvincingly.

"Perhaps you saw my secretary whispering to me during the meeting?"

Charlie grinned, and nodded his head. "She certainly looks....ah...extremely efficient."

Trevor laughed, "I thought you might have noticed. Actually, she is as dumb as a rock, but almost anyone can learn to answer the phone."

His grin disappeared as he continued "She told me we were just advised by your Embassy that one of their staff members over in the western Kazakhstan fields was found with his throat cut. They don't know why, or who did it, but they are pretty much on edge, and wanted to warn us as well," Trevor concluded with a slight shudder.

"My God Trevor, that's terrible. Throat cut. Who do they think did it?" Charlie thought it was better not to mention he learned about the dead agent the night before.

He had been uneasy about the project even before he left home. He heard about the armed uprising in Kyrgyzstan the day before he left Chicago. Emmett's calls had not made him feel any better. Now, the dead agent, and Trevor's analogy about dancing on top of a volcano had not eased his mind either. But, what could he do? It was far too late to back out now, and backing out had never been part of his character. His father once told him "The Irish never back out, and never back down." Of course, he reasoned, that maybe why they have so damn much trouble.

The two men chatted a few minutes longer about their respective families. Trevor gave Charlie his direct number and left the room so Charlie could use his phone to call his wife.

Things were fine at home, and he felt better about his journey as he rushed downstairs to the waiting Land Rover.

6

Washington

Emmett Valentine was in a Russian mood. Definitely a Russian mood. He selected Rimsky Korsakov's Scherezade from his file of CDs. It was his opinion that Korsakov, as a former officer in the Imperial Navy, knew how to write music that appealed to a man. None of this stuff that you have to turn up the volume to hear.

The music flowed through the small office as he studied the pictures received that morning of his dead agent. Terrible—just terrible. A bad way for a good man to die. Throat cut from ear to ear. Blood all over the bed. No sign of a struggle. Did he know the attacker? But, how did they know he was an agent? What was it he had learned that someone did not want known? Wanted it so badly they had to kill him to keep him quiet. He recalled once again that in the past, during the Cold War, the protocol among the players of the game was that you did not kill an opposing agent. Imprison him maybe, but not kill him.

But, that was the old KGB Emmett concluded with considerable rancor. He never thought he would be referring to that era as the good old days. Now, in Vladimir Putin's Russia, and the Putin managed presidency of Dmitry Medvedev, the FSB (Federalnaya Sluzhba Bezopasnosti or Federal Security Service) had been given free rein to do whatever they wanted to do —however they want to do it--with their over 200,000 highly paid personnel.

Their purview had expanded from the original responsibility for domestic security to controlling security for Russia's borders; as well as conducting security operations anywhere else they thought was a threat to Russia's sovereignty. As a result of their wealth, influence, and ability to strike fear in anyone that might oppose them, the FSB's people had become the country's new nobility.

Their responsibilities now range from countering the terrorist threat from the Chechens, to presumably running the agents that were recently apprehended and released in the United States. Now they don't have to worry what anyone—inside or outside of Russia might feel about them.

Emmett's experience was developed primarily during the Cold War. He often joked that men like him and Vincent were the original *"Mad Men"*, earning their spurs during a time when the prevailing national strategy was one of Mutually Assured Destruction. Then, both sides participated in a lethal arms race, balancing one side's technology against the other. Now, it is just a phrase applied to the hucksters of Madison Avenue who spent their Cold War lunching on dry martinis, and banging their secretaries.

However, his mind wandered. Now he had to focus on the task at hand--as undesirable as it might be. It has to be them, Emmett decided. It has to be the Russians, but how the hell did they learn about poor old Barry? Did he unconsciously reveal something about himself that had tipped them off?

Highly doubtful he decided. Durand was a consummate professional who had been around for a while. He first worked in Europe during the last days of the Soviet Empire, leaving just before The Wall crumbled. Then he transferred to China where he fell in love and married an Asian woman. She soon divorced him for being too circumspect and uncommunicative. Imagine that, an agent that does not talk very much. The Agency reassigned him to Almaty when the divorce became final.

If he hadn't revealed himself then, the only other conclusion that Emmett was able to reach was there must be a mole someplace who had access to information they should not have. Perhaps here in Washington, or more likely somewhere in Kazakhstan. That must be the case, Emmett concluded.

He had asked the staff, the *shadow people* they were called, sitting behind their desks, to prepare a summary of moles who were uprooted in the past that had used their position to acquire information and had sold out their country to a foreign power. Emmett flicked slowly through the pages, hoping for a clue from their history that might have previously eluded him.

Perhaps the most recent of them was good old Robert Philip Hanssen. They even made a movie of his defection. As a high-level FBI agent, he had provided his Russian handlers with sensitive national security information for well over 20 years. He was so trusted that the cousins at the Bureau had never given him a lie detector test, even after they knew that someone among them was providing top-secret information to the Russians about their activities. They were eventually able to uncover his identity by using fake information as a trap, and tracing it back to him as the source.

Emmett remembered the case very well. Hanssen was a practicing Catholic—even a member of the ultra conservative Opus Dei--who spent a lot of his money on an exotic dancer; and videotaped his own sexual encounters with his wife, to be watched later by his best friend. What a consummate bastard, Emmett thought. He sold out his country, church, and family.

The CIA, of course, has had its own moles. Boy did it ever, Emmett thought. Aldrich Ames may have been the most famous of them. He was a counter intelligence official who, along with his wife Rosario, passed the names and covert identities of at least nine U.S. agents, along with their counterintelligence techniques, to Moscow from 1985 to 1994.

The Agency was aware that someone was betraying its people for a long time before suspecting the source. Even when they knew that Ames had a severe drinking problem, drove very expensive cars, and spent far more money than he could have ever earned on his CIA salary, they still had not given him a lie detector test. They finally planted false information in a dead-drop he was using, and when he went to pick it up, they arrested him. Ames is serving a life sentence in a federal prison for his betrayal.

Reading through the file, Emmett tried to become more comfortable behind his large desk. The highly polished surface was devoid of any personal items that usually help characterize most other men. There were no family photographs, expensive pen sets, calendars or other correspondence waiting to be read and answered. In addition to the file he was reading, there was only a blank pad of paper, and an ancient abacus positioned precisely in the center of his desk. It was if the old man could leave at any moment, and no one would ever know that he had been there at all.

Apparently, defection has become an equal opportunity obsession Emmett concluded seeing the name Sharon Scrange on his list of moles. He remembered her, and the case. It had taken the CIA a long time to uncover her, as well. They never believed that a woman could be a mole. Yet, working as a CIA support employee at the American Embassy in Ghana, she was sleeping with a relative of the Ghanaian Prime Minister, against Agency regulations of course. Even after the CIA became aware of the relationship, they unwisely left her in place. She rewarded their generosity, or stupidity, by providing the Ghanaian Government with the names of all the American agents that were in-country. They were summarily removed, eliminating any future ability of the CIA to gather information in this critical country.

Emmett chuckled as he recalled that Ghana was also the country the Reagan Administration sent Shirley Temple as Ambassador. Poor Shirley. He wondered what she had done to be assigned to such a God-forsaken place. You had to give her credit though. She handled her assignment with dignity and never complained.

Of course, there was also old Edward Lee Howard. What a beauty he was. When Howard was finally suspected of spying, the former disgruntled CIA officer eluded the FBI agents, who had come to arrest him, by leaping from a car driven by his wife. She then immediately propped up an inflatable dummy in his place, and continued on her way as if nothing had happened. He ended up safely in Russia. Several years later, he died there at the bottom of a hill with his neck broken. People often wondered if was at the hands of his Russian handlers who got fed-up with his drunken arrogance, or the CIA getting even.

You can't trust anyone were the watchwords agents lived by. Sometimes your allies become your enemy. Look at Jonathan Pollard, serving life in prison. He pleaded guilty in 1987 to passing information to the Mossad while holding down a highly classified job for the United States. The Israelis are still trying to bargain for his release.

Emmett was becoming terribly discouraged. So far, he was able to conclude only that it took a very long time to uncover anyone, man or woman, who buried themselves in a secret life. In addition, the motives seemed to vary all over the place. Money—sex—ego whatever. Damn near anything you could imagine.

The only consolation was the Agency had occasionally been able to penetrate the Russian KGB. Of course, the public rarely heard of these successes, which was a constant cause of organizational frustration. Occasionally though, something that was done right did become known. The most recent success, gradually receiving international notoriety, was that of Colonel Shcherbakov.

Emmett snorted with pleasure when he thought of him. The Colonel was a longtime member of Russia's Foreign Intelligence Service. The daily *Kommersant* newspaper reported he was the informant who alerted the Americans to the sleeper cell with Anna Chapman and her fellow Russian spies. It seemed that he planted them, and then dug them up. What a crazy business this is, he concluded.

He sat back in his chair reflecting on what he had learned. Certainly, nothing definitive. What could he do to find out who had taken out old Barry?

His mind drifted to James Jesus Angleton. What a name. You couldn't make-up a name like that. Old JJ had started his career at the same time as Emmett—and pretty much in the same location. James Jesus grew up in Europe, the son of an American executive with the National Cash Register Company. He attended Yale, and subsequently graduated from Harvard Law School before joining the society-conscious OSS in the early stages of WWII. Like Emmett, he had learned his craft from the British. After the war, the CIA sent him to Europe as an undercover cold warrior.

Later, he returned to Washington where he became the Agency's principal counter intelligence authority. *Chief Mole Whacker* many called him behind his back—but never to his face. He was universally feared and often hated around Langley, and was the reason a number of agents' careers had ended prematurely. However, he seemed to never uncover a proven traitor within the Agency's hallowed halls.

The downfall of Angleton's own career came as a result of a close personal friendship with Kim Philby, who was one of the top men in England's MI6. Philby was so trusted by the Brits he was rumored to be in line to take over the top job at the organizational counterpart to the CIA. They assigned him to Washington as liaison to the Agency.

Philby and Angleton had many interests in common, and worked closely together on counter intelligence problems. During his assignment, the British finally became suspicious of Philby after providing him with information they knew eventually reached the KGB. When they were on the verge of recalling him to London for questioning he learned of their intent and fled to Moscow. Safely in Russia, they gave him a medal and a pension for his long-term service to their country. Old Philby lived there comfortably and peacefully until he eventually died of alcoholism and old age.

James Jesus was the smartest and most dedicated man Emmett had ever known. If he was unable to uncover a spy under his very nose, what chance was there of finding someone in Washington, let alone Kazakhstan, who was killing his agents?

Scherezade had finished some time ago. Now, Emmett decided, what he needed was thinking music. He replaced Korsakov with Debussy, and the mellow tones of Claire de Lune filled the small office. Always liked Debussy he thought, reaching into his desk for his old meerschaum pipe. Soon foul smelling smoke engulfed his head.

Emmett finally decided there was only one way he could be successful in his search. There was not enough time to study the records of all the possible agents; or rely on random lie detector tests. From what he had learned from reviewing the records the most effective way would be to set a trap. It would have to be in Kazakhstan. The Washington office was far too vast. He would gamble that the leak was in Kazakhstan. But, if you want to set a trap you need something to use for bait. What kind of trap could he set, and what to use as bait?

A polite tapping at his door interrupted his contemplation. "Ah Roger, how are you? I was just thinking about you. Come in. Come in young man. Sit down." Smiling benignly, Emmett welcomed Roger to his office. "We need to talk about the next step in your career."

7

The Silk Road

The two 4x4s formed a strange caravan, slowly wending their way along the northern branch of the ancient Silk Road, heading toward the Tekili mining community. The rust colored dust somehow managed to seep through the tightly closed windows, and every other crevice of the relatively new cars. In the back seat of the lead Rover, Charlie gingerly rubbed the back of his neck. He thought he might be getting a headache; not helped at all by the frequent deep ruts in the road's neglected surface. The rolling steppes of eastern Kazakhstan's arid moonscape went on endlessly. Charlie had given up cigarettes years ago, but occasionally had a desire to begin again. This was one of them, as time seemed to pass on leaden shoes.

It was still too early for any sense of companionship to develop among them. They were virtual strangers to each other, with different professional and cultural backgrounds. As a result, there was very little banter that might have otherwise served to pass the time more pleasantly.

Charlie shared the back seat with Henry Butts. The accountant stared out the window oddly mesmerized by the endless expanse of nothingness, apparently fixated by the passing landscape. His concentration seemed curious since the passing scene was completely devoid of vegetation, with the occasional exception of a scrubby tree or anemic shrub. He wondered what Henry found so engrossing, staring out the window seemingly lost in thought.

Andre Malott dozed fitfully in the front seat he shared with the driver Sammie Wang; the self-described GBC's man Thursday. The trip from Santiago to Almaty had worn him out, and the grey haired engineer needed all the rest he could get.

The other Land Rover trailed behind, driven by the red-haired Nadia. Dave Dieter sat beside her, helping to navigate from a dog-eared road map printed years ago by the Russian Government.

Elaina dozed in the back seat, worn out from spending the night with her boyfriend, and welcoming the opportunity to catch up on her sleep. She didn't care that she was shoe-horned among the suitcases and boxes of groceries for the mine. The hotel, where the group was staying, had been empty for some time. There was no longer any reason for visitors to meet with the mine's management. The Kazakhstan Government representatives had given-up on their visits that were proving to be an exercise in futility.

The cleaners and cooks operating the hotel had been inactive, and now needed food staples and cleaning materials to accommodate the immediate needs of their new guests. The Bank took responsibility for the per diem covering their representatives lodging and meals, and it wanted to make sure the hotel had enough supplies to tide them over until the local staff could better accommodate their guest's requirements from nearby markets.

The two Land Rovers had begun the trip together, but Nadia had decided to make a quick detour to make sure the two Persian cats, that condescendingly shared her apartment, were adequately cared for during her absence. Rushing inside, she was relieved to find that the young woman hired to care for her pets had dropped by on her way to school as she promised.

Nadia attempted to catch-up with the others, by driving faster than she should. They passed Panfilov Park, oblivious to the crowd forming outside of Zenkov cathedral. The century old wooden church was one of the few remaining tsarist-era structures in Kazakhstan, and was built entirely without the use of nails. Stalin had been hard on the onion-dome churches of the Soviet Union, converting many of them into warehouses, barns and grain silos.

This church had been more fortunate, and was used as a concert hall during the Soviet period and reasonably well maintained. The Kazakh Government returned it to the Russian Orthodox Church soon after independence, and it became a daily place of gathering by the more devout among the local Russian community.

Nadia concentrated on her driving paying little attention to the long line waiting to gain entrance for the daily services.

East of the Cathedral, increased traffic forced her to crawl past the fierce looking WWII memorial dedicated to the Almaty infantry unit whose men died, outside of Moscow, fighting-off advancing Nazi tanks. Russia had conscripted thousands of Kazakhs and forced them to fight in some of the deadliest battles of the war. Afterwards, they erected the memorial hoping to salve the feelings of the Kazakh descendents.

Once past the Park, Nadia was able to pick-up speed again and soon left the city traffic behind. Eventually, she was able to regain her former position behind the lead Rover. Nadia honked briefly to let them know that she was there.

Sammie Wang tried to pass the time by providing his passengers with information regarding some of the more interesting locations along their route. "Over there," he waved broadly "is Semipalatinsk. During WW II, old Joe Stalin moved a lot of his Russian factories to Kazakhstan to keep them out of reach of the German army. He set up a series of Gulag labor camps and rounded up thousands of ethnics from all over the USSR. They piled them into hundreds of freight cars, and shipped them out here. Most of the deportees had never done anything subversive, but Stalin was afraid they might, and needed the workers. This way he solved both problems with one massive sweep.

"One of the unlucky bastards was the author Dostoyevsky. You've heard of Dostoyevsky haven't you?" Not waiting for an answer he continued, "The poor old guy spent five years there, and later placed his fictional characters in his book, *Crime and Punishment*, in one of those damn Gulags.

"It is also the same area where the Russians built a secret town they used as a test-site for their early atomic bombs. Stalin was desperate to catch-up with the West. He gave orders for tests to be carried-out at a rate of 12-15 a year up until they were ended in 1990." Shaking his head he added, "The poor people still bear the scars. Cancer rates are the highest in the world, and there are a terribly large number of mutations among the people attributed to the tests."

It didn't seem as if Sammie cared if anyone was listening or not. In fact, he appeared to relish his role as local expert.

"Before independence," he continued, "the Russian economy was so hard-up they tried to turn the area into a tourist location. Maybe a nuclear theme park," Sammie laughed, turning to his passengers to see if they appreciated his humor. Apparently, they missed the point.

Waking-up, Andre pointed to a group of ramshackle buildings alongside the road. "What's that up there?" he asked.

"Rest stop," Sammie announced, suddenly turning the wheel to pull off the road. It was a mistake a driver unfamiliar with the top-heavy configuration of a Land Rover might make, and the vehicle careened dangerously into the small roadside park.

Unexpectedly thrown against the door, Andre exploded with a French curse.

A family of Kazakhs in their native garb already occupied the area. The weather had turned cold and their toddler, bundled in padded trousers and brightly colored jacket, reminded Charlie of the Pillsbury doughboy. Gaining permission from the parents, Andre gave the child a piece of candy as the family began to climb into their dilapidated truck to continue their trip to Almaty.

It was immediately apparent to the travelers why the Kazakh family had been eager to leave. This was not the type of modern facility's presently dotting America's US 80. It was more reminiscent of those sparsely scattered stops along Route 66 during the early 1930s. The stench enveloping the two outhouses was overwhelming. They were the Turkish type where you either stand or squat, and even fouler than expected.

While the travelers waited their turn, a dilapidated pickup truck pulled into the stop, and disgorged a half dozen fierce looking, heavily bearded, Asian men who waved to Sammie. The smell of the facilities, combined with the threatening look of the new arrivals, encouraged the travelers to return to their cars as quickly as possible, eager to put distance between themselves and the rest stop.

Back on the road, Sammie resumed his responsibility as the self-appointed tour director. "Over there," he nodded in the direction of a new set of rolling brown hills that looked exactly like the others, "is the Baikoner Cosmodrone, which is the headquarters of the Soviet space program. All Russian astronauts landed there, and that's where much of their research took place. They wanted to put it in an out of the way place where they could keep their activities secure. They figured this was as far out of the way as they could get," he chuckled. "Now they lease it from the Kazakh Government."

Rounding a curve, Sammie suddenly slammed on the brakes, simultaneously shooting his arm across Andre's chest like a caring mother with a small child. Andre exploded with another curse. The other passengers tried to brace themselves to keep from sliding off their seats. The trailing car was able to stop just short of ramming into the Land Rover's rear bumper.

Inside the car, they all stared in disbelief as a herd of double-hump Bactrian camels casually crossed in front of them, indolently gazing at the foreign interlopers in their modern conveyance. A single camel-herder, on horseback, vainly attempted to hurry the gawking beasts out of the path of the waiting autos.

Sammie and Andre fumed in the front seat, eager to get on their way, while Charlie and Henry watched with curiosity as a circus-type parade, from out of the past, unfolded before them.

It is doubtful if any of the travelers considered how absurd their situation was. Britain's best iron had just been brought to an abrupt halt to accommodate the passage of an abbreviated caravan that was very much like those traveling the trail centuries before them.

After the last camel finished crossing the road, Sammie irritably jammed his Rover into gear and sped away. The grinning herdsman jauntily waved his fur cap in farewell, happy for any diversion to his routine life.

The sun that seemed to be following them began its daily descent, bringing the temperature along for the ride. The fading light suddenly dissolved in a cloud of red dust, kicked up by the old pickup truck that shared their rest stop earlier in the day. As it sped past, the men bouncing around in the truck's bed glared at the travelers as if they were unwanted interlopers on their land. In a matter of minutes, the vehicle disappeared up the road.

"There they are again. See that pass through the mountains?" Sammie suddenly pointed to a tiny cloud of dust in the direction of Tien Shans. None of the riders could. Andre, seated beside him, felt obligated to nod in acknowledgment.

"Through that pass is Uremkie the capital Xinjiang Province in China," Sammie told them. "The name Urumqi means beautiful pasture in English," he added as further explanation.

"That's the home of the Uighurs. At one time, during the Soviet period, that road was wide enough for a landing strip.

Now the Russians have gone, and the Kazakhs are afraid that the Chinese will swamp this country, so they destroyed it."

In the backseat, Henry nudged Charlie, not too gently, and whispered, "What, what the hell did he say? Home of whom? Home of the Uggers?"

"No-no not Uggers--Uighurs. It sounds like We-gers, but is spelled U-i-g-h-u-r," Charlie replied in sotto voice.

Unaware of the conversation behind him, Sammie continued, "It is a province the world ignores. It's a Muslim area, made up of Turkic people who hate the Chinese, and want their independence. Beijing has recently reinforced its military there to put down the uprisings, and throw the instigators in prison. Everyone knows about Tibet, but no one ever hears about the poor Uighurs.

"Not too long ago there were only a few thousand Chinese in that province. Now they outnumber the Uighurs. Thousands of new Chinese immigrants are shipped in each week, and they are destroying the local culture. The Uighurs hate and fear their Chinese oppressors, and the Kazakhs who see what's happening are afraid it could happen to them. They have tried to establish a buffer zone between the two countries, but it is a failure," he added unsympathetically.

"How the hell did a bloke from the land of the Golden Arches know about the Uighurs?" Henry whispered to Charlie, unmindful of Sammie's portrayal of the plight of the neighboring people.

Charlie laughed at the reference. He was glad to see his companion less depressed than before. "During the early days of the Afghan war, our CIA captured a group of them who were training with al Qaida. They were Muslims who had traveled there to learn how to be terrorists so they could go back and cause problems with the Chinese military controlling their province. We brought them back and put them in Guantanamo.

"The Uighurs never had it so well, but when President Obama was first trying to close down the facility, he thought the easiest prisoners to start with would be them. He miscalculated. No other country would take them, and he was afraid to send them back to China for fear they would be killed."

"Why did he care?" Henry asked, now more curious than before.

"Well I guess he didn't want to offend the international community. We have become very sensitive to that lately."

"So what happened to them? Are they still in Guantanamo?"

"No, not quite. We took four of them and sent them to Bermuda. Bought them a house, and found them a job."

"You're pulling my leg," Henry exclaimed incredulously.

"Honest to God. We sent a couple more to some small island in the Pacific. I wrote my congressman and volunteered for the program, but never got an answer. My wife and I love Bermuda."

The Brit snickered. "Sounds like the kind of dumb thing we would do back home in Londonstan,"

Unaware of the conversation in the back seat, Sammie continued telling Andre how the Kazakhs had given up trying to guard the pass, and the Uighurs continued to come and go pretty much at will.

Further up the road, the steppes suddenly fell away, revealing a valley surrounding a small town. Trees with a few remaining leafs clinging to their stubby branches partially masked a scattering of small buildings. The bleak structures seemed huddled together for protection with their backs turned toward the surrounding mountains hoping to be shielded from the elements. A meager road snaked from the village to a gaping wound in the mountainside that apparently served as the mouth of the mine.

8

Tekeli

By the time the travelers reached Tekeli, the sun was disappearing behind the mountains. Riding through town, Charlie could occasionally catch a glimpse of a face, unknowingly exposed by the lights within, furtively peeking through shabby curtains. Their car passed the barbershop, then the tavern, a village hall, an icehouse, and a lot filled with dilapidated heavy trucks that appeared to be rusting out from lack of use; finally drawing to a stop at the foot of a small hill. "We are here," Sammie announced unceremoniously.

The tired travelers piled out of the two Land Rovers, and began brushing the dust off each other. It was cold. A bitter wind whipped through the branches of the surrounding trees, stealing their last leaves and scattering them across the ground, partially hiding the path that led to the box-like hotel at the crest of the hill.

The structure reminded Charlie of some of the barracks he had lived in when he was in the military. A light shone dimly in only two of the windows on the second floor. The rest of the building conveyed an unwelcoming darkness.

Sammie began pulling the bags from the cars; then helped Andre struggle with a large duffle. As it was, the Frenchman gasped for breath as he trudged up the steep incline to the hotel.

Following behind, Charlie became curious about a clinking noise coming from the duffle. He finally concluded that it must be some kind of special instruments the mining expert required for the project.

The hotel's office was on the second floor. A slender woman, apparently the hotel manager, looked down on them from the top of the stairs. After a perfunctory greeting, she took their names, entering them into an empty register. Charlie received his key, and began to search the narrow hallway for his assigned room.

A single low wattage bulb cast a pallid glow creating distorted shadows as he walked. The flooring creaked from unaccustomed weight until he was able to make out his room number on a partially ajar door.

The room was small, but adequate. A musty odor permeated the area, but he was used to that from his travels in SE Asia. A bulb, hanging by a bare black cord from the ceiling, provided faint light to the room. There was also a small reading lamp on the desk, squeezed alongside a large black and white television set. After making room for his laptop, he adjusted the lamp's faded shade. The ancient springs groaned their defiance, as he tossed his travel bag on the bed.

The manager had informed the group that the staff would be serving dinner shortly. He washed in the chipped porcelain sink, attempting to get the red dust from his hands, arms, and face.

Entering the combination kitchen/dining room, he was surprised to see his traveling companions already seated around a long table. The hotel manager introduced herself once more before launching on a series of introductions that included the two female Kazakh cooks with unpronounceable names, and a houseboy of uncertain origin.

"Tonight," the manager explained, "we plan to welcome our international guests with a true Kazakh dinner." After a nod to her staff, they obediently began taking large plates of food from an iron oven, and distributing them to the waiting guests.

It became apparent what Andre had been carrying in his duffle as he reached under the table and brought up the first of what ultimately seemed to be an almost inexhaustible supply of Chilean wine.

"*Salud,*" Andre roared, raising his glass in a toast to his companions.

Henry responded with "Cheers," wearing a thin smile.

"*Buena suerte!*" Charlie offered in response.

"*Nostrovia*!" chorused Nadia and Elaina.

"Hopefully we won't need good luck," Andre replied with a grin. "But more realistically, we probably will," he added more seriously.

All the diners were pleased with the wine, except Sammie. He had already taken the cap off a large bottle of white liquid in preparation of passing it around the table. "Its koumiss," he exclaimed with pleasure. "Fermented mares milk," he added as further explanation. "It's the staple of the Kazakh nomads, and the Kazakh national drink."

Charlie recalled the statues of golden maidens in the lobby of the hotel. He was once told that koumiss was what they were supposedly offering in welcome to the newly arriving guests.

As the bottle made its way around the table, the two women interpreters poured a small sampling into their glasses.

Upset by the unenthusiastic response, Sammie added, "It is said that Tolstoy drank eight liters a day, and recommended it to all of his friends as a cure for depression."

"Eight liters a day, that's preposterous," Dave Dieter exclaimed without thinking. In spite of his placid appearance, he had a quick tongue, which was often the cause of some regret. This was not one of those times. He proceeded unabashed. "If the old boy did drink that much, it sure as hell would eliminate any depression he might have. Along with his liver," he added in a failed attempt at mollifying Sammie.

By now, each of the diners had received their plates, along with a large serving bowl, placed in the center of the table. The woman interpreters began eating rapidly. It had been a long trip, and they were hungry.

The men, on the other hand, stared quizzically at their overflowing plates, and then at each another.

The silence was finally broken by Andre, "What in the bloody hell is this?" he asked making a face.

"It is *beshbarmak*" Nadia explained. In English, the word sounds like **besh**-bahr-mahk. It is the national dish of Kazakhstan and it is made of boiled mutton, beef, horseflesh, and noodles."

"Horseflesh?" the men chorused in dismay.

Dave turned toward Charlie with a rictus grin. "I guess we ain't in Kansas any longer Toto," he announced with a giggle. Dave may have had more wine than he was accustomed to.

"What did he say? What did he say?" Henry inquired. "What the hell does that mean?" Everyone ignored his question. "This looks like a bloody shepherd's pie," he added with finality.

"We usually serve it along with dumplings or bread," Nadia continued. "Tonight the manager is serving it with Kazakhstan Rice. She has made it especially for you with ground beef, almonds, dates, prunes and some other things to add to the taste."

That sounded less offensive, and the men ate the rice dish, while poking cautiously at whatever it was the manager had called the other dish.

Charlie made a mental note to ask Nadia to speak to the staff about their future meals. He also chuckled to himself wondering if a wine enthusiast would consider the Chilean Sauvignon Blanc to be the proper choice to complement horsemeat.

Dinner was drawing to a close, and everyone was in good spirits. The rapport had not come immediately. They were a strange mixture of nationalities representing a variety of professional backgrounds. In spite of their different personalities, they began to talk with each other with more relaxed familiarity as the meal progressed,

Dessert that night consisted of bright red apples. "Apples are originally from Kazakhstan," Sammie explained. An assortment of strange looking candies and figs surrounded the apples in an attempt, by the kitchen staff, to make the simple fare more appealing. After dessert, one of the local women serenaded the guests by playing the dombra and singing Kazakh folk songs in a high-pitched, but oddly appealing voice.

"It is a lot of sound from a two-string guitar," Dave said leaning toward Nadia.

"It is a lute," She explained.

Dave roared with laughter. "That's exactly what I said. It's a lot."

Nadia exchanged glances with Elaina. Henry tried to slide Dave's wine glass away from him. Charlie concentrated on his plate.

Following dinner, the discussion centered on the next day's meeting. The men were all aware they would be speaking to a hostile audience of Russian mine managers who were opposed to them being there, and were reluctant to cooperate. The men were aware that the miners feared the project would end in a recommendation for their mine to be placed on the international market. If that did occur, the workers were worried they could end up working for the Chinese, the Swiss, or some other organization less sympathetic than their fellow Russians.

The men decided that Charlie would begin tomorrow's meeting, followed by Henry who would describe the type of data he needed. The mining experts would summarize their backgrounds, and discuss their plans for the project.

Charlie would close out the discussion, and then open it to questions and comments from the assembled managers. The purpose of the meeting was to try to acquire as much cooperation as possible from the assembled group so they would provide the required operating information.

Nadia would serve as the translator, and the informal conversation that evening provided an opportunity for her to become accustomed to the pronunciation and cadence of each of the men.

Returning to his room, Charlie began the job of unpacking, and trying to find a place for his clothes. When he finished, he took a large tube of Colgate toothpaste from his ditty bag and carefully inserted a small penknife to apply pressure under the top rim. It flipped off easily before falling to the floor. He then turned the tube upside down and shook it vigorously. A slender blue barrel of a 22-caliber pistol slid out. Before leaving Chicago, he had taped the gun's small cartridge cylinder to his electric razor, making it slightly longer than the Norelco Company had initially intended.

Placing the barrel and cylinder on the table, Charlie foraged inside his bag and removed a pair of English wingtips. Taped inside the right shoe, just above the leather heel, was the gun's small bone grip. He was well aware of the consequences of hiding a gun in checked luggage, but decided the airport inspectors were not that attentive and the contents of his bag could probably get by without detection.

Charlie abruptly returned to the doorway peering down the hallway. Relieved by its emptiness he returned to his task of assembling the small Beretta.

Real gun owners derisively referred to a small caliber revolver as a pussy pistol. Not at all like the Glock 19, currently in favor among handgun enthusiasts. Charlie didn't care. This one was easy to conceal, and would be powerful enough to wound a person, and possibly kill at close quarters.

He had scattered the cartridges throughout his bag, carefully tucking them among different items of clothing. He soon found them all, and inserted each into the cylinder before spinning it. Satisfied with the sound of the action, he carefully set the safety.

The next thing was to find an acceptable hiding place. The room was bare—monastically so—not many places to conceal a weapon. Finally, he stood on the chair, and stretching, positioned the gun carefully on top of the armoire. Judging from the thickness of the dust, there was little worry the housekeeper would find it while cleaning his room.

Charlie had never carried a gun on his trips. It had never occurred to him that he might need one. Now he felt rather foolish about his precautions, but the last project in Ukraine had changed his mind about many things.

9

Kiev

It began peacefully enough, Charlie recalled. Everything happened accidently, seemingly driven by a series of weird coincidences, as such things often occur. After he retired, and became bored with his humdrum existence, Charlie began sending out resumes to organizations that were looking for part-time consultants with special skills. The Soviet system had imploded. The Berlin Wall had decayed, physically and morally, and then finally collapsed. Torn down by the East Germans who for many years had longed for the type of freedom their relatives on the other side in West Berlin enjoyed. Afterwards, the remaining countries that had been contained within the Soviet bloc began to fall like dominoes. Russia, no longer had the economic strength, or perhaps the will, to enforce themselves on their far-flung empire that encompassed a wide range of nationalities and ethnic groups.

Once these countries regained their political independence, it became vital for them to acquire a level of economic independence as well. Many were attempting to achieve this by converting their government owned industries to privately held companies, referring to this as privatization. Along the way, these industries were finding it necessary to become familiar with operating in a free market society instead of a communist controlled economy. As a result, nongovernmental organizations in the West were employing consultants to assist these new governments and their businesses to make the difficult conversion.

With Charlie's background in the private sector, he was able to get assignments with the World Bank, and agencies of the UN in Lithuania, Belarus, and Kyrgyzstan. The General Bank Corp was looking for someone to work in Ukraine, and picked-up on Charlie's resume.

Ukraine was like the other former Soviet countries he had been to--only more so. The country, through the centuries, had lived under the thumb of a number of foreign governments, with only a brief taste of independence, lasting about as long as a hiccup, after WWII. Russian apparatchiks had controlled the entire government structure with Ukrainian nationals relegated to only the more subservient roles. As a result, there was no cadre of experienced Ukrainians to take control when the time came.

John Perryman, GBC's man in Kiev, told Charlie when he checked in, "The country is like a giant matryoshka doll. When you take out each doll they get smaller and smaller. After you finally get to the center there is nothing left but corruption. Either you learn to deal with it or you fail."

His assignment was in a small city in southwestern Ukraine by the name of Ivano Frankivsk. It was what was previously described as a "closed city." For years, the Russians had isolated the town because of a concentration of ICBMs concealed in the surrounding Carpathian Mountains. There were also a number of secret military electronic factories within the town itself.

Charlie's assignment was to assist one of these plants in converting their military offerings to a more market oriented consumer products line.

When he arrived, he was the first person from the "outside" most of the people had ever met, and certainly the first from their former enemy the United States. The assignment was a difficult one. There was considerable resistance by the factory management to his recommendations. Most of them were looking forward to the improbable return of the Russians in order to regain their previous position of power. Not unlike the situation he expected to find tomorrow among the management of mine.

It was after he finished his project and returned to Kiev that he ran into Karen. Fall was in the air, about the same time of year it was now in Kazakhstan he recalled with surprise. The chestnut trees that lined the avenues were beginning to lose their leaves, and they swirled aimlessly in the air.

The Orange Revolution was in full gear, and the Ukrainian students had been demonstrating daily against the corrupt government. As his cab passed Mayden Square, he could see an island of pitched tents and young men and women standing on discarded egg cartons attempting to protect their thinly soled sneakers from the concrete. He could see them singing and waving their orange banners in noisy defiance of the Kuchma government.

After several weeks of eating in the factory cafeteria, he was looking forward to a leisurely dinner before spending the next few days finishing his report, and writing his recommendations for the GBC.

Like all single diners, he was led to the restaurant's most obscure table, next to the clatter of the kitchen. At the far end of the dining room, he noticed a woman who appeared surprisingly familiar. She sat among a large group of men, some of whom looked to be Ukrainian, while others were dark complected, wearing gray business suits with black and white checked Kaffiyehs over their heads. Occasionally, one of them would turn to her as if they were seeking an explanation or advice.

He would recognize her anywhere, even though it had been several years since they last met. She was still a striking woman, tall and angular, always in command of her surroundings. Her dark brown hair was now blond, more fitting for a woman in Ukraine. She was well occupied, devoting her attentions as evenly as possible between the two groups—who seemed almost to be competing for her attention.

Charlie's table was some distance from hers, surrounded by a group of Japanese tourists, almost obscured by their large party.

He had first met Karen Kinkaid when he was a traveling Vice President of International at Apex Electronics in Chicago, and she was the local CIA representative there. She had come to the office and suggested that his knowledge could be helpful to the Agency and that she would like to "pick his brain" so to speak from time to time.

He had been agreeable, and they met from time to time. One day, she contacted him and asked if he would do the Agency a few small favors, occasionally during his travels. Nothing much. A meeting with a contact here, or an envelope dropped there. It would "of course never interfere with his job," she assured him. They wanted someone with no traceable ties to the CIA, and Charlie was perfect for the job. He did as Karen asked. No harm. No foul.

After awhile, Karen faded from the picture, and he was dealing more directly with the people in Washington. Charlie never heard from her again.

He learned later from Emmett that some people at the Agency believed she was turning over secrets to the Russians. When they went to pick her up, she vanished without a trace. Now here she was in Ukraine. He never believed that she would betray her country. Emmett had told him that he did not think so either.

He decided to see what she was up to before contacting the Agency. When the party broke-up, he followed her. Apparently, she had been away from the business long enough to become complacent, and she was easy to follow through the dark cobblestone streets of Kiev. He recalled that it had begun to rain, which made it easier. Everyone walked with their collar turned up or were hidden behind their umbrella.

Karen turned into an old apartment building, and Charlie watched from across the street. He soon saw lights go on up on the third floor, and decided to see what she was doing in Kiev. After going to her room, it turned out that she was working for the Ukrainian Government. She was of Ukrainian decent and had studied Russian at Sarah Lawrence. With her knowledge of armaments, she was perfect for them. They didn't ask any questions about her past, other than to know she had previously worked for the American Government before returning home—as she told them.

She acquired increasingly more responsibility, and soon earned the complete confidence of her superiors. It is easy to trust an attractive woman even in Ukraine. Eventually, they assigned her to help in their negotiations with the Islamists. They were interested in purchasing Russian Kh55 missiles that were previously stored in Ukraine, and abandoned by the Russians as they hastily vacated the country. Karen realized they were eventually intended to be used, one way or the other, against the United States or Israel, but she didn't know what to do about it--until Charlie crossed her path once more.

With the help of the CIA Station Chief at the American Embassy in Kiev, Karen and he were able to find and destroy the blueprints and manuals that the Russians had prepared. Without them, the Kh55s were of no use to Iran, and the deal fell through. There was just one problem. The Ukrainian Government was furious, and had a good idea what happened. They blocked the airport and the railroad stations while they looked for Karen.

The Station Chief at the Embassy helped them with new passports, and booked them on an Intourist cruise ship, leaving that night down the Dnieper River for Odessa.

On board, they thought they were safe, and began to relax and enjoy the trip. Until they stopped at a small town along the way, so the tourists could visit the Cossack Glory Museum and attend a horse show.

When they returned, a local KGB agent had joined the group, following-up on an alert that had been issued for Karen.

He began searching the cabins and eventually found her. He pulled his gun, just as Charlie entered the room. A look of sheer unmitigated hatred consumed the burly man's face when he saw the two of them together. The two men fought, and the gun discharged killing the agent.

That night, under a starless sky, they threw his body overboard. The two of them were in Odessa and on their way out of the country before the KGB goon was missed.

Karen caught a freighter to Tel Aviv where she knew some people in the Mossad who would help her. Charlie never heard from her again. He vowed then that he would never get mixed up with the Agency or their people ever again.

~~~

That was then. Now, here he was in an out of the way hotel room in an out of the way country geographically and culturally on the edge of the world. Still in contact with Emmett and the Agency, and hiding a gun he had smuggled through Customs. It seemed that he had learned nothing. It is crazy how time has the ability to lessen the impact of bad situations. They say it heals all wounds. He didn't know about that, but he had become well aware that memories seem less taxing as time goes on.

He would like to have become the callous practitioner he thought as he looked glumly around the light starved room, but he had never managed to keep from caring, and now it was probably far too late to change.

He took a small shortwave radio from his bag, and switched it on. He had carried it for years. It could be helpful in countries where the only news available was in a language you didn't understand. He had tried the black and white television on the desk, but could get only a blurry picture, which would come and go at will.

The electromagnetic field in the area was too strong to allow stable communications. Even if the TV did work
~~~

properly, he would be unable to understand anything the people were saying.

He fiddled with the dials on his radio, and listened to the world's hum. A shortwave isn't like a normal radio. It is more finicky and you have to play with it, particularly when you haven't used it before in a particular country. The same broadcasts don't always appear at the same time on the same position of the dial. You have to find them, and then remember where they were when you want to use them again.

He heard an English broadcast from China, soon replaced by NHK from Japan, before recognizing the chimes of Big Ben announcing the BBC.

A British soldier had been kidnapped in eastern Iraq, and there was an arrest of some terrorists in London who were planning to blow up the underground.

He would have to remember that spot on the dial. Finally, he found the Voice of America. They were playing music from the past. He liked that, and placed the radio close by on his nightstand.

Before going to bed, Charlie glanced out his window. A half moon cast a faint light on the yard below, forming a lacework of eerie shadows around the deserted motor vehicles in the nearby lot. Looking more intently, he thought he could see a moving silhouette leaving the hotel and heading toward the 4x4s. He wasn't sure, and turned away. He paused, and then turned back again. A cloud had covered the thin moon, and the shadow had disappeared.

As he drifted off to sleep, the radio was playing a song he recognized from a long time ago. Dinah Shore's voice came out of the small speakers and plaintively floated around the room.

Faraway places with strange sounding names, faraway over

The sea.

Those faraway places with strange sounding names keep calling,

Calling me.

Going to China and maybe Siam, I want to ....

Charlie finally fell asleep without fully appreciating the irony of Dinah's lyrics.

10

A sound on his window awakened Charlie from a troubled sleep. He checked his alarm and discovered he had failed to adjust it to the local time zone before going to bed. It was later than he liked, but nevertheless he began his morning routine of sixty pushups. They seemed a little more difficult than usual, and he paused at thirty-five before beginning again.

Glancing out the window he could see that it had begun to rain. A torrent of raindrops formed refracted rivulets down the grimy windowpane. Great! That was all they needed. An introduction to a hostile group of out-of-work miners on a cold rainy day.

The bathroom was directly across the hall from his room. During the night he occasionally could hear a shuffling of feet, and the bathroom door opening and closing.

Inside there was a small shower/bath combination; a sink, a mirror, and a reasonable toilet. Thank God, it wasn't a Turkish toilet as he had half expected. He had enough of those round holes in the floor on the project in Ukraine.

It was obvious that others had been there before him, judging from the stack of soiled towels piled haphazardly in the corner. He found a clean towel in a small cabinet by the sink and hurried through his shower before the tepid water turned cold.

While shaving he thought of home. During the night he had attempted to call Beth, but with no success. He had even been unable to make contact with an operator. It was not a surprise. He and his wife's relationship had been marked by a frequent inability to communicate, literally but not emotionally. They had become familiar with long separations as he traveled the world, and she capably managed the family. He sometimes thought it had drawn them closer together. What was that about absence and the heart. Maybe it was right.

He had noticed, however, that his character seemed to gradually change after he had been gone for awhile. He seemed to become Charlie the traveler rather than Charlie the husband and father, as the thread binding him to his family became more tenuous with the passage of time.

Returning to his room, he decided on his navy camel hair blazer and white button-down shirt. He wanted to look successful with an air of informality. The miners would expect a seasoned executive representing the Bank, and he had no intention of disappointing them.

He caught up with Andre in the hallway. "I hope to Christ it isn't going to be a Kazakh breakfast of warmed over besh—besha--beshamak," he stammered, "or whatever the hell that stuff was called last night."

Fortunately It wasn't that. Instead it was left over rice and frankfurters. The two men looked at each other and grinned. It could have been worse.

The other men and the two interpreters were already seated around the table, and Charlie took an empty chair between Nadia and Henry Butts.

The accountant leaned toward him. "Last night I got hungry," he whispered, "and I thought I would see if I could find something to eat. You know that bloody mess we...well anyway, when I got here I saw our man Sammie bonking the dombra player--stretched her out on the dining table. She was making a lot sweeter music than she had last night at dinner," he snickered.

"On this table?" Charlie asked, trying to reconstruct the scene in his mind. "Sammie?"

"Oh yes Sammie--it wasn't that dark, and they must have been sure we had all tucked in. Apparently, our man *Thursday* is active on other days as well. The cheeky bugger."

"Where Is Sammie?" Charlie asked turning to Nadia, trying to change the subject.

She didn't appear to hear the question. The interpreter was busy writing on her ever present pad--*bonk, bonked, bonking*. She looked puzzled, then began to smile. Sammie? Sammie? She giggled.

The hotel manager heard Charlie's question and interrupted her supervision of the breakfast service to reply that he had received a late night call, and had to return to Almaty.

"On that road? Late at night?" Charlie asked incredulously.

"He is very familiar with the area. He has been here many times," she replied as she continued to clear the table.

The group wanted to see the conference room before the mine management arrived. They huddled in their coats against the cold rain as they formed a line from the hotel to the administration building.

The building was impressive even on a dank day. It was a large two-story structure fronted by four giant Doric Style Roman Columns supporting a high peaked roof. They were all surprised that the Russians had constructed such an elaborate building in such a remote and gritty location.

The expansiveness of the lobby did nothing to dispel the gloom of the mostly vacant offices. Their doors were open, and an occasional clerk could be seen sitting idly behind a large desk, or lounging in front of a stack of dusty filing cabinets.

The ground floor was made of expensive marble. A curved mahogany staircase led to the second floor where the conference room was located. There was also a series of additional vacant offices on the second floor, fanning out on each side of the larger room.

Elaina elected the largest, with the most equipment, and began to set up shop. The others proceeded to the meeting room. Inside rows of metal folding chairs faced a small stage with a lone speaker's podium.

The night before the men had agreed on a sequence of events. Charlie would make the initial introductions, followed by the individual speakers. As the men reviewed again the principal points they felt it important to make, Nadia nervously circled the stage to find the best location to stand. She finally selected a position below the podium where both the speakers and the audience could best understand her.

On the wall behind them a large photograph of the President of Kazakhstan glumly surveyed the room's activities.

The miners began to straggle in. They were a broad shouldered, square jawed, sullen lot. There was no conversation or forced congeniality among them that would usually mark a similar gathering in the Western world. They were apparently knowledgeable of where each would sit by virtue of their pre-established organizational level.

The general manager occupied the first seat of the first row, followed by the assistant general manager, and then the individual directors.

As the miners settled in, a faint odor of stale vodka and tobacco smoke quickly permeate the room. Their mood seemed to fit the weather, and the flickering fluorescent ceiling lights did little to improve the bleak atmosphere. Tension filled the room.

Once the men settled in their hardback chairs, Charlie took the podium, and scanned the room. These bastards really do hate us, he decided.

Charlie stretched his body to its full height, lowered his shoulders to relax, and pointed his finger towards the photograph on the rear wall. "President Nursultan

Nazarbayev, he began, "is confident that with the proper investment and technology Tekeli can once again become an important and profitable mineral resource for the country of Kazakhstan."

Charlie paused, waiting for Nadia to begin her translation. He was painfully aware from past experience that not all interpreters are qualified. Some were good--some were bad--some active--some passive. They were like a machine with an electrical connection from mind to mouth. Charlie had dealt with all kinds in his travels. Nadia appeared to be one of the good ones. She seemed to be applying the proper emphasis, with a more masculine tone, and hopefully the correct Russian pronunciations.

"He has therefore asked the Global Bank Corp. to assist him in evaluating this resource, and provide..." As Charlie spoke, he studied the audience attempting to determine if any of them were listening, and if what he was saying was having any visible effect. The miner's faces were devoid of any expression.

Charlie's palms were becoming damp, but he pressed on "....and he would like you to cooperate with us so that we can provide the best recommendations possible."

Brevity was important, he reminded himself. Hell it was a god-damned necessity with this group. At least, he consoled himself, it can't get any worse.

"I would now like to introduce Henry Butts who is our financial expert, and who will describe the type of information that will be needed for him to complete his financial analysis."

Charlie sat down, and Henry took the stage.

Nadia continued to translate. Her face expressionless as she mentally converted from Charlie's American English to Henry's British English, and then subsequently weaving the words and phrases into the most palatable Russian vernacular she could possibly derive.

Henry squinted at the audience, attempting to convert their fuzzy features into sharper focus. "I appreciate the opportunity to meet with you, and to return to Kazakhstan, the place of my youth," he told them with a forced smile.

Charlie had been trying to think how he could better reach these hostile miners to enlist their cooperation, but what was it Henry had just said about the home of his youth? Had he heard that correctly? He must have because the accountant was continuing to explain his previous exposure to the country.

Henry continued to speak, occasionally awkwardly inserting Russian phrases between his English terms. His lips began to quiver and his words became less distinct. Then, tears began to cascade down his wrinkled face. Suddenly he was seized by deep uncontrolled sobs, accompanied quickly by a flood of tears. A dark shadow had descended and engulfed him. His former placid demeanor had been replaced by one of deep sadness and melancholy. He began to sob uncontrollably.

Nadia turned toward Charlie, a shocked expression on her face. The two mining consultants stared in disbelief. Charlie would have liked to pull his sport coat over his head, and sneak out of the room.

Instead, he bolted to the podium thinking, 'Oh my God it did get worse.' What must these hard headed miners think of the consultants that had come to solve their problems?' One thing people like these hate is a show of weakness, and Henry was displaying that in spades.

Placing his arm protectively on Henry's shoulders he led him rapidly from the stage, Charlie attempted to explain how his companion was so overcome with joy on returning to Kazakhstan he was temporarily having difficulty containing his exuberance. It wasn't a good explanation, but the best he could think of at the time.

As Henry returned to his chair, Andre quickly joined Charlie on the platform and began to tell the group, in his rough masculine voice, what he was planning to do for his part of the project.

Nadia regained her composure and implacably began to weave her linguistic way through a minefield of technical jargon.

Henry sat silently, once again withdrawn into himself. In a short while he, almost unnoticed, left the conference room for the solitude of his hotel room.

When Andre finished Dave Dieter replaced him, and began talking about how his responsibility was to evaluate the concentrator's efficiency before recommending any logistical improvements in the utilization and scheduling of the mines trucks and railroad cars.

Nadia converted seamlessly from Andre's slight French accent to the nasal tones of the Midwest. When she was unfamiliar with any of his technical terms, she merely repeated them as best she could, hoping they were universally understood in the mining community.

When the presentation ended, Charlie asked for questions. There were none. The general manager stood, and perfunctorily thanked the consultants for coming. The rest of the men rose in unison and began to file out of the room.

Charlie leapt from the podium and approached the general manager, hoping to establish some form of rapport. The Russian ignored his outstretched hand and turned to leave. Charlie considered following him and trying again. Nadia recognized what he was attempting and took a position by his side.

Before Charlie could continue, one of the assistant directors inserted himself between the two. The man's eyes were runny, and his breath foul. "*Nazdorovia ya sons ze beeches,*" he laughed, shoving Charlie backward while running calloused hands down his chest. Charlie was a tall man with broad shoulders and an aggressive temperament.

He had never been good at faking his feelings or shielding his emotions. Too much Irish perhaps. He sucked in his breath before cocking his right arm in preparation to give the miner more than he had received. Nadia's hand on his wrist provided a more rational restraint. Before he could reconsider, the miners had finished filing out of the room.

"Sorry," Nadia apologized.

"You were right, of course. Let's get the hell out of here." Charlie was furious. Not at Nadia, but at Henry, the miners, and the entire impossible situation.

Returning to his room, Charlie immediately tried to use the private number that Trevor Gunn had provided. Surprisingly it went through.

"Gunn here."

"How the hell could you have provided us with a twitchy accountant," Charlie roared, ignoring the cheerful greeting on the other end of the line.

"Whoa, whoa there, hold on old boy, what is going on up there?"

Gunn's composure infuriated Charlie even more, but after a moment he realized that there was no benefit in giving Gunn hell, and began more coolly to recount what had happened at the meeting.

"So he broke down sobbing in front of the miners. Good lord man," Trevor exclaimed, "that's very un-British I must say. Very dodgy. Very dodgy indeed. Why do you think that happened?"

"Don't know. He started out by talking about how he was glad to be back in Kazakhstan, and the more he talked the more he sobbed. Then Andre and I took over. Did you know he had been here before Trevor?"

"Not the foggiest. Nothing on his CV. But, unfortunately there is nothing that we can do about it now. We could never get someone up there in time to replace him. Try to find out what his problem is. You fellows keep an eye on him. I am sure you can work it out.

"Your confidence is deeply appreciated," Charlie replied with veiled sarcasm.

"By the way old man," Trevor hastened to add before closing the conversation, "I understand that we will be getting another American at your Embassy here. He is going to be replacing your fellow Durand. You know, the one that got murdered over in the oil fields. Do you know a Roger Pembroke? He is going to be the new Assistant Cultural Attaché."

"Never heard of him, but then I have never been too culturally inclined."

"Charlie—be careful up there, and keep in touch. We need to finish the project on schedule but we want you all safe as well."

"We will try to oblige Trevor."

After the call with GBC was completed, Charlie thought for a few minutes about how best to proceed. He wasn't sure, but one thing was certain. He needed to have confidence in the people with whom he was working. They all seemed competent, but then so had Henry. Sure he had a few quirks, but who doesn't he thought, opening his laptop.

He quickly composed an email to Emmett Valentine using a secure address. It listed the names of the people on the project, and to the best of his knowledge, where they came from. Emmett would know what to do with it. He had worked with the Agency long enough to know and they had extensive resources when it came to background checks. After hitting **Send** he knew that the message would travel the atmosphere like a phantom, first to be encrypted, then decrypted, and eventually placed on Emmett's desk, flagged for a rapid response.

The next thing was to find Henry and determine what his problem was, and what to do next. Andre and Dave were already in the lounge.

Charlie went down the hallway to Henry's room. He hesitated, and then tapped on the door. "Let's talk."

11

Karaganda

Henry had stopped crying. He seemed to have regained control of his emotions; but with his rumpled suit, tousled hair, and red-rimmed eyes he appeared, for all the world, like an accounting artifact from hell.

By the time the two of them entered the lounge, Andre was uncorking some of his Chilean reserve, and Dave had managed to scrounge-up four clean glasses from the kitchen.

"Que pasa mi amigo?" Andre inquired pleasantly, passing an overflowing glass of white to Henry. He took it gratefully, and drained it before speaking. "Oh my God, I am terribly sorry. I had no idea that would happen. I thought I could get through it without a problem." He handed his glass back to Andre who quickly refilled it.

The men were silent, then Charlie finally blurted, "what the hell was that all about?" As soon as the words were out of his mouth, he felt badly. He knew he should have been more tactful, more indirect.

"I don't know where to begin," Henry mumbled, "my name is not really Henry Butts. I changed it when I came to England. It is really Henry Butofski. I was born in Poland before the war. My father was a mathematician. When the Russians rolled through our town, they rounded up all the Jewish families they thought could be helpful to them and tossed us into freight cars-- They packed us in like kippers in a can. At first there was no food no water, no toilets--it was terrible. The worst was the cold. Oh my God the cold!" His voice trailed off.

Andre refilled Henry's glass once more.

"Anyway....." Charlie said, encouraging him to continue.

"Well anyway," Henry picked up the thread. "We traveled for days. For weeks. I don't know. Finally, we ended up in Kazakhstan. Kazakhstan for God's sake! None of us had ever heard of the place. Even my father, who was an educated man, had never heard of Kazakhstan.

"What happened then?" Dave prompted sympathetically.

"They put us in these camps, Gulags they called them. Do you know what Gulag stands for?" Henry asked, his voice full of bitterness. "It is a Russian acronym for the Chief Administration of Corrective Labor Camps that ran the system. The Russians had camps everywhere.

"Karlag was the name of the Gulag network in Kazakhstan. We were *zeks.* That is what they call convicts—criminals in Russia. We were criminals to them. We were just zeks—just ciphers."

The little accountant paced back and forth in the small lounge while he described his family's terrifying experience at the hands of the Soviets. As his story unfolded he became increasingly agitated, and his pace quickened.

"I believe they planned to use my father and his mathematical training on their nuclear program. But, it was wartime. The main thing was to get people who might be harmful to them out of the way. Kazakhstan was the most God forsaken place they could think of. Somehow, the paperwork must have got bollixed up, and they sent us to Karaganda to work in the mines. Men, women and children. We were like the donkeys that pulled the wagons out of the tunnels. The only reason they didn't starve us to death was that they needed the ore."

Henry paused, lost in his thoughts.

Andre refilled his glass, although this time it was not nearly close to being empty.

"Before the war, people thought that the area was uninhabitable," Henry continued. The Russians figured that would be the perfect place for a dumping ground, and they needed a supply of minerals for their war effort. The camp ran for miles. I can still remember how they drove us from the train—we rode and rode. Along the way, I could see areas where there was nothing but mounds of dirt. I learned later they were mass graves."

Nadia slipped into the room, unnoticed by Henry, and took a place on the couch next to Charlie. He slid his untouched wine glass toward her, but she shook her head with a faint smile.

Henry took a sip of wine, and cleared his throat. "There were people from all over Europe at the camp. People from Hungary, Poland, Lithuania--Germany, of course. The Germans were treated the worst—if you can imagine that. We had schoolteachers, scientists, artists, the whole goddamn gamut of occupations and professions.... except those like doctors that would be more valuable at the front.

"My mother died within the first six months. My father lasted a year. Another Polish couple, without children, adopted me—if you can call it that. They tried to take care of me as best they could. They shared their rations, and tried to comfort me over the loss of my parents."

Henry's eyes began to fill up again. He paused for a moment and blew his nose before continuing. "After the war was over, they didn't need us anymore, and we were told that we could leave or stay—whichever we wanted. No one wanted to stay, but how to leave, where could you go? Eastern Europe was occupied by the Russians, Germany was in shambles, France was trying to recover from the occupation.

"Somehow, the Vatican was working behind the scenes attempting to arrange homes for some of the children by claiming they were Catholic. I don't know how I got chosen. Just luck I guess. I had to sign a certificate stating I was Catholic. The Polish family had to sign it as well.

"The Church was able to get us to England, with the help of some relief organizations. They placed me with a Catholic family. There are Catholics in England you know."

No one answered.

"I got an English education, and was raised a Catholic. So you see standing before you a Catholic Jew or a Jewish Catholic. I am never sure which. Anyway, I became an accountant, and eventually set up my own business."

"What brought you back to Kazakhstan?" Nadia asked gently.

Her question seemed to startle Henry. Apparently, he had been so lost in his recollections he had not seen her enter the lounge.

"You must hate the Kazakhs and the Russians," she added.

"Why did I come back here?" he replied puzzled. "That's a good question. Eventually, I sold my business in England and started doing consulting work. I think I mentioned back in Almaty that I had worked for the World Bank on some projects, and when I heard that GBC was looking for an accountant for a project in Kazakhstan I thought it would be interesting to see what the country was like now. I guess, now that I think about it, I really wanted to confront my own demons. The terrible dreams—the night sweats. I always had trouble getting along with people for any length of time. My wife left me after just a few years.

"It was a terrible mistake coming back. I realized that on the ride up here. The deeper we got into the country, the more I regretted coming. Then when I took the podium today, and looked out on all those Russian faces, everything came flooding back, and I was overwhelmed. I could almost feel the cold, and smell the odor of death, and I just lost control.

"But that's over now. It's out of my system. I know it is. I will be all right. I guarantee it." Henry stared at his associates imploringly with his red-rimmed eyes, begging for their acceptance.

"You must still hate the Kazakhs and Russians?" Charlie repeated Nadia's question. It was important to get a feeling for Henry's emotional stability. He knew the miners had no time for the visiting consultants. That was accepted, but if Henry was on some kind of a vendetta that would really make their task impossible.

Henry pursed his lips. "No-- no I don't. Surely, nothing was the fault of the Kazakhs, he added "They just happened to live in an out of the way place that was rich in minerals that could provide a dumping ground for the perceived enemies of the Communist Party.

"The Russians? Well, that is another thing. I hated the Communists. That's a certainty. Now I'm over it. It was a long while ago. No problem now. I will be all right. I know my job, and I can do it better than most. I want to stay and finish the project. I am sorry I broke down. It won't happen again." He looked at his associates, who nodded their acceptance.

Henry drained his glass, and started back to his room. "I need to get some sleep," he told them. "I'll be fine in the morning."

Halfway through the door, he paused. "Did you know that Solzhenitsyn was a zek in Kazakhstan? That's where he wrote *One Day in the Life of Ivan Denisovich.*" The significance of his parting statement was lost on the group. But, it was obviously important to Henry.

After he had left, Charlie thought about what he had just heard. He still had many questions running through his mind. He wanted to respond but instead turned to the group. "What do you think? Can he do the job?"

Each man looked at the other. Finally, Andre offered, "What is our option? What is the alternative? I am not an accountant, and I don't think any of you fellows are either. They never could find someone else, and get him up here in time to meet Trevor Gunn's schedule. We have no choice."

"Agreed," Charlie muttered.

"You know that Elaina is pretty good with numbers," Nadia offered. "That is what she did in the office at GBC. She obviously doesn't have the level of experience that Henry does, but she can back him up if need be."

Charlie considered her suggestion. There really wasn't much choice, but with Elaina as support, and doing most of the interface with the mine staff, it might work.

"OK let's stick with him," Charlie offered. The others nodded their agreement.

Andre left to inspect the mine, and the others drifted back to their rooms.

Charlie began to change for dinner. He was drained. The others must be worn out as well. You had to give Andre credit to go into the mine so late in the day.

He took off the blazer and hung it carefully in the armoire. His shirt was damp and it stuck to his back. As he peeled it off and tossed it onto the bed, a small piece of paper fluttered to the floor. "What the hell was that?" he wondered, stooping to pick it up.

Carefully unfolding the soiled, blue-lined paper, he tried to figure out how it got into his pocket in the first place. He recalled the shirt was fresh from the laundry when he unfolded it that morning. It couldn't have been in there then.

He replayed the day's events. The note couldn't have been in his shirt when he put it on, so how in the hell did it get in his pocket. If not then how? The only answer he could come-up with was that the miner who shoved him at the meeting might have slipped it into his pocket when he ran his hands down his chest. Perhaps—just perhaps, but why?

The note had a diagram of some sort. He could make out two vertical lines leading to a series of horizontal ones running in divergent directions. At several points on the diagram, there were crudely penciled Russian words. He could tell that much, but he didn't understand the drawing, or what might be written on it. It must have been important to the miner, but he had no idea why that might be.

"Nadia," he shouted, but she had already returned to her room.

12

Almaty

Roger stared bleakly at the soul crushing sameness of the cinder block architecture his cab was passing on its way from the airport to the American Embassy. He was shocked when Mr. Valentine called him into his office and told him he would be leaving immediately for Kazakhstan. He could still recall, with considerable clarity, and some concern, Mr. Valentine telling him 'this is not a training mission Roger. We do not have the time, or the available personnel, to break you in slowly. It's *o-p-e-r-a-t-i-o-n-a-l*,' pronouncing the word very slowly to convey all the risk inherent in such an early assignment.

Hell! The only time he had even traveled out of the country before was when he and his friends would go down to Cabo San Lucas for spring break. Now he was in Central Asia. Join the CIA and see the world--that was part of the allure the Agency offered to its new recruits.

But Kazakhstan for God's sake! The only thing he knew about the country was from watching Sacha Baron Cohen's movie *Borat*. He had seen it twice when he was in college, and thought it was hilarious. It was obvious from what he had seen so far the movie bore little resemblance to reality. He knew the country was an emerging petro-power, and it was possible in the future it could become one of the world's major producers of oil and gas. They had at least told him that before he left, but he could see little evidence of that as his cab raced through the gray early morning streets.

He was nervous. There was no denying it. He knew eventually he would be going into the field. It was what he wanted. That was what all the new recruits wanted. It was just that he thought it would be later rather than sooner. He was shocked when Mr. Valentine told him he was replacing a murdered agent. Shocked hell, he was scared stiff after he had time on the plane to think it over. But, this was his big chance. He was well of that, and he did not want to screw it up.

The taxi pulled to an abrupt stop in front of the American Embassy. Roger paid the driver, and grabbed his bag out of the trunk. A tall iron fence separated the building from the street. He showed his passport to the Marine guard at the gate who, after glancing at his picture, waved him through. The embassy was in an old multi-storied Russian style box building with a reflective dark coating on all of the windows.

Once inside, Roger approached another Marine, a sergeant with three rows of "fruit salad" on the chest of his dress blue tunic. He was a powerfully built man with a wrinkled world-weary face, situated behind a glass-enclosed desk, centered under the official print of President Barak Obama.

"Roger Pembroke for Michael Perlman" Roger announced, handing his passport through the small opening on the counter.

"Ledger," the Marine pointed to an open register with signatures of recent visitors.

"Wait over there please," the sergeant, drawled, pointing to a cluster of overstuffed chairs surrounding a glass table on the other side of the lobby. Roger saw the Marine pick-up the phone as he took a seat and selected a copy of last month's Time magazine from a stack strewn haphazardly across the table.

As soon as he opened the magazine, he heard his name called. Looking up, he saw a small Asian woman approaching. "Follow me," she smiled pleasantly, leading Roger down a long poorly lit hallway past several unmarked closed doors.

The young woman's high-heeled boots tap-tapped a quick cadence on the hallway's highly buffed surface, while fluorescent lights cast eerie shadows along the empty hall.

"In there" she pointed to the door on his right. "Mr. Perlman is expecting you."

The office was large. The Cultural Attaché was a small dour looking man seated behind a highly polished walnut desk. Despite his size, he was a powerful looking man with broad shoulders, and a large baldhead that glistened in the bright fluorescent light. He had narrow slits for eyes, like someone who had spent too many hours gazing into the sun, but his pallid complexion gave a lie to the story his eyes told.

Pearlman's most distinguishing feature was a deep red scar that ran across his forehead and down his cheek, past his cold grey eyes before disappearing into the man's bushy Calvary officer's mustache. He rose and extended his hand. "Ah my new man-- sit down. I was just looking over your papers. You know anything about culture?" he laughed.

Standing, the station chief looked older than Roger had first thought. The lack of any eyebrows, combined with the bristling mustache gave the man's face a rather macabre appearance.

"No not much," Roger replied nervously clearing his throat.

"Not a problem. As you know, it is just a cover. My principal role is CIA Station Chief. The culture thing gives us an opportunity to move around the country. Meet people, attend parties, hold poetry readings, and all that culture crap.

"The Agency always believes that if they bury their people in some pussy job at the embassies—something like commercial or cultural attaché, no one will know that they are actually spooks. Of course the people that matter—the opposition—they all have a pretty good idea. But, what the hell, maybe it keeps them guessing for awhile. It also seems less offensive to friendly governments who get uneasy about having CIA guys fooling around in their country.

"Anyway, you just met my assistant who brought you in here. She is pretty good—Chinese type Kazakh—lived here a long while. Used to be secretary to the ambassadors wife, but wanted a job with more substance. The ambassador asked me to take her, and she has been a lot of help. I am also head of embassy security and she had already been cleared by the ambassador's staff so I was glad to get her. She knows her way around the country, and her husband works across town for the Global Bank Corp. So don't get any ideas," Pearlman added jokingly.

That had been the furthest thing from Roger's mind, but now that it was mentioned, she was damned attractive. Dark black hair, graceful walk, and small round breasts. Damned appealing in an exotic Byzantine Asian way.

"You work for Emmett Valentine. Right?"

"That's right, Mr. Pearlman."

"Michael, OK?"

"OK Michael," Roger replied, relaxing a bit. I have worked for him for several months. Started right after I finished training at the Farm. It was a good introduction to the workings of the Agency. When he learned that Barry Durand got eliminated, he wanted to fill the vacancy as quickly as possible. I guess I was available."

"I've known Valentine for a long time," Pearlman offered. "Knew him when he was with the Agency the last time. They called him the maestro. Always playing music," he chuckled. But, he is one hell of a man. He has forgotten more about gathering intelligence than most people ever knew. I am sure he would not have sent you here if he didn't think you could do the job.

"So now, we have to think about how we are going to work you in here. We have an embassy party tonight so you can attend and meet the ambassador and his people. They are entertaining some American oilmen who are in the country eager to meet and greet the Kazakh officials. Later we will work you around town a bit to get you acquainted. Get familiar with some of the NGOs. USAID, World Bank, GBC and the entire alphabet of development organizations that operate in Almaty.

"By the way Roger let your hair grow."

"My *hair* grow?" Roger asked puzzled.

"Yeah, let your hair grow longer. Maybe get some glasses. Tomorrow we will send you over to see the embassy's doc. He can fit you with some clear glasses. Yeah that's a good idea," Pearlman added, complimenting himself on his ingenuity. "You don't look too cultured. Too athletic. Did you play some type of ball in school?"

"Lacrosse," Roger replied, taken off-guard.

"OK—OK long hair and glasses." That will make you look more cultured," he laughed. "That will do it. Then later today we will get you a weapon."

"What do you use here?" Roger asked. This was more like it.

"Well we—hell, I am partial to the Glock 19. It packs a hell of a punch, but the base model is only about 6 inches long. It comes with a 15 shot magazine. You can also get an extended clip that will hold 33 bullets. Of course, that won't be necessary unless the embassy comes under attack," he laughed.

Strange sense of humor, Roger thought to himself, but smiled in acceptance.

"Have you ever used one of them before?"

"In training," Roger replied. "They tried to acquaint us with all kinds of weapons we might have to use."

"Good, we have a small range in the basement here if you ever want to practice. The jarheads guarding the gates like to keep in practice and some of us go down there sometimes to keep our hand in.

"We try to provide them with as much diversion as possible. Usually it's only the older marines assigned to the embassies. There was a problem a few years ago at the Moscow station. One of the guards—a young stud—got bored and started fooling around with a local Russian broad. Ended up feeding her all kinds of classified information. He's serving time now, and the State Department is more careful about who they assign.

"In a couple of days, after you get settled," Pearlman moved on to a different subject, "we will start moving you around the country. Over to the oil fields, of course, but maybe that can wait for a while, all things considered. We don't want you ending up like Durand. At least not right away," he chuckled. "It would make me look bad to lose another agent.

"That quickly," he added as an afterthought.

His comments didn't seem overly reassuring.

"Do you have any idea what happened to him?" Roger asked.

"None—nada—zip—I have been going over our system here, but no idea. I reviewed our approach with headquarters, and they have been no help. No surprise. Someway, his name got leaked to the opposition, and we don't even know who or which opposition we are dealing with. Could be the Russians or..."

"Mr. Valentine thinks it was the Russians."

"Emmett always thinks it's the Russians," Perlman laughed. "And who knows maybe he is right. We are sure they were the ones fomenting the problems in Kyrgyzstan a few weeks ago."

"Really—what makes you think that?"

"Well there was this newspaper guy—Syrgak Abdyldayev, or something like that. He reported in the local paper that there was a large group of Russian-speaking specialists that arrived to advise the Kyrgyz government. Shortly afterwards, President Bakiyev began to look to Russia for financial support, and then he began ignoring any of the opposing local factions. The reporter referred to the Russian's assistance, "as oxygen for a sinking submarine."

"That was pretty colorful prose," Roger observed.

"Too damned colorful for his own good it appears. In no time, three men with metal pipes attacked the poor bastard as he left his newspaper office. The goons broke both his arms, along with his ribs and a leg, and stabbed him 26 times in the ass."

"Whew," Roger exhaled. "That would certainly make a believer out of me."

The two men looked at each other. There was nothing more to add. They both knew they were in a tough business.

"I also want you to get up to the Cosmodrome sometime," the station chief continued. *"By the rockets' red glare,"* he hummed to himself, looking into his desk for a file. "Ok, ok, here it is" he exclaimed, taking out a dog-eared manila folder from his top drawer. "Tomorrow I got to get organized. That would be a good job for my assistant," he added. She was good looking, he thought to himself. It would be nice to have her close by working on those files. "Here is a list of contacts we have developed up there. You can look them over before you go."

"Don't you keep those locked up?" Roger asked incredulously.

"Yeah—yeah sometimes. Problem is, everything we got is classified, and the safe will only hold so much. Anyway, no one would know what the names represent. For all they know they might belong to the cleaning service.

"You understand, these are not our people, they are our *joes.* We have recruited them. We pay them. We buy and sell them. They're kind of like a rent a spy.

"For one reason or another, they are willing to provide us with inside information—at least they claim it is inside information—our job is to verify it—on what the Russians are doing, and sometimes even what the Kazakhs are doing. But, we have to be damned careful about that. It wouldn't do to get our asses kicked out of the country. Langley wouldn't like that at all.

"That's going to be part of your job here," Perlman explained warming to his job of indoctrinating the new man, "to develop contacts. Build up a stable of your own joes. They can be priests, peasants, parolees, politicians, or perverts. Whatever gets the job done, as long as they have access we could care less," he added with unveiled cynicism.

"That's what Durand was doing when he got erased. He was very good at running joes. He had a lot of experience at that before he got here."

"Anyway, I think maybe we will scrub the Cosmodrome for now, a good place for you to start would be going up to Tekeli. That should be a reasonably safe place to start. You know Charlie Connelly?"

Roger nodded, startled at the change of direction. "Yeah, I have heard of him. Mr. Valentine told me about Connelly. He is kind of a friend of his. Worked for him before I guess."

"That's right. I have never met him, but Emmett says he is one of the best amateurs he has ever seen. He has him hidden on the GBC privatization project. I don't think that Trevor Gunn, who runs their office here, knows he is doing double duty—so we have to be careful."

"I understand," Roger assured his new boss. "Mr. Valentine warned me about that. But, he did want me to establish contact. Apparently, you can't be sure when he might need some help."

"Everyone is pretty familiar with the oil and gas reserves here," the station chief explained. "All the countries are trying to get their part of the action. At the same time Kazakhstan has important mineral resources other countries need. Particularly now their industries are picking up and converting to new technologies. We are surrounded here by other stronger countries that would do anything to get their hands on some of these reserves. This always leads to corruption and turmoil, and the lead and zinc reserves are right in the center of their scopes."

He was interrupted by his secretary announcing, "Mr. Pearlman, the man from the newspaper is waiting in the lobby to see you about the male chorus that is touring the country."

"Thank you Mei Lyn. Go bring him in."

"Good to meet you Roger, and welcome to Kazakhstan," Michael Pearlman brusquely dismissed his new agent before moving on to the less interesting aspects of his job.

13

Tekeli

It was obvious to Charlie that he would need Nadia to translate the Russian words if he were to make any sense out of the puzzling diagram, but he wasn't sure which room she was assigned. "Nadia, Nadia" he called loudly as he walked down the hallway.

A door opened at the far end, next to the kitchen. Nadia, wearing a white loosely-fitting robe, peered out of her doorway, curious to see who was calling her name. The light from the room behind her, presented a distorted silhouette in the dim hallway.

"I was just getting ready to take a shower," she offered embarrassed.

"I need your help," Charlie told her, passing by her in the doorway, stepping over her discarded clothes and lingerie littering the floor.

Nadia's blush burned through her normally light complexion, as she stooped to pick up her discarded clothes..

The room was considerably smaller than his was. It contained a bed, a desk, one chair, a small sink below a cloudy mirror, leaving little unoccupied space.

"Take a look at this," he told her sitting on the edge of the bed.

Nadia took the folded paper from him, and peered at it, seemingly as perplexed with the rough diagram as Charlie was. She turned away to retrieve her glasses from the top of her desk.

While she studied the diagram, Charlie recognized that it was an awkward situation, and he tried to set her at ease. "Nadia," he began, "I think you did a great job of translation this morning, under very difficult conditions with a hostile audience. I have used many of them around……"

"What is it?" she asked, sitting beside him examining the crumpled paper, ignoring his attempted compliment.

"Don't know. It fell out of my shirt pocket when I was changing my clothes. The only thing I can figure out is that the wild-eyed miner who shoved me must have slipped it into my pocket. I can't make any sense out of it, and thought you might understand the words."

Nadia rotated the paper holding it up to the light. The diagram bore circles, numbers ranging from 1 to 3 digits, parallel and squiggly lines, and arrows leading in different directions. It must have been difficult for a man's hand to squeeze so much onto such a small scrap of paper.

Nadia handed the diagram back to Charlie. "He is obviously not an artist," she observed blandly, returning to her desk. She picked up a well-worn Russian/English dictionary, and withdrew a note pad from a desk drawer before returning to the bed.

Charlie held the diagram so she could see it as she began to make a list of the translated words. Minutes before, she was a blushing embarrassed young woman, tightly clutching her robe around her. Now she had become transformed into a Germanic style super-organizer, translating barely intelligible scribbles into words that might be better understood by her foreign associates.

Pursing her lips, she wrote on her pad:

concentrator,

repair and machine works,

mouth,

"What are you getting?" Charlie asked.

Nadia shrugged and continued studying the diagram completely engrossed in her task.

cage,

shaft,

ventilator,

As she bent over her note pad, attempting to translate unfamiliar terms, Charlie couldn't avoid noticing her increasingly exposed breasts.

She unconsciously adjusted her round thick spectacles, that were reflecting the glare from the fluorescent overhead light. Probably Russian Government issued. No make-up. Tough but vulnerable. Considerably younger than Charlie. No nonsense here he concluded. She's all business.

underground supervisor's office,

tunnel 1,

wagon track,

Can you make any sense out of it at all? Charlie asked impatiently.

"Not a lot," she answered, adjusting her robe before handing him the list of terms she had completed. "I think it is probably the location of the mine, but we already knew where that was. Look here, this must be the entranceway, and this looks like it may be the lift, but after that I have no idea what it shows. See these arrows. They must be showing direction. But then, these symbols—what could they mean? Look here at these four or maybe five—they're badly smudged—parallel lines. I have no idea what most of these other things are—either in Russian or English."

"Or why the hell the guy would make such an effort to give the note to us without anyone seeing him." Charlie added in frustration. "He must have thought it was important, but to whom? To us or to him?

"Supper's ready in a few minutes," the hotel manager announced primly, poking her head tentatively through the open doorway, surprised to find Charlie there.

"We'll show it to Andre, maybe he can figure it out," Charlie decided, as he left for the dining room.

The meals were improving. Nadia and Elaina had been advising the cooks on dishes that were more acceptable to foreign tastes. The group had also learned that it was better to refrain from asking "what's in this?" The dining area was also better lighted than before. Some of the burnt out bulbs had been replaced. The staff also seemed friendlier, but the dombra player had not reappeared.

Of course, it also helped that Andre seemed to have an inexhaustible supply of Chilean wine. "This is one of my favorites," he told them enthusiastically. It's a Cono Sur Sauvignon Blanc, and it is as good as any of the French, and not nearly as expensive. You know," he continued "some people refer to Chile as the Bordeaux of South America. Recently, it has been attracting some of the Old World grape superstars like Chateau Lafitte Rothschild, Paul Pontallier of Chateau Margaux, and Robert Mondavi to name a few."

As Andre expounded at length on his favorite subject, he seemed completely oblivious to the mine dust on his shoulders, and peppering his silver hair.

As Andre's voice droned on, Charlie's mind wandered back to the note in his pocket. He continued to try and understand its importance, and why it was given to him.

Once the hotel staff began serving the meals, the attention of the group turned to their food. Only small talk went on among the diners who studiously avoided any further discussion of what had happened during the morning meeting.

Henry apparently had regained his composure by temporarily shelving his emotional breakdown in the same manner he might have previously dealt with an aberrant account.

The approach seemed successful since he approached his meal with obvious enthusiasm, eating more than usual.

Finished, the group filed out of the dining room, Charlie tugged at Andre's sleeve. "I have something I want you to look at," he said handing over the diagram.

"Where did you get this?" Andre asked.

Charlie related his theory about the wild-eyed miner.

"I didn't see him do that, but I left before you did. What do you think it is?" Andre asked turning it over slowly in his hand. He was obviously unsure which was the top and which was the bottom.

"We hoped you could tell us," Nadia told him after joining the two men outside the dining room.

"Nadia translated the Russian terms into English," Charlie added, handing Andre the list. "See if that helps."

"The Tekeli Lead and Zinc Combinat," Andre explained "includes a number of structural units. The Tekeli underground mine; the Tuyuk underground mining site, the concentrator plant, a railway shop, maintenance shops, the motor transport shop, an energy plant, a special repair shop—that's by the construction and underground erection area—they also do chemical analysis there. Then there is the fire protection building, a cafeteria, and a mini brewery. Can't have a mine without a brewery" he grinned, "especially a Russian mine."

Your diagram shows the concentrator plant, so I guess this is the Tekeli shaft and not the Tuyuk. It is the bigger of the two. I was down there this afternoon. I can recognize some things, but not others.

Your miner obviously thought that it was important you have this, so there must be some significance to it. Not just some childish drawing," he added not fully convinced, looking more closely at the crude markings.

"That was what Nadia and I decided when she finished her translation. We hoped you could figure that out."

'Sorry amigo," Andre grinned. "There is only one way to find out. Tomorrow, the three of us go down there. Have you ever been in a mine before?" he asked.

Charlie and Nadia looked at each other. This was obviously not the answer either one wanted to hear.

"You think that is the only way huh?" Charlie asked. "What about.....? His voice trailed off.

"Yeah, what about it. Look at it as a learning experience" Andre suggested with a broad smile on his face. "I need to go back down anyway. I want to take some samples and see if Dave is able to analyze them with some of the gear he brought along. Some of the sides of the shafts look like they might contain something other than lead or zinc. The stuff looks odd. It is probably just some anomaly, but I don't recognize it. Anyway, we won't be getting in anyone's way, the mine hasn't been worked for weeks," Andre added attempting to be reassuring.

Back in his room, Charlie sent an email to Beth, to tell her about the meeting earlier in the day, but omitting the part about the note or what they planned to do tomorrow. Afterwards, he stretched out on the bed, not listening to the orchestra he had tuned-in on the shortwave. His mind was on the following day—on the damned mine. He wasn't afraid to go underground, he told himself.

He wasn't claustrophobic. Not really. He had MRIs before, where they put you into a narrow tube and bang your eardrums with high velocity sound. It hadn't bothered him---*much*. It did some people though. Some people had to take a sedative. Not him. But, the idea of going a mile below the surface of the earth, that was an entirely different thing.

The problem was he had very little confidence in third world maintenance programs and their equipment. There was that time when Beth and he had gone to the top of the Rock of Gibraltar in a cable car. The damn thing swayed in the wind. Back and forth. *Back and forth.*

The beat of the orchestra's music on the radio seemed to him it be in sync with his mental image of the swaying gondola.

On the way down the cable became stuck. The operator tried to make it swing to get the cable back on track. Back and forth. It didn't catch. Then he opened-up a trap door in the top of the cab, climbed out, stood up, and jumped up and down. He jumped up and down on the roof, while they swung back and forth thousands of feet above ground. The cable finally caught, and they continued their descent. When they reached the bottom, the manager turned away the waiting crowd, telling them they were shutting down for routine maintenance. *Routine my ass.*

He also recalled some of the dumpy third world airlines it had been necessary for him to fly as part of his job. Air Brunei—Aero Peru—Ecuadorian, Air Surinam and Garuda immediately crossed his mind. He hadn't wanted to use them, but it was the only way he could get to where he was going. The equipment was all right, but he was sure the bozos who ran the airlines weren't spending any more money than they absolutely had to on maintenance, and they didn't have too much money to start with.

But, he had survived. No big deal. And, he got the job done. That was the main thing. That was what they paid him to do. That was what kept the kids in college and food on the table.

Maybe this would be all right too. Probably would be. Nadia didn't seem to have any qualms about going down there--how could he?

Then again, he thought, this whole damn thing could be a diversion to get them spending their time mucking around in a dead mine, rather than finishing the project they were sent to do.

On the other hand, he suddenly realized, it could even be a trap. Get some of those smart-ass yahoos down there and knock them off. *That would finish the project all right.*

Now, the miners know these foreign guys are a soft touch. They even break down and cry during an opening speech.

Oh to hell with it, he decided. Whoever said, earlier in the day, that 'we have no other option' was right. I *have* to go down in the mine with Andre and Nadia.

Charlie clicked off the radio, punched his pillow, and tried to shut off his mind and get to sleep.

14

The morning was crisp and clear. A deep sleep had effectively banished Connelly's profound concerns of the night before. After completing his daily number of pushups, he felt refreshed and renewed, prepared to face whatever the day required.

After breakfast, Henry and Elaina went to the Administration Building to set up their procedures, and pore over the information that Sammie had acquired during his previous visits to Tekeli.

Dave went back to his room to finish calibrating his equipment.

Charlie, Andre, and Nadia returned to their rooms to get their coats before setting off on foot for the mine.

"It's not too far," Andre assured them as they began their trek to the mine.

They passed the dilapidated heavy vehicles parked in the lot close to the hotel. The streets were almost deserted, with only an old woman inspecting her garden, or a slight flutter of a lace curtain in a home as they passed. An occasional gray column of smoke rose from several of the houses, suggesting they were not as abandoned as they might initially appear.

Walking along the street, the three of them did present a rather peculiar procession Charlie had to admit. A silver topped Frenchman with a ruddy complexion, flanked by a red haired Russian woman wearing a heavy leather jacket and a matching fur trimmed hat, escorted by a gangly American in a

Burberry trench coat. No wonder some of the villagers could not resist monitoring their progression.

They paused for a moment to study a large lead sculpture of a miner prepared for work, dressed in miners cap, coat, and boots. The Russians had a talent for erecting sculptures of fierce fighting men or heroic male or female workers glorifying one occupation or another.

It was still too early for the brewery to open, but there was a small group of men already waiting to be welcomed by the manager. They stared curiously at the passersby before hastily turning their attention back to the brewery's locked door. The barber sat idly in the shop's only chair, focusing her attention on the newcomers, and perhaps potential customers. Her regular ones were few and far between as their income had gradually dwindled.

Andre chose a path through a stand of silver birch that defined the outskirts of the village. The wind sighed through the trees as they walked. "It's shorter this way," he assured them, brushing a slender branch from his face.

They soon left the small forest behind them, and the mouth of the mine came into view. It was a gaping hole in the side of a hill. A thick growth of underbrush was beginning to fill in the gaps between the rusting tracks that led to the mine's entrance. A single metal tub remained on the rails that once bore the ore to the nearby compressor.

There was no gate or obstruction limiting entrance to the area, nor a fence surrounding it. Only a few of the shoddy buildings appeared locked. Several had broken windows, their panes rattled in the breeze creating an eerie form of wind chime. One of the larger shed's roof was collapsed, and birds flew in and out of the vacant building at will.

"In here," Andre told them, entering the building nearest the entrance. "I found this yesterday. I couldn't get the damned generator going so there are no lights underground. We will each need a lamp," he advised, as he walked to the back of the ramshackle building. Along the wall, there was a series of large shelves holding rows of brightly colored metal helmets. Crowning the top of each yellow helmet was a large battery powered lamp.

Charlie eventually found one that seemed to fit. When he turned to look at the others Nadia giggled. "You look like a gigantic Cyclops from another planet," she told him, ignoring the effect that the yellow hat had on her own appearance.

"And you of course look very debonair," he replied with a broad grin.

They looked at each other to make sure their lamps worked before entering the mine. Once inside, the outer light began to fade the further in they got.

"This is a deep one," Andre warned. "If closets make you uneasy you may want to reconsider going down. Once you get below, it might be hard to get back up quickly enough."

Well, this won't bother me, at least that was what Charlie told himself, halfway hoping Nadia would decide to bow out. He glanced at her. She nonchalantly shrugged her lack of concern.

The three entered the open cage. Andre took the controls. "Last chance," he laughed, pushing a large red lever forward. His gallows humor was lost in the clang of the warning bell. The cable screamed, then caught and the cage began to drop into the hell of a deep mine.

The wire enclosure started to descend slowly down through the concrete lined upper mouth of the abandoned shaft, passing into a beehive of steel and timber lining the walls of the narrow passage. The mesh enclosure had a strong odor of diesel fuel mixed with body odor left over from generations of sweating men.

It quickly picked-up speed, now dropping so fast Charlie could feel his breath rushing from his lungs. Miner's pay doesn't begin until they check in on the floor of the mine, and they don 't want to waste any time along the way.

Charlie was certain that the lift was going to drop like a rock--but it did not. Not quite.

It was black as pitch above them, and equally as opaque beneath. The lights from their helmets cast faint illumination on the walls of the mine as they passed.

Once, Charlie thought he could make out an older abandoned landing but they speed past so fast he was not sure. He could feel the jerking and grinding of the cable in the pit of his stomach, and he fought back nausea. A single bead of sweat trickled slowly down his side, causing him to repress a slight shiver in the cold air.

"How deep is this damn pit?" Charlie asked, more out of nervousness than curiosity.

"Oh maybe a mile *mas or menos,*" Andre replied off handedly.

"Would that be more than or less than a mile?" Charlie pursued the question.

Andre ignored him, concentrating on the controls.

After an eternity, Andre slowed the rate of decent. The lift shuddered, and then came to a grinding stop. The door opened and Andre leapt out, followed more cautiously by his less eager companions.

They stood in front of a small open office marked by a dust covered metal desk. Huge pneumatic drills lay strewn about the floor of the mine; as if someone had shouted *get out* and the miners abandoned their equipment in the same position that it was now.

"This is where the miners check in," Andre explained. He held out his hand to Nadia, pointing toward the crumpled diagram she had forgotten she still clutched tightly in her fist. She had been afraid of losing it during the drop to the bottom.

Andre spread out the map on the desk, placing small pebbles on the corners so they could focus their lamps on the faintly drawn lines. Looking closely they could identify multiple tunnels leading from the Under-supervisors office. They squinted in an attempt to determine which one they were to follow.

"This way," Andre finally pointed to the tunnel leading to their right. "If you hear noises hug the wall."

"Why?" Charlie and Nadia asked in unison.

"One of the dangers miners face is falling rocks. Occasionally it can signal a cave-in. If it does, you are pretty much screwed. Mostly it's just that--falling rocks."

"Of course," he continued, almost to himself. "*Just* falling rocks can also be a problem if one is big enough and lands on your head, or on your foot--it could cripple you. That's why the miners wear steel toed boots."

Charlie looked down at his tassel loafers--their soft leather and thin soles. He had not planned on becoming a spelunker on this trip he thought with some bitterness.

"Deep mining isn't easy," Andre continued, "the deeper the mine goes—and this is a deep bugger—the more risk there is from underground earthquakes, rock bursts, gas discharges, and flooding. And for the miners, the deeper they work, the conditions get progressively more uncomfortable from the heat and the cramped spaces.

Visions of the recently trapped Chilean miners flooded Charlie's mind—and his fears--as they tried to find their way along the tunnel.

He also noticed that the three of them had unconsciously slipped into the miner's stride: a half-crouch with the head up, unconsciously measuring the length between the ties of the track that the tubs traveled. The irises of his eyes had dilated so that dark had become shadow, and shadow took on form.

Andre stopped so they could better focus their lamps on the map.

"Looks like we are going all right, but it's hard to tell how far this tunnel runs without some type of scale," Charlie observed.

Andre shrugged in agreement. "I wasn't down this way yesterday," he told them, picking up the pace. "This is a totally new seam."

Their lamps cast weird silhouettes on the walls as they went. They reminded Charlie of the shadow-puppet show he and Beth had seen in Jakarta. He was curious then who was pulling the puppets strings, and he wondered now who was manipulating theirs to get the three of them in this hellish hole.

"Where is the zinc?" Charlie yelled to Andre attempting to slow their progression.

"It's all around you," came the muffled reply. "At least it should be. I took some samples yesterday and left them with Dave Dieter. He promised to see if he could analyze them when he gets his equipment set-up. I can't tell, but it looks to this old miner like the seam is still strong. If I am right, I am puzzled why the men refuse to mine it. After all, it is their life. Their bread and butter so to speak," he shouted back, amused by his own witticism.

Water had seeped through the walls, and mud sucked at their shoes as they continued along the dark, dank tunnel. It was now clear to Charlie why the miner of the statue wore knee-high rubber boots.

He had to stop momentarily to scrape the soles of his loafers against a rock he had stumbled over. He leaned against the tunnel's side to support himself—it would not do to fall over here he thought. Straightening up, his gaze focused on a narrow fissure in the tunnel's wall he had not seen before. He moved his head back and forth, making his lamp shine down a narrow tributary leading to even greater darkness.

"Hey hold-up a minute," he shouted at the backs of his companions as they began to disappear in the gloom. At the sound of his voice, the two of them turned immediately, and were soon standing at his side.

"Look here," Charlie pointed. "I could have walked right past, and never known this opening ever existed.

"We already had done that," Nadia told him, re-examining the diagram. It was hard to read in the dim light. The poorly drawn lines were confusing enough, but the weird symbols had become even more difficult to interpret in the murky light.

"Do you think Andre....?" she asked letting the sentence trail off.

"Hell, I don't know."

All three of them studied the map. There was something drawn across the line they had been following.

"Screw it," Charlie told them. "We have come this far not knowing what we were doing, we might as well keep at it a while longer.

"Just one thing Andre, are you certain you can find your way out? I am miserably lost."

"The miners tell you to keep the wind at your back, and when you want out, keep it in your face. Only problem is we left the wind a way back. But, don't worry, laddie. I always get out. Or I have so far," Andre added less convincingly.

Their path plunged deeper, and then turned sharply to the right. It became narrower, so that Charlie's shoulders sometimes brushed against the sides.

His Burberry was filthy. He had worn it on many trips to over a hundred countries. The old coat may have to be retired after this one he thought, as they moved more slowly along the path. There were no tub rails along this route, so the seam probably had not been worked enough to warrant them. I should have kept my mouth shut he decided, beginning to gasp for breath in the stale dust filled air.

Occasionally, they would stop at the sound of an abandoned timber brace creaking under the pressure of its load. "Don't worry," Andre assured them. "The sound gets much louder if it is about to collapse. It's one of the reasons that miners prefer wood braces to steel."

"Phewie," Nadia exclaimed, clutching a handkerchief to her nose. "What is that odor—smell—stink? "she asked, attempting to find the right English word for the noxious odor that was filling the narrow passage.

"Damned if I know," Andre replied. "I think it's coming from here," pointing to a break in the wall.

Andre directed his light to the opening, then began to squeeze through.

"Oh my god! Oh my dear god! Come in here Charlie."

Connelly squeezed through the narrow opening, followed closely by Nadia. Inside a crypt-like room were the remains of five bodies, in varying forms of decomposition. They were laid out in manner resembling the coarse lines drawn on the diagram they were following.

Charlie bent down, shining his lamp on the bodies. Their sightless eyes looked back at him. "Look here Andre, look at their necks." Around each man's neck was a small leather cord.

"It's a garrote. I saw this once before in South America. It is a leather thong that permits a man to sneak up behind someone and quietly strangle his victim by surprise.

"Down there they refer to it as the great equalizer, because it enables a smaller man to attack a much larger one and choke him to death before he can shout, turn, or do anything to defend himself. It's lethal as a gunshot, and a hell of a lot quieter. No wonder the miners thought this hole was haunted."

"We can't just leave them here," Nadia whispered, trying to regain her composure.

Charlie was bending over closing the men's eyes, and searching for identification. There was none. He had seen death before, but it was in combat. Somehow, this was different. Regardless of the cause or manner of death he had never become hardened to the passage of a man's soul into the hands of God.

Standing up, Charlie turned toward her, "Yes we can Nadia," he told her softly. "There is no way we can get them out. We might be able to roll one of the tubs in here, but it would be impossible to get them to the lift. Besides, I am not sure we want it known that we have found them. Someone has gone to a lot of trouble to hide these bodies, and they might not take too kindly to whoever finds them.

"What do you think Andre?"

"Absolutely, and I'm too damn old to push a tub full of rotting bodies up to the lift. They must be miners, so let the miners take care of them. Meet Jack Black?" he asked holding out a silver flask to Nadia.

She took it gratefully, and swallowed thirstily. "Ahh!" she choked. "I thought it would be wine."

Charlie took as deep a swallow as he could from the small flask. Wiping his lips on his sleeve he returned it to Andre.

"It's Johnny Walker Black Label Scotch,"Andre explained to Nadia who was still making a face and clearing her throat. "It has a taste you have to cultivate," he explained.

She tilted her head and looked at him quizzically. "Really?"

"Let's get our a...let's leave here *now*," Andre directed, beginning to squeeze through the narrow opening once more.

"Wait a minute," he told them retuning to the enclosure. Once inside he took out a large Swiss Army knife he carried and scraped-off some of the stone wall. "This stuff looks different from what I took out yesterday," he replied depositing the sample in a large handkerchief before returning it to his pocket.

"Stuff?" Charlie asked.

"It's a technical term we miners use," Andre replied. " You city boys wouldn't understand."

The three of them moved along the dark underground pathways, progressing faster going back than they had going in. Their breath came in gasps, and their faces were coated with dust.

The lift that earlier in the day had seemed so menacing to Charlie now appeared as a form of salvation, transporting them from an underground hell to a welcoming heaven.

Once on top, they gasped the fresh air like drowning people. The sky had never looked so good to Charlie and Nadia. Even Andre seemed relieved to be on top once again.

On the way back to the village, they discussed how best to approach the problem of the dead bodies they had left behind. While the question of who killed the miners was in all of their minds, the most immediate problem was "how to get the poor bastards out" as Andre so poetically phrased it.

"Easy enough," Charlie told them. "Let their friends do it. after-all isn't that what friends are for," he joked lamely.

"It is?" Nadia asked seriously.

"Well not exactly Nadia, It was a bad joke. But, how do we get in touch with the men?" Charlie wondered, thinking aloud. "They obviously make every effort to keep out of our way."

"That's easy," Andre told them. "Look in the brewery. If I know miners---and believe me, I know miners--they will be in the tavern this time of day."

Andre was right. Inside the brewery, the three of them looked around the smoke-filled room until they found a face they recognized. They actually found two faces. One was the mine manager and the other man seated close by him was the man Charlie believed stuck the diagram in his pocket.

The miners sat at wooden picnic-like tables. Before the mine was abandoned, the brewery served as the company cafeteria, and a place where beer was both made and sold. Charlie, Nadia, and Andre squeezed in across from the mine manager. Andre began to explain to the dour Russian what they had found (as Nadia translated) without relating how they had stumbled on the dead bodies. They had agreed beforehand to not reveal anything about the diagram, only to say they were exploring the mine to get a better idea what was involved in their project.

At first, the Russian manager glowered at the intrusion into his cloistered retreat. The alcohol he had already consumed seemed to have fogged his comprehension and required considerable repetition.

Nadia nervously flicked a wisp of red hair from her face as she was forced to cope with the complex and unfamiliar technical jargon of the mines, directed to a highly unresponsive audience.

As she soldiered on, it soon became clear her effort was unnecessary. Andre knew how to speak the universal language of the miners. Gradually the words began to pierce their alcoholic fog. The manager's frown turned into a look of increasing comprehension, and then considerable shock.

While Andre related their experiences, Charlie focused his attention on the man to his right. The man whom he thought had passed him the diagram. If he was the one, it certainly was not apparent from his reaction. It mirrored the expressions of his boss.

Perhaps, Charlie thought that is the role of the assistant. If so, the man with the watery gaze accomplished it superbly. Charlie acquired no clue from his reaction, and was no clearer as to the man's motive than he was before. If indeed, he actually was the one who slipped the note into his pocket the day of the disastrous presentation.

The miners conferred amongst themselves, and decided to go down the shaft and bring up the bodies. Andre would lead the way. At first he thought that Nadia should come with them but noticing her reluctance he reconsidered.

"I will go with you.....if you need me. That is my job," she told him. But.... her voice trailed off.

Charlie certainly didn't blame her. He would also have gone with Andre, but they obviously didn't need him, and he wanted to get in touch with Trevor to tell him what they had found at Tekeli.

It was decided then that Andre would go back with the miners, and Charlie and Nadia would return to the hotel.

As the group of miners was about to leave, Andre turned to Charlie, pulling his handkerchief from his hip pocket. "Give this to Dieter," he winked. "He will know what to do with it."

15

By the time Nadia and Charlie left the brewery, the sun had begun its daily descent in the western sky. It was late October, but the chill in the air heralded the beginning of the transition from autumn to the long and bitter Kazakh winter.

The two of them were almost unrecognizable from the well-groomed couple who passed through town earlier in the day. Dust from the mine covered their coats, and would take considerable effort to remove. Never the less, they both pulled their soiled collars up around their necks in partial protection from the late afternoon chill.

The old babushka who was cleaning her garden, earlier in the day, had long ago abandoned her effort and gone inside to the warmth of her hearth.

The window curtains in the small houses were back in their ordinary arrangement, as the self-appointed monitors of the street diverted their attention from a possible passersby to the more productive preparation of the family's supper. The statuesque lead miner looked on impassively at the two passing strangers, unaware of the fate that had befallen his working comrades.

Once back in his room, Charlie experienced considerable difficulty placing a call to Almaty. After the third attempt, he was relieved when he heard "Trevor Gunn here," at the other end of the line. Charlie began to describe what they had found in the mine.

"Five men? Oh my God. How did they get there? Who killed them? Garrote you said. I have never heard of that."

These were the same questions Charlie had asked himself countless times during the day. While he was sympathetic to Trevor's concern, he wasn't much help in providing answers. He did, however, tell him about how he had found the note.

"It fluttered to the floor when you took off your shirt?"

"Yes, it must have been placed there by one of the assistant managers who wanted me to find it, and follow the diagram to the bodies."

"Why on earth would he have done that?" Trevor asked for a second time, in a slightly different way than before.

Charlie repeated what he had said earlier. "I can't imagine. Perhaps he had been close to one or more of the men and wanted them found, without letting any of the others know he knew."

"Why would he do that?"

"For fear of ending up the same way the others did. And, he might not have any idea who killed them, and didn't' want any of the others to know he knew. He chose me because I was new on the scene, and he could be relatively certain that I had no hand in it."

"Makes sense, but you are still left with who did it, or as your countrymen might say *who done it?"*

"Precisely."

"Let me see," Trevor pressed, "if I have this right. One of our consultants had a breakdown—yesterday was it? Then someone slipped the map of the mine secretly into your shirt pocket. Right?" Trevor continued before Charlie had a chance to answer. "Now today you follow the map and find five dead bodies.

"Ah well old boy, one thing is abundantly clear."

"Which is?"

"You cannot let this little puzzle distract you from our main objective. You cannot let the wheels fall off our wagon now. You have to finish the project on time with cogent and concrete recommendations."

Always the good soldier, Charlie thought. We could all be strangled in our sleep, and old Trevor would be primarily concerned about the impact on his project. What the hell, he decided, he might very well be the same way under similar conditions.

"We are still on schedule and forging ahead," Charlie assured him. "Andre is down in the mine now with some of the Russian managers in order to show them where the bodies are hidden. He has, however, already extracted some samples he wants Dave Dieter to analyze. Andre believes this operation can still be productive.

"It looks like the miners thought the shafts were haunted because their friends were turning-up missing. Maybe they were turning up missing so the miners would be afraid to work in the mine," Charlie thought aloud, his mind working in circles.

"But who and why," Trevor interjected. "For what reason?"

They both paused in their conversation. The discussion had led them back to the beginning, and now that they were there they had nowhere else to go.

"Anyway," Trevor started on a new subject. "I was going to call you. You are about to have a visitor."

"Who? Why?" Charlie asked. The last thing he needed now was someone else to interrupt his work. In his experience, visitors were always trouble, or at the very least an unwanted distraction.

Trevor ignored his concern. "Not to worry old man. This one is one of your own. A yank by the name of Roger Pembroke. We got a call from your embassy last night. He is a new cultural attaché, and they want him to visit the mine."

"What for?" Charlie asked, surprised at the request. "We ain't got no culture hereabouts."

Trevor paused for a moment, and then chuckled. "That's what I told them. I may have used somewhat better phrasing, but we always want to keep on good relations with our American associates. Sammie is driving him up tomorrow. He will stay with you, and Roger will drive the car back tomorrow night, or the day after."

"Whatever you say Trevor. Ours is not to reason why. Ours is just to ...."

"Yes, yes I know old sport. I will be sure and make a note of that in your permanent record. Have a good night." The line went dead.

Before going to find Dave and Henry to alert them to what had happened that day, Charlie decided he should first advise Emmett Valentine what was happening at Tekili. Perhaps he could figure out what was going on. The old man certainly had more experience at these types of things than anyone else he knew.

Opening his laptop, he recalled the encrypted address that led him into a secure line, and tapped out a brief summary of the day's events. He re-read what he had just written to make sure it was clear before hitting **Send**. Instantaneously a series of obscure numbers and letters scrolled rapidly across the screen, destroying the ability for anyone to intercept the automatically encoded message, or trace it back to the originator. The screen then immediately faded to black.

Charlie stared for a moment at the blank screen, in hopes it might somehow provide an answer. Of course it did not. He quickly shut down the laptop, and headed for the lounge.

It had been the men's practice to gather there after work to discuss the day's progress, and pool any *libation,* as Andre referred to it, they might have available.

Charlie picked up the bottle of Stolichnaya he had bought at the hotel in Almaty. It wasn't a Bombay martini, but then you had to make do with what you have. An old traveler's adage he thought, and he was certainly an old traveler.

Dave Dieter relaxed behind his liquid companion from America, Jim Beam. Henry Butts sipped a cup of tea. Charlie found some ice in the kitchen before offering his bottle of vodka to Henry, who looked quizzically at the bottle, made his decision, and pushed aside his cup and saucer.

Once the three of them settled in, Charlie began to relate the events leading up the excursion to the mine, and ended with what they found.

In telling his story, he attempted to assume a tone of false detachment. The last thing he needed was to spook the two of them, and as a result have them so frightened they would be distracted from their jobs.

His fears were unfounded. After the usual questions, followed by his inadequate answers, the two consultants seemed satisfied. They apparently saw little immediate impact on their own situation. The mine did seem far removed, in both distance and in culture, from the relative safety of the old hotel.

Charlie was not as complacent. He too often had seen relative innocent beginnings cascade into events that threatened anyone in the vicinity. Regardless, if they were innocent or not, and involved or not. There is no such thing as the innocent bystander in this type of work, he knew. They are the ones that lightning invariably strikes—sometimes twice.

Dave, the consummate technician, quickly put aside the day's distractions to focus on his own activities and challenges. "I took the sample Andre gave me yesterday, and after I finished setting up my….."

Charlie jerked, reminded of the samples in his pocket Andre handed him before leaving the brewery.

"……equipment," Dave continued, "I began assessing its mineral composition. The tests are very basic, you understand. I brought this equipment more for portability than quality, so the tests are only rudimentary." He cleared his throat, more for effect than necessity. "But, I am reasonably certain that the samples contain a relatively high level of minerals--some lead--some zinc—that would allow a reasonably productive mining operation here."

"So you conclude then that this can be a profitable operation, after all?" Charlie inquired hopefully.

"Can't be certain. I will need more samples, but the evidence is leading in the right direction."

"Before Andre went back to the mine with the Russians, he asked that I give you this," Charlie told him quickly unfolding the handkerchief on the table in front of Dave. "He got it from the shaft where we found the missing miners. He thought that it was different from the other stuff—that's a technical mining term," he added with a smile, "and he wanted you to take a look at it tonight. Can you do that?"

"Not without another blast of my old friend Mr. Beam," Dave laughed, finishing his drink and refilling his glass.

As they were about to return to their rooms and clean up for dinner, the men heard Andre's heavy footsteps trudging down the hallway.

"Well I am back," he reported with an obvious sense of relief. "I showed the miners where their missing friends are. They seemed as shocked as we were. I couldn't understand what they were saying among themselves, but I gather they were just as baffled as we are."

"What are they doing now?" Charlie asked.

"They had begun to carry the remains—it was a gruesome business—from the area where we found them. Some of the others were moving several of the tubs as close as they could get them. It looked like they were going to load them into to the tubs, and roll them along the tracks back to where they can be lifted to the top.

"Once they got the process started, I bowed out. There was nothing more I could do," Andre concluded. The *jaife*—the boss did shake my hand before I left. I think they were grateful that we found the men, and led them to where they were."

"Hand me that bottle of Stolie--please." Andre asked, spotting the bottle on the table.

"God, I needed that," he roared. "It has been one hell of a day."

"What do you think they will do with the bodies?" Henry asked, pouring himself another drink.

"Beats me," Andre replied. "I thought I heard one of them say something about the *ice house,* but I couldn't be sure. It could make sense."

Henry swirled the ice floating in his glass, and shuddered.

16

After a breakfast of bland cabbage and spicy wieners, André returned to the "hole," and Dave headed out to look in at the vacant concentrator plant.

As they were leaving, Charlie asked Dave "what is it that a concentrator actually does?"

Dave explained as briefly and patiently as he could as they walked down the stairs. "The concentrator operation includes four industrial units at the plant site: basic production which consists of crushing and filter-drying, reagent and grinding at the flotation site, maintenance services, and tailing facilities.

"Its major activity is the processing and concentration of lead-zinc," he droned on "and lead barite ores, resulting in the production of lead, zinc, and lead-barite concentrates."

Charlie began to regret he asked but, like the infomercials that seemingly never end only to continue with *wait there is more*, Dave felt obligated to provide further information.

"These concentrates are then shipped to mineral processing plants and smelters in Kazakhstan. One of them is in Chimkent, over in the west, and Oskermen up north of here."

Like most technical people, Dave liked to be asked what he did; and like all non-technical people, Charlie ended up as bewildered as he began, drowned in a verbal deluge of incomprehensible terms.

The two men separated to go their individual ways, and Charlie hurried to catch up with the two interpreters and Henry who were straggling over to the Administration Building.

Inside, a few clerks sat idly behind large desks, staring at each other, or gazing off into a world of their own making. They had given up the pretext of artificial activity months ago, and now lived in a dark realm populated primarily by despair and desperation.

The sound of the interpreters' leather heels on the marble stairs echoed through the deserted hallway. The uncommon noise caused several of the office workers to divert their attention from staring at the tops of their desks to peer quizzically at the strangers who were disrupting their solitude.

Elaina and Henry had established a temporary office next to the conference room, while the others were exploring the mysteries of the mine. Charlie found an empty desk and began to draw a grid that restructuring consultants use that is often referred to as a SWOT analysis. Using a blue-lined pad, he wrote column headings across the top:

STRENGTHS	WEAKNESSES	OPPORTUNITIES	THREATS
Product demand	Over staffed	Outside capital	Complete closure
Quality of ore	Single customer	Foreign owner	Impact on town
Low labor rates	Cost of funds	Increased production	Exhaust ore

Charlie spent the next two hours thinking about, and then scribbling appropriate diagnostic components in the vertical columns under the major headings relating to the future viability of the Tekeli mine. The grid would provide a method of analyzing the comparable merits and disadvantages of various elements that governed the potential of the mining operation.

When the grids were completed, the girls would convert his rough graph to a presentable form containing both Russian and English headings. This would later serve as a simplified tool for presenting his findings to a group of Kazakhstan government officials.

Charlie was absorbed in his work when he felt a gentle touch on his shoulder. Startled, he turned to see Nadia standing beside him. She really is quite attractive he thought.

"Mr. Connelly, there is a man waiting outside to see you. He just arrived from Almaty along with Sammie. "

"Thank you Nadia. I was expecting him," he told her as he rose to leave.

Outside, Charlie saw a young man standing expectantly beside his overnight bag, and Sammie heading into the hotel.

"Roger Pembroke," he grinned, extending his hand.

"And I am Charlie Connelly. Trevor Gunn told me you would be coming up here, but I guess I didn't expect you this soon."

"Actually Mr. Connelly...."

"Charlie will do."

"Actually Charlie, I am the new Assistant Cultural Attaché at the embassy in Almati, but it was really Mr. Valentine that wanted me to see you. I work for him—as well as for the embassy. The job there is only for cover."

Charlie attempted to conceal his surprise. "Really, why did Emmett want you to see me?"

"He has a good deal of respect for you. He seems to have known you for some time."

Charlie nodded. "Yeah, that's right. Too long I often think."

Roger smiled, understanding what he meant. He sometimes felt that way himself, and he had only known Mr. Valentine for a short time---not nearly as long as Mr. Connelly.

"What is going on down there?" Roger asked, as both men turned their attention to a procession leaving the icehouse. The sound they heard was a Gregorian funeral chant led by a long bearded Orthodox priest in a flowerpot hat, who was holding a large ornate golden icon high over his head, as he led a long procession down the dusty street.

Trailing behind the priest was a line of pallbearers carrying five roughly hewn wooden caskets. In the group, Charlie recognized the mine manager and his ever present assistant. Directly behind the caskets were five women in black widow weeds. Their high-pitched wails mingled with the deep-throated lament of the similarly black clad priest.

A chilly wind picked-up, creating dust devils that twirled unnoticed around the mourners, causing the priest's robe to flap treacherously around his long legs as he strode through town.

The widow's grief punctuated his chants and amplified their wails.

Soon the grieving procession evaporated like bleak specters into the birch forest surrounding the cemetery. The chants and the wails trailed-off in the wind.

Returning his attention to the visitor, Charlie replied to his question more brusquely than he intended. "I will explain later," he said, steering him toward the hotel.

"You were telling me about Emmett Valentine," Charlie reminded him.

"Yes that's right. You sent him an email with a list of people with whom you are working here. He called me at the embassy on their secure line to let me know what he found, and he wanted me to fill you in."

"Why didn't he call me himself?" Charlie asked, as the two of them walked toward the hotel. Emmett had never been hesitant about calling him before--regardless where he was at the time--or whatever time it was where he was.

"Have you heard about that bastard Assange and WikiLeaks up here?" Roger replied bitterly.

Charlie was surprised at the rancor in the young man's voice. "Yeah even up here. I listen to the BBC and the VOA on my shortwave. They have been covering it pretty thoroughly."

"Well, as you can guess, it really has Washington in turmoil. Everyone is suspicious of each other. The CIA will no longer trust the FBI with information for fear it will be leaked. Not that there was a great deal of trust between them before.

"Mr. Valentine told me once that there has been a long antipathy in the Agency toward the Bureau. Our *cousins* in the FBI, as he refers to them. It dates back to the days of "Wild Bill" Donavan and J. Edgar. Anyway, people thought that after 9/11 the animosity would fade. Everyone spent a lot of time trying to iron out the wrinkles. Now it is back as bad as it was before."

Roger seemed pleased that he could provide the older man with inside information.

The two of them reached the door of the hotel. A flock of doves feeding by the walkway burst into flight. Roger jumped, and then laughed at his own nervousness.

Walking up the stairs, Charlie explained, there was a small lounge where they could talk without being disturbed.

"Outstanding," Roger replied.

My God Charlie thought, was I ever that young. It was a common reaction people had when they first encountered Roger Pembroke.

Finding a seat in the empty lounge the young man continued. "To make things worse, the Department of Defense learned that a foreign spy agency breached the Pentagon's computer network by inserting a flash drive into a U.S. military laptop in the Middle East.

A "malicious code" on the flash drive spread undetected on both classified and unclassified Pentagon systems, establishing what amounted to a digital beachhead that enabled the foreign agency to transfer any information they wanted to servers under their own control. So now, both the

CIA and the FBI are afraid to transfer information to each other; and to the Pentagon as well. It is one hell of a mess," Roger concluded with considerable conviction.

Charlie had to agree, but remained curious. "So what does this all have to do with me?"

"Several things. First, Mr. Valentine wanted me to tell you what he found-out about your associates rather than sending you an email that might get intercepted. The other thing is to show you a more secure way of corresponding with the Agency."

"Before we begin Roger, I should have asked you how was your trip?"

"Oh my God," Roger laughed. "Riding with Sammie was like having your own tour guide through *wonderland.* By the way, who *are* the Uighurs? They must be the world's most oppressed people, and I have never heard of them."

"We got the same lecture. Old Sammie really has a bug about them."

"So what did Emmett find out about my associates here?" Charlie prompted him.

"Well, not a great deal really. Andre has an interesting past. Did you know that his wife was murdered by The Shining Path terrorists in Chile?"

"The *Sendero Luminosa*? He never mentioned it."

"Yes that's it. How did you know about them?

"I ran into them when I was doing business in Peru. "They were referred to as the Shining Path because they would drop in on a mountain village with lightning-like speed, wiping out any government troops, or anyone else for that matter, that had the misfortune of getting in their way.

They started out in the Andean town of Ayacucho, before morphing into a more militaristic style gorilla army. They later branched out into all of Peru and Chile.

"A radical by the name of Abie Guzman led them. He was a follower of Chairman Mao. Ironically it was at a time when the Chinese communists were moving toward capitalism," Charlie laughed, "and the terrorists were moving in the opposite direction."

As he was explaining the radical movement in South America to Roger, Charlie recalled that it was because of the Shining Path that he first became actively involved with the CIA. Before, his participation was limited to only answering their economic questions about the locations he visited. One day he was sitting in his office when he got a call from this contact who asked if he would deliver an envelope for him when he traveled to Lima. It seemed innocent enough at the time, although he wondered how they knew he would be going there.

It turned out the envelope was stuffed with thousand dollar bills that he was supposed to covertly pass to someone he was to meet in a park in the center of the City. The money was to be wrapped in a copy of the Wall Street Journal. The cash would then be used to fund the Peruvian Government forces opposing the *Sendero Luminosa*.

He recognized later that he was the designated *cut-out.* Someone with no discernable ties back to the U. S. Government.

He was to sit on a bench in the center Plaza de Armas with the Wall Street Journal at his side. On his way to the park, he practiced what little tradecraft he knew. It entailed finding a busy street—not a difficult task in overcrowded downtown Lima—but one with stores and restaurants with large angled windows which can provide an adequate mirror that would allow a reasonable glimpse of a possible tail. He did this, and eventually decided he was clear, and alone.

The park was directly across from the Palcio de Gobierno the official home of El Presidente. As he watched, red and black uniformed guards with gleaming gold Roman style helmets began their daily slow goose-stepping ritual marking the changing of the palace guards.

While his attention was diverted by the colorful ceremony, he was surprised to feel a slight brush against his hand. He jerked away, instinctively clutching his cash filled envelope more tightly. Turning, he saw a Catholic nun cloaked in a full-length black habit, adorned with a veil and scapular collar. She picked up the paper after whispering the word he was told to expect. He watched in amazement as the nun rose quickly, and glided away on hidden feet; the paper already concealed somewhere within her flowing robes.

Later the same day, still on the Agency's dime, he caught a cab directing it to take him to the *La Rosa Nautica,* as they had told him to do. It was an oceanfront restaurant he was familiar with from his previous trips to Lima. It was early in the evening, but it was already beginning to fill with the important makers and takers of Peruvian society.

He pushed his way through the crowd, and found a seat at the long bar. He ordered a Pisco Sour, and watched the sun begin to dip below the coastline. Suddenly he felt a touch on his shoulder and turned to see a tall attractive brunette, with flashing dark eyes, who was fashionably dressed.

There were no words. Nothing!

She slipped him a note, then quickly turned and made her way toward the restaurant's door. Many eyes followed her exit, but Charlie concentrated his attention on the note he had just received. It was a signed receipt for the money he had delivered earlier in the day.

He finished his drink, and afterwards often wondered if the two women he had met were the same one in different clothing; and if so, which was real and which was not.

That was his introduction to the world of mirrors where nothing is as it seems. If he had been smart, that would have been the end of his association with the Agency and Emmett.

Too late now, he decided turning his full attention back to what Roger Pembroke was telling him.

"They killed his wife?" Charlie asked, forcing his mind to the situation at hand.

"Kidnapped and shot her," Roger replied, "while they were up in the mountains working at a mine."

"Mr. Valentine says that the Brit is clean," Roger continued scanning his notes, "although it was impossible to trace him back further than when he originally came to England.

"That's OK, I know about that," Charlie assured him.

"Well anyway he has a BSC Economics London," Roger continued undeterred. "He was an auditor for Arthur Young in London. He went from there to Ferro-Mag Electrical, then opened and closed his own accounting business.

"The expert from Illinois is also clean—totally clean," Roger continued. "He got his degree from the Colorado School of Mines. Worked as a Technical Director for the Dravo Corporation, and finished up as Senior Minerals Engineer for the Illinois State Geological Survey specializing in mineral processing."

"So there is no problem then?" Charlie asked."

"Well not exactly," Roger told him turning a page of his notes. "The men seem all right but, Mr. Valentine thinks there could be a problem with one of the interpreters. Let's see," he added referring to his notes. "You have two…..

"Which one?"

"The one you call Nadia Okh…." Roger stumbled over the pronunciation "...lopkev—Nadia Okhlopkev," he finally decided, attempting a flawed phonetic pronunciation.

"Nadia----that can't be. She is invaluable to us. Solid as a rock. You must mean Elaina. If it is one of the two, I would guess Elaina."

"No, no, not her, she is clean. There is nothing to suspect there. Mr. Valentine sent along a picture of her. She's hot. Will I get to meet her," Rodger grinned.

"You will tonight at dinner. But why Nadia?"

"Well she *is* Russian. Mr. Valentine always suspects the Russians----and he is usually right. On top of that, she comes from a long line of Russian military offices. Her grandfather was a colonel in the Cossacks when he first came to Kazakhstan. Her father was a general who led a Kazakh battalion in the Second World War. At that level, they are always tight with the KGB. They are both dead of course, but….

"Ok, ok, I get the picture." Charlie had heard enough. He would think about it, but was highly skeptical. Sometimes he thought that Emmett had fought too many battles, and may be ready to ride-off into the sunset.

"…..she was working over in the Caspian Basin as an interpreter in the same area, at the same time, as Barry Durand."

"Coincidence---just a coincidence."

"If it were not for coincidences there would be no conclusions," Roger replied dogmatically.

"What in the hell does that mean?" Charlie demanded.

"Damned if I know," Roger admitted. "They drummed that into us when I was in training at Camp Peary. I wondered about it myself at the time, I just thought I would throw it into the conversation here, but it sounded funny to me after I said it."

Charlie threw up his arms in dismay.

""So now Roger what else…..," but Roger wasn't paying any attention to him. His eyes focused on the hallway where Nadia and Elaina were walking arm in arm to their rooms.

The two women looked into the lounge, and smiled as they passed.

"Roger---Roger, what else did Emmett want you to tell me?"

Roger turned toward him and winked. "She *is* hot."

"Is this room clean?" he asked, changing the subject, and looking around the small lounge with its antiquated overstuffed furniture.

Charlie knew enough to recognize the young man was not asking about the sanitary condition of the dusty room. "We haven't swept it for bugs , if that is what you mean. We don't have the equipment to debug it, and it is highly unlikely that anyone would have wanted to install listening devices in an old hotel in an out of the way town."

It doesn't take long for them to become paranoid he thought—it must come with the job.

"You're probably right," Roger agreed. "I know that you can put the damn things anywhere -in a thermostat, a telephone, a TV speaker—anywhere. You could never find one without the right equipment. Anyway, why would they do it here? As you say, why would they do that here?"

"Have you ever heard of a one-time pad?" Roger continued, seemingly satisfied that their conversation was not being recorded.

"Not recently. What is it?"

"It is a secure method of communicating with Langley," Roger told him, going into the hallway and looking up and down to see if anyone was within earshot. Returning to his seat, he pulled out a Kindle looking type of device.

"The Agency used these a lot, but gave it up with computer encoded internet messages. Now with WikiLeaks they are going back to them for use in the field. The Station Chief in Almaty gave me this one for you. Said you might need it, if you get in trouble."

Roger moved from his chair so he was sitting beside Charlie on the sofa.

"They operate on the mathematical principal of matching sets of random numbers *once* between the sender and the receiver in small groups in a coded message. The matching set then become your source code."

"Sounds awfully complicated," Charlie interrupted, his eyes already beginning to glaze.

"Not really, you will get the hang of it."

Roger seemed pleased with himself. He had learned about these when he was in training at The Farm, and was glad he could describe the complicated process.

"Once the groups are in the message they can be translated into words by referring to a non-reusable key. But, they can only be used *once.* That's the secret of them, and of course that is the reason they are called one-time pads," he concluded looking to Charlie for a sign of understanding and appreciation.

Charlie had begun his career in the computer industry and had some understanding of random number generators so he was not completely lost. "I will think about it," he assured Roger slipping the device into his coat pocket.

Charlie looked more closely at the young agent sitting across from him, and decided that aside from his interest in women, he could be more serious than he had first thought.

His closely cropped hair, struggling to grow-out, and an apparent stubble on his chin provided a profile in progress of a young man with a choirboy face. However, Roger had deep-set blue eyes that seemed to penetrate and record everything in view. He had an athlete's shoulders tapering to a slender waist atop powerful legs.

He may be all right, Charlie decided—when he has been around a while longer.

"Good," Roger exclaimed. "Now what was it with the funeral?"

Charlie told him as briefly as he could how they had found the dead miners the day before, and then led the mine managers to their bodies.

"Good God, That's significant. Have you told Mr. Valentine about the dead miners?"

"Yes, Emmett *and* Trevor Gunn. But I am not confident there is a direct connection between them and what we are doing here."

"Don't bet your life on it Charlie. It is obvious someone doesn't want your mine mined--for whatever reason they may have. Your project, as I understand it, is to see what the prospects are of operating Tekeli in a way that would attract new investment."

"Well, you are right about that," Charlie conceded, "either for new investors or the government of Kazakhstan. I suppose that any number of people could be opposed to that."

Andre came into the lounge carrying his evening's supply of wine. He was followed almost immediately by Henry, and Dave Dieter.

Charlie made the introductions telling the men that Roger was with the American Embassy and was there to become familiar with the area. He avoided mentioning that he was the new Cultural Attaché.

Before leaving for the dining room, Charlie showed Roger where he would spend the night. Madam Manager had put the unexpected visitor in a small room at the foot of the stairs she occasionally used in an emergency.

While Charlie helped Roger get settled, the young man confided he had met a Kazakh woman at the Embassy in Almaty whom he found extremely appealing. He was going to try and get to know her better when he returned. Roger seemed confident that all good things come to those who try.

At dinner, Roger managed to position himself next to Elaina. Charlie watched with amusement as the young man struck up a conversation with the interpreter. He couldn't blame him, Elaina was a very attractive young woman.

While Madam Manager and her assistants were serving dessert, Charlie was surprised to see the dombra player reappear. She began to play what Nadia described as a Kazakh love song about a young woman abandoned by her lover.

The woman had positioned herself directly in front of Sammie, and seemed to be directing her song toward him.

The strange but appealing music filled the room. Charlie watched Roger and Elaina exchange glances, as the other men focused their attention on the musician. All Elaina knew about the young visitor was that he was from the American Embassy, and was greatly interested in Central Asian culture.

Charlie could not keep from wondering if Roger was destined to become a latter-day Lieutenant Pinkerton; finding his love on his first visit to a foreign port, only to abandon poor Madam Butterfly when he returned home.

Charlie poured another glass of Andre's wine. Drinking sometimes made him reflective. Tonight he wondered if any woman could become accustomed to living with a man who told lies as part of his job description.

Emmett had once told him that not everyone could be an effective spy. According to the old man, in order to be a good agent, a CIA officer must spend much of his life pretending he is someone he is not. Persuading others to turn against their own country and then convince them to become a traitor by committing espionage. The agent has to always be certain how he feels on the moral issues...and so do their wives, Charlie concluded.

How could a woman knowingly accept that kind of husband? He knew Beth could not. Even his tenuous association with the Agency was an anathema to her. She was continually trying to get him to promise that he would sever his relations with Emmett. He *had* promised her that he would do that--several times.

After the others left the table, Charlie told Andre and Henry about the funeral that took place earlier in the day. He was the last to leave the dining room. Entering the darkened hallway, he caught a glimpse of Elaina's shadow trailing down the stairs to the first floor. A slender sliver of light beckoned from Roger's open doorway.

17

In the morning, a few flakes were beginning to fall, and already a slight coating of white covered the ground. Charlie remembered to give Roger the samples Andre had scrapped from the side of the tunnel where they found the dead miners.

Roger assured him that once he reached Almaty he would take them to the Embassy and they would rush them to Mr. Valentine in a diplomatic pouch. There were people at the Agency who would be able to perform an analysis of them very quickly.

Charlie watched Roger and Elaina exchange scraps of paper during breakfast. They now gave each other a perfunctory peck on the cheek before Roger jauntily climbed into the Land Rover for the drive back to Almaty. Before he could start the engine, the dombra player came running from the hotel, her instrument wrapped in a cloth cover, and slung over her shoulder.

As she approached the car, Roger looked puzzled and rolled down the window. The two exchanged a few gestures before the young woman climbed in beside him. There was a grinding of gears as the car leapt forward, and Roger left Tekeli in a cloud of dirt that was kicked-up by the oversize tires.

The SUV bounced over the old road, as it sped along the ancient route. Roger was surprised, but pleased to have a passenger. It was a long trip, and he was unsure of the road. The young woman spoke no English, and could only gesture to point out places she thought he might find interesting. In spite of the inability to communicate, she provided a pleasant diversion from the bleak landscape. He was even more surprised when she began to point to the old roadside park with its dilapidated building. He first thought that she wanted to visit the facilities, and was astonished to notice an old pickup truck parked under a tree. She ran toward it, and jumped in beside the driver. She gave him a wave of her hand as the truck headed for a path over the mountains.

Wow! That is strange, Roger thought pulling back on the road. How did they know I was coming this way this morning?

It was a boring drive. Not much chance of getting lost, there was only one road between Tekeli and Almaty. The landscape was desolate. He had previously expected something more exotic. Tekeli wasn't a hell of a lot better.

That Charlie was interesting. A little long in the tooth perhaps. All those guys up there were—but they seemed to know what they were doing. He was curious how a corporate guy had ever got involved in intelligence work.

Actually, he had asked Charlie just that when they were alone in the lounge. He had replied that that there were certain similarities with both activities. They were both working in an arena where things were constantly changing. Kind of like an ocean with currents running one way then the other, he said. Sometimes they run together, and other times they diverge. You establish your goals or objectives, then you work like hell to achieve them, regardless which way the current takes you.

At the time, Roger recalled, Mr. Valentine telling him that one of the things that made Connelly a good agent was his unrelenting drive to successfully finish the job—whatever the job might be—or whatever might happen to distract him.

"Problem is," Charlie had continued warming to his subject, "you never have enough facts to make a decision, and you have to learn to operate with insufficient information—that's where your gut comes into play. Both the Agency and the corporation require intense competitors. Academics find competition abhorrent. They could never survive in such a constantly changing environment."

Maybe he was right Roger thought. That Connelly is an interesting dude...He would have to think about what he had to say… later.

To kill the time as he drove, Roger began singing to himself an old college glee club song he liked.

To the tables down at Mory's

To the place where Louie dwells,

To the dear old Temple Bar

We love so well

Sing the Whiffenpoofs assembled

with their glasses raised on high.

Roger, whether he was aware of it or not, was a walking talking tribute to the Agency's Ivy League mystique that had dominated the CIA since its inception. At one time almost 50% of the personnel had attended Yale. More recently, as the Agency found it necessary to expand and become more diverse, the Ivies had diminished in numbers, but not in influence. It was no wonder then that Charlie and Dave, with their Midwestern backgrounds, seemed to be somewhat *foreign* to Roger in their approach to problems.

Suddenly, Roger hit the brakes and pulled over to the side of the road. In the distance, he spotted a man on horseback, accompanied by a large dog, herding a string of grazing camels across the steppes. That is one hell of a picture he thought. *The camel cowboy of Kazakhstan,* he chuckled, throwing the Rover into gear and resuming his journey.

Maybe this place isn't as bad as he first thought. That Elaina was something else. She was hot. He really dug those almond eyes and olive complexion. Not at all like the women at Sarah Lawrence, or Wellesley. They were icebergs compared with little old Elaina. What can be sexier than almond eyes and black boots? Now that's real culture, he decided grinning broadly. He would have to give her a call when he got back to the Embassy.

Eventually, the outskirts of Almaty came into view. The city looked a little different to him from when he left. Perhaps the sun shining helped. The buildings didn't look nearly as grim as they had when he was leaving the city. Now children seemed happy as they played their games in Panfilov Park. Couples held hands as they posed for their wedding pictures in front of the bronzed soldiers of the Panfilov Division.

Maybe this assignment will be better than he originally thought.

He was smiling as he pulled into the entrance of the embassy compound. A new marine guard was at the gate. He was a little younger than the one there before. After flashing his ID, the guard waved him through.

Parking the Rover in the visitor's slot, he looked back over his shoulder and saw the young marine already flicking through a copy of Playboy magazine.

Michael Pearlman was in his office, and rose to welcome his new assistant. "Hi kid good to see you. How is life in the mines?"

Roger quickly told him about the people he had met at Tekeli. Most of them at least. He also went into some detail recalling the death of the five miners, and the unusual funeral he witnessed.

"That's quite a story. I thought it was going to be a classic boondoggle sending you up there, but the old man insisted. Does he know about the dead miners?"

Roger assured him that he did, and handed him the envelope with the samples Charlie had given him before he left for Almaty.

The station chief put the samples in a thick manila envelope, and addressed it to Emmett Valentine. "Mei Lyn," he bellowed through the open doorway.

The young woman entered almost instantaneously, as if she had been outside awaiting a command. "Get this in today's pouch to Langley," he ordered. The young woman smiled at Roger as she turned to leave.

"She's been asking about you," Pearlman told Roger after she was gone.

"Look there has been a slight change of plans concerning what we do with you," he added more seriously. "I had a chat over the secure line with Emmett after you left. He is becoming increasingly concerned over what is going on in Kazakhstan, and how it fits into the entire international scene right now."

"And that is?" Roger prompted, surprised by the new course of events.

"Well to put it bluntly everything is going to hell. The Mideast has caught fire with the conflagration spreading from Tunisia to Egypt, then on to Bahrain, Yemen, and now Libya.

"They are referring to it as *the Arab Spring*. You know the government has to have a name for everything, or they think that no one will know that it actually exists.

At the same time, the shadow of a nuclear Iran looms over the entire region and we still haven't figured out what to do with that. Aside from hoping it just goes away.

"The intelligence community was caught flatfooted again, and now we are trying to catch-up. They have formed a thirty-five man task force at Langley to try and determine where the hell the fire will break out next, and what we can do to respond. We should be trying to figure out how to prevent it, of course, but it is a little too late for that."

Roger was taken off guard by the station chief's candor. He was not used to hearing someone criticize their own family. "What does it mean for us here?" he asked becoming concerned for his own position.

"To put it very bluntly, Emmett needs a success. He thinks it may be possible here in Kazakhstan. The country is becoming increasingly critical to the United States.

"Since becoming independent, President Nursultan Nazarbayev traditionally has been our ally. It has massive oil fields, when oil is becoming an endangered element. We need a secure supply, and the Kazakh fields could be a tremendous benefit. At the same time, the country contains profound mineral resources that are becoming increasingly critical to commercial and military development. That mine up there at Tekeli is a good example of important mineral deposits…if they can figure out how to produce them as they did before."

"Sure Connelly knows that," Roger assured him, rising from his chair and beginning to pace around the room. "All the men up there know it, but someone may be trying to keep the mine from developing. Why would that be?"

"Any number of people, for any number of reasons," Pearlman replied taking his feet off his desk and standing to face Roger. "Perhaps they want to keep the mine from being owned by someone other than themselves. Russia and China are the most likely culprits. They could want the minerals to maintain their commercial production and market expansion. Or they may need it for their own military developments.

"Emmett told me that we are entering a new paradigm where a country's natural resources are the real portal to power. You know how the old man talks," Pearlman told Roger smiling affectionately. "He thinks that we may be entering a new form of Cold War for natural resources. But, he is afraid that America has become too damn *green* to win it."

The station chief returned to his desk, and began fumbling through the top drawer. He found what he was looking for and offered Roger a glass half filled with smoky scotch. "Talking so much always makes me thirsty."

"Ok, Ok," Roger replied, accepting the drink and returning to his chair. "So now how does that impact me, and the change of plans?"

"Emmett wants you to stay here in Almaty for awhile until we can figure out what the hell is going on. We first thought that we would send you over to the oil fields to nose around…maybe figure out what happened to Durand. Now he has decided that before we do anything drastic with you, we build your cover a little bit more. With all the focus on the Mideast now he can't afford to lose you. He could never get a replacement."

"You have no idea how comforting that is to me," Roger observed wryly. "And?" he prompted.

"And you are going to become an honest to God Cultural Attaché' starting now."

"Now?"

"Yes now!" Pearlman bellowed. "We have a Navy choral group coming through here. They are going to be putting on a concert of *sea shanties* for the Ambassador's party. Then they have a concert at Al-Farabi University. You are going to be their baby sitter. I'm pretty sure I could come up with a little better term for your job description, but right now I can't think of one." Pearlman poured himself another drink from his bottle before returning it to his former hiding place.

"So what will that entail?"

"You mean what do you do? Well kid it's like this. Your major role is keeping them sober, and getting them to their appearance on time. Before they get there, you check the microphones, you check the stage, You check the toilets in the room to make sure they work properly, then you make sure the curtains work, but most of all….now hear this…you keep the sailors away from the punch bowl, and the embassy wives. Later you make certain that none of them try to bang the university coeds. Got it? This is, after all, a predominately Muslim country."

Roger understood, but it didn't sound like what he expected a foreign intelligence agent would have to do. They had told him at the Farm that an agent's life would be composed of hours of tedium, occasionally punctuated by moments of sheer terror. This didn't seem to fit either category.

"By the way, you will need a date for the party. Why don't you take Mei Lyn?" Pearlman suggested. She is a good friend of the Ambassador's wife, and could make you look good.

"Me too maybe," he added with a smirk.

Perhaps this will not be as bad as he first thought Roger decided leaving the office.

18

Tekeli

After waving goodbye to Roger, and his unexpected passenger, Charlie turned and walked toward the administration building. On the second floor, he found the file he was working on the day before. Andre had returned to the mine, and Henry and Elaina were reviewing the payroll records they had received from Sammie. Dave Dieter sat with his boots on the desk. The results from his test samples were spread across his lap, as he gazed distractedly at the snow falling outside the window.

Things were once again resuming a rhythm, with the consultants doing what consultants do---working on their final report. Business produces and sells products. Consultants, on the other hand, produce and sell reports--with heavy emphasis on length and secondarily content.

Before Charlie left Chicago, the General Bank had mailed him a folder of economic data describing Kazakhstan's position in the world economy. Today Charlie pored over the pages relating to the lead and zinc markets.

The minerals were experiencing resurgence in their importance. During the 1990's, the market was considerably depressed. More recently, there had been an increase in their importance, due to an international expansion of industrial markets. Another factor driving up their value was the military expansion in China, and Russia, as well as in the U.S.

Now, as America became more deeply involved in the War on Terror, basic armaments such as warheads and bullets, as well as X-ray facilities, isotope containers, and shielding in nuclear power stations required increasing amounts of ore from mines such as Tekeli.

Charlie rubbed his eyes. Pretty dull stuff, but that's was consultants do...pretty dull things. He looked back blankly at the data tables spread across his desk,

Elaina attempted to stifle a yawn, giving up any effort to conceal her fatigue.

Henry glanced at her irritably, before returning to his task of attempting to make some sense out of the erratic and incomplete payroll records he had been studying.

Charlie rose and stretched. Noticing Dave gazing out the window, he walked toward him, and took a chair beside his desk. Startled, Dave turned toward him, a sheepish grin spreading across his weather-beaten face. He laughed, "This is really at the end of the world. It is even bleaker than southern Illinois in the winter."

"Have you any idea what the samples might be. The ones that Andre gave you to analyze."

"Oh those. No, not really, I think I told you that my equipment is less than perfect for determining unusual substances. I hadn't expected to be looking at stuff like that," Dave said apologetically.

"They are unusual then?"

"Yeah, yeah, pretty unusual."

"Want to hazard a guess what they are? I won't hold it against you," Charlie assured him.

"Do you know what rare-earth is?"

"Never heard of it."

"It isn't an *it*. It's a them. There is a whole bunch of them."

"Whole bunch? Is this another technical term that we poor peddlers are not intellectually equipped to comprehend?"

Dave looked at him before responding. "Exactly, that is why I am about to enlighten you--my uninformed associate. Rare earth minerals are a grouping of 17 chemically similar elements that are usually found together in ore, and then are later refined and split apart. Their primary use is in magnets and semiconductors, and a lot of other technologies that have both military and commercial applications.

"To give you an idea of their importance," Dave continued, warming to his subject now that he had captured Charlie's full attention. "They are sometimes referred to as "21st Century gold because of their importance in such high-tech applications as laser-guided weapons, and hybrid car batteries."

"Where is this stuff? Or that stuff---or however the hell you refer to it --found?" Charlie asked.

"Just across the border from us, China controls more than 90% of current global supply of rare earth metals, and they are making damn sure they stay that way by establishing tight export quotas. Which, by the way, they usually decide to ignore. It has been widely reported that storage facilities built in recent months in the Chinese province of Inner Mongolia can hold *more* than the 39,000 metric tons the Chinese released last year."

"So What?"

"Well I will tell you what. Putting restrictions on exports of this *stuff,* as you refer to it, will increase costs for companies in lots of critical industries around the world reducing their ability to compete with China. It could also restrict America's development and production of products critical to our national defense."

"Damn clever these Chinese. In other words Dave, demand is artificially created to exceed supply."

The engineer paused for a moment. "Well yes I guess you could put it that way, if you want to."

"Do you know Dave, if any of these elements are available in the United States?" Do we produce any rare earth?"

"Not really. The U.S. and Australia have deposits, but lack the expertise in extracting and refining them....at least in a manner that satisfies the environmentalists. Mining in our country and other places fell off several years ago, primarily because of ecological concerns. A further problem is that a new mine can take a decade to develop and a process for refining rare - earth elements can take almost the same amount of time.

"Those crazy greenies again huh?"

"Yeah, I guess," Dave replied more cautiously. "Rare-earths have a clean, futuristic image. The problem is extracting and processing them can be dirty, dangerous work. They tend to blacken the soil around the mine with waste and pollute the water with hydrochloric acid, while at the same time filling the air with radioactive dust, so they may have a point"

"So if our pit here contained one of these elements, in addition to lead and zinc, it could make its ownership and control far more valuable than we first thought?" Charlie asked.

"Well yeah...yeah...yeah I guess you are right. I never thought of that exactly in those terms... Maybe it could."

Charlie studied his friend's serious face. "To China?"

"Sure, of course, but not just China. They are pretty close to us, but so is Kazakhstan. If this country knew that this mine also contained rare-earth they would sure as hell want to retain control over the place. It could make the mine as valuable to them as their oil.

"Really?"

Well maybe. That might be something of an exaggeration, but pretty damned important. And don't forget Russia," Dave added.

"Russia?"

"Sure, they need rare-earth elements as much as anyone. They are increasing their military development again, and also gearing up their industrial production. It would also be valuable to them. And they are just up the street, so to speak. Russians already manage the mine, so it would not be much of a stretch for them to step in with both feet. Then they would have better control of the output.

"And don't forget the good old USA," Dave added as an afterthought. "I am sure that the U.S. would love to have a reliable supply of some of the rare-earth elements---other than China. I remember that some time ago the Santa Fe Gold Corporation signed a joint venture agreement with Kazakhstan to explore over three million hectors in the northeastern part of the country not very far from here."

"So what do you think, Dave?" Where does all this leave us?"

Dave rose, stretched, and looked at his watch. "You know what I think. I think its happy-hour time. We have solved enough of the world's problems for the day."

They approached Henry, who was still bending over his columns of payroll numbers, and patted him on the shoulder. He looked-up startled.

"Come on, its quitting time for Brits. Let's have a drink before dinner." Charlie suggested.

There was no argument from him, and the three men left for the hotel together.

Nadia and Elaina watched them leave, looked at each other, and returned to their work.

19

The men were surprised to see that the lounge was empty. Usually Andre was the first one there, spread across the yellow plastic leather chair, wine glass firmly in hand. After brushing the snow from their coats, they began to speculate where he might be.

"Probably still in the mine," Dave offered, returning from the empty kitchen.

"No,' Henry countered, "He is probably taking a nap. That's' what I should have done."

"Too close to dinner," Charlie concluded, coming from his room with the bottle of Stolie he had opened earlier.

Andre remained among the missing at dinner. "See I was right," Henry told them. "Sound asleep. Do you think we should wake him?"

"Let him sleep," Dave suggested. "He can catch a sandwich when he wakes up."

There was not the usual banter among the men. As the meal progressed without Andre, a sense of apprehension was beginning to settle over them.

Time seemed to have stopped since they sat down. Charlie glanced frequently at his Zenith chronograph. It had enough dials and buttons to tell him many things, but it gave no indication of the time Andre might appear.

"Where is Sammie?" Nadia asked, counting heads.

"Maybe in the mine with Andre," Henry suggested.

"Sammie left earlier this afternoon," the manager remarked, as she began to clear the dishes in preparation for desert.

Charlie was surprised. "Where did he go? How did he get out of here? Pembroke took the Rover back to Almaty."

She shrugged indifferently. "Some people came in a pickup truck, and Sammie left with them. He comes and goes regularly."

Peeling his apple, Charlie mulled this over in his mind. Suddenly he put down his knife. "Nadia, would you please check on Andre-- just to be certain he is all right. If he is asleep, leave him alone."

She returned a few minutes later "Not there. The bed has never been disturbed. I also listened at the bathroom, and it was empty."

"Thank you Nadia."

"This is not good," Charlie told them. "I think we had better check on him."

"How? Where? Not In the mine?" Henry asked, astonished at the turn of events. "Do you really think that's necessary?"

"Damn it Henry, I don't have the foggiest idea where he might be, but if he is not in the hotel it would seem that the mine would be the most likely place to look."

"You Americans are so relentlessly logical," Henry replied sheepishly. "We Brits always wait for a miracle to save us from having to make an undesirable decision."

Charlie was not as certain as he sounded. Going down that damn hole was the last thing in the world he wanted to do, but something had to be done.

"Dave, why don't you come with me? Henry you stay here, if we are not back in a couple of hours try and get some of the miners to come and help. And stay away from the vodka" he chided him, attempting to lighten the mood.

Henry slumped in his chair without offering an argument..

"Do you mind if I come along?" Nadia asked. "Maybe I can help somehow."

Charlie looked at her. She certainly had nerve. On the other hand, perhaps Emmett was right. She could be a mole, only trying to keep track of things for the Russians

"Bring the diagram," he told her getting up from the table.

After putting on their coats, Charlie found a flashlight in the pantry. Outside, the snow was falling more steadily than when they returned from the administration building. He looked around outside of the hotel, but there were no footprints. It was too dark, and the snow made it increasingly difficult to see anything very well.

The three of them moved tentatively through the birch trees lining the path to the mine. The snow-filled branches brushed against their faces, dumping cold flakes down their upturned collars.

Finally, they reached the buildings at the perimeter of the pit. Each of them stomped their feet before entering the equipment building. It created a hollow sound that echoed ominously through the old building.

Charlie aimed the flashlight at the cabinet with the helmets. The yellow hats lined along the shelves reflected the beam, casting an eerie glow among the gloom. Each member of the search party hurried to select one that would fit.

Turning on their headlamps, they checked to make sure all the lights functioned properly. This time there was no laughter at each other's outlandish appearance. They all knew it would be pitch-black in the tunnels, and they would need all the lighting they could get.

Dave checked the generator before prying open the creaking gate to the cage. Charlie and Nadia squeezed past, taking their place in the rear. The lift shook violently, then shivered as it began its uneven decent.

Dave gave out a feeble laugh. "This thing is as cold as we are, but it will get us where we are going."

The bottom of the shaft came sooner than Charlie wished. He glanced at Nadia as they were leaving the cage. She was expressionless. That is one cool broad he decided, a little short on looks, but long on nerve. He envied her composure. He didn't feel that way at all. His palms were moist in the cold air, and his underarms felt clammy. An occasional gust of wind would funnel down the shaft creating a banshee-like sound that unnerved him.

Dave was more accustomed to the surroundings, and ignored the noise.

"Let's go this way," Charlie suggested, heading toward a tunnel he thought looked familiar. Charlie had spent half of his adult life trying to find his way in foreign places. The murky mineshaft was the strangest by far.

Their headlamps transformed their shadows into giants as they groped their way down the reinforced passageway. The light from his flashlight would occasionally illuminate opaque eddies of suspended dust. I hate mines he decided, as he steadied himself after stumbling over a loose pile of rock.

"Let me see that damned diagram again," he said turning to Nadia. The three of them huddled together studying the rough drawing they had used to locate the dead miners.

"It looks like we can go a little further down this way," Charlie decided, groping his way through the narrowing tunnel. "We will cut off to the right in a little.....oh my God!" he blurted as the beam revealed the crumpled form of a man.

Nadia screamed, as she stepped in puddle of blood. "Is it---is it Andre?" she whispered.

"I don't know," Charlie replied, praying that it was not. "Dave, give me a hand here," he asked as he struggled to roll the body over.

The light from their helmets centered on the man's face. It stared vacantly upward, contorted with fear, sheathed by white blood streaked hair.

"Jesus!" Dave exhaled reverently. "It is Andre. Oh my God! Poor old Andre."

"The poor man. Is he dead?" Nadia sobbed.

Charlie leaned over, attempting to find a pulse in his neck. He could not find one. He brushed the eyelids closed, and then turned away, sadly shaking his head.

"We can't just leave him here," Dave told them. "How the hell do we get him out?"

Charlie took off his coat. "He is too heavy to carry as far as the lift. Help me roll him onto this. Maybe we can drag him out."

Nadia led the way holding the flashlight.

Charlie and Dave dragged their dead friend along the path they had just come. The air was heavy. They had to stop frequently to catch their breath, and reposition Andre's body on Charlie's Burberry. The shadows seemed even more ominous. Each of them realized that whoever killed Andre might be waiting for them hidden behind the next turn.

"Perhaps he was struck by a falling rock," Nadia suggested.

"Charlie strained to provide a positive response. "Yes perhaps that *was* what happened," he said, hoping to reassure her.

After he had rolled the body over, he had stolen a furtive glance around the area. There were no loose rocks anywhere near. He was sure whoever killed the miners had also killed Andre, but this didn't seem to be the right time for that discussion.

The lift was a welcome sight. Nadia boarded first, and then directed her beam of light through the gloom toward her trailing companions.

The men carefully placed André's lifeless body on the floor of the enclosure.

"Ready?" Dave asked, turning to see if everyone was properly located before starting the lift.

The ride to the top seemed to take much longer than it did coming down. Both men were sweating heavily from their trek. They shivered violently when the frigid outside air whistled down the shaft.

"Now what?" Nadia asked, turning to the men who were struggling to pull André's body from the cage.

The wind had picked up considerably since their decent into the mine. Drifts were beginning to form around the mouth of the pit. Their approaching tracks had been entirely wiped out.

It was cold. Damn cold Charlie thought, shivering without his coat. The wind seeped through every seam of his cashmere turtleneck. He had read once that the one indispensible item a traveler needs is a black cashmere turtleneck. That advice had never been more correct, he thought grudgingly.

"Now what? Dave asked echoing Nadia.

"The ice house," Charlie answered. That's where we took the miners, and it's close to the hotel.

Dave was thrashing his arms to keep warm. "Take my coat awhile," he offered Charlie.

"Thanks, but let's get on our way. It will go a little faster now that we are sliding him on the snowy ground instead of the floor of the mine."

Nadia led their way, shining the flashlight in front and behind her. The beam sliced the night like a narrow knife.

They finally saw the ancient structure a short distance ahead.

The icehouse door had frozen shut. Dave backed up and gave it a resounding kick that reverberated like a gunshot through the night. The door did not budge. He tried again, with the same result.

"Wait a minute," Charlie told him. "Let's try shouldering it open--together." The two men backed up.

Nadia counted, "one—two—three."

At the count of three, the men flung themselves against the door. It groaned and creaked, opening only slightly.

"Once more," Charlie shouted.

Nadia repeated the count. One—two—**three**!" she screamed.

The door swung open, and the men stumbled through. After pausing to catch their breath, they lifted Andre's body onto a large block of ice. It was an ignominious bier for a good man.

Charlie removed Andre's wallet, watch, and an opal ring he always wore. He then picked-up his coat from the ground and flung it over his lifeless friend. Shaking from sadness and cold, Charlie made the sign of the cross over the Frenchman's prostrate form. "May God have mercy on his soul," he whispered. In the numbing cold of the frigid icehouse, it was all he could think to say.

The three turned away, and began the slow journey through the driving snow toward the warmth and protection of the hotel. Charlie led the way back, half-running, half stumbling, wildly beating his arms against his body as he went. Nadia trailed behind him, her boots making a path for Dave who followed her.

Henry was waiting in the lounge, pacing nervously back and forth. Dave told him what they found, while Charlie and Nadia went directly to their rooms.

Charlie's hand shook as he took the vodka bottle from his desk drawer. He fumbled with the cap until it fell to the floor, rolling under the desk. It was of little concern to him, as he poured the stained water glass half-full of Stolichnaya.

Downing the fiery liquid in two large gulps, he hurried across the hall and the soothing affect of a steaming shower.

After the shower, he felt much better, and returned to his room. Sitting at his desk, he opened his laptop and addressed a message to Emmett's secure address.

> *Sorry to tell you that your old friend Andre Malott died suddenly today, while inspecting the mine. Will inform later regarding funeral arrangements. Signed CC*

Hitting **Send** Charlie felt confident that even WikiLeaks would not have an interest in such a distressing personal message.

Charlie poured another drink, before picking up the phone. He knew he should call Trevor Gunn to tell him about the death of his mining expert. He also knew that even the diligent Englishman would not be in his office this late in the day, but he hoped his recorder would be working.

He was right. The recorder *was* on, but the phone line was breaking up. The storm, Charlie decided. He told Trevor about Andre's death as briefly as possible, hoping to convey by his tone his concern for the project and the plight of the isolated experts.

Finishing the call, he hung up and dialed again, repeating what he had previously reported. Perhaps Trevor could put the two messages together to obtain one coherent description of what was happening at Tekeli.

He knew Trevor must do several things. After notifying Andre's family, if he had any, he would have to make arrangements for getting the old man's body returned to them. Charlie knew that he would also have to immediately alert corporate headquarters in Vienna that there were serious problems facing the Tekeli project.

Charlie poured himself another short shot of Russia's best before removing Andre's personal effects from his pockets. Spreading them across the desk, he thought that they represented pitiful evidence of a long life. There were a few credit cards, some family pictures, and a folded, yellowed article from an English language Santiago paper.

Charlie's hand began to tremble again as he read a description of how the Sendero Luminosa had brutally murdered Andre's wife after attacking the small mountain village where the two of them lived. At the time, Andre was consultant for a nationally owned silver mine, and he and his wife were living in the small mining community. The Maoists shot his wife, and then hung her upside down in the village square as a warning to others.

The article told how Andre was in Santiago, meeting with the government's Bureau of Mines. The local authorities never found her killers, although the Chilean Government later convicted the leader of the Maoists for other crimes. Charlie carefully refolded the article before replacing it in Andre's wallet.

Rising from the desk, he took the billfold, pictures, and ring and locked them in his travel case. Satisfied they would be secure, Charlie went to the hallway. It was empty. The light at end of the aisle glowed weakly, providing enough light for Charlie to find his way to the lounge. Everyone was in bed. The kitchen was empty.

He tried Andre's door. It was unlocked, and he glanced around the small room. The lamp on the desk cast its light on the room's masculine disarray.

Charlie quickly searched to make sure there was nothing left of value. He found Andre's carefully written technical notes in a desk drawer, and hurriedly collected them to carry back to his room. Satisfied he had located everything of value he opened the door to leave. He paused in the hallway and turned back. He quickly located what he was looking for in the closet, and removed Andre's heavy anorak. There was a tinge of guilt, but the hooded coat could replace the Burberry he left in the icehouse. It was like a trade, he rationalized.

Charlie flipped the lock, and returned to his room carrying Andre's papers with the heavy coat flung over his shoulder.

It had been a long day. A hard day. A very long hard day. He was exhausted, but there was one more thing to do before turning in for the night. He knew very little about the details of intelligence work. And even less what a field agent does, but he knew enough to know that in order to figure out who might be behind a series of events it was necessary to try and shrink the pool of suspects. It was the same thing that a corporate planner does in order to reduce the number of alternatives to his business plan.

Charlie found the list of names he had sent to Emmett for a background check, and began to pore over it hoping to reduce the list of possibilities. He first crossed Andre's name from the list. He recalled that Nadia, and Elaina were working in the administration building with Henry and Dave while Andre was in the mine. It would have been impossible for them to have anything to do with his death.

The manager had told them that Sammie had left earlier, so he crossed that name off his list. Now, there was only the kitchen staff as a remote possibility—and the miners. He stared at the paper, still searching for an answer. It must be one or more of the Russian miners he concluded. They had a motive and the opportunity. Perhaps Emmett was right. The Russians must be behind all of the deaths.

Charlie was too drained to think clearly, but still had difficulty sleeping. He tossed and turned, unable to get Andre's face from his mind. During the night, he awoke soaked with perspiration. He rose stiffly from the bed and looked outside. It was jet black, but he could see that the snow was continuing to fall.

He watched for a few minutes longer before returning to bed. The shortwave radio was on his nightstand, and he spun the dial. The Voice of America was featuring Porgy and Bess, and a young woman was extolling the virtues of a *summertime when the living is easy*. Charlie had already fallen asleep, unaware of the lyrical irony of the song.

20

The storm intensified during the night. The wind howled against the side of the old hotel. By morning it had moved on, but it had driven deep drifts against anything obstructing its path.

Looking out the window, Charlie was amused to see several miners were already beginning to shovel paths from their homes to the brewery. He checked his watch, and hurriedly finished dressing.

Nadia, and Elaina, were already at the table, whispering to each other. Henry sat across from them, deep in his own thoughts. As Charlie found his chair, the manager announced, "We are snowed in. There is no way in or out of here right now. So we will have to make do with what we have for awhile." She turned to leave, and as an afterthought added, "our phones are also dead."

Henry looked up from the table. "When will the snowplows come through?"

She laughed, and returned to the kitchen.

They all looked at each other.

Henry removed his glasses, inspected them, and nervously cleaned them with his paper napkin. Satisfied, he returned them to the bridge of his nose, and carefully straightened them, before studying the other diners. "What in the bloody hell can we do?"

"We are trapped here!" Elaina sobbed.

"Don't worry," Charlie tried to assure her. "There really is not much we can do about it. We weren't going anywhere anyway," he added.

Suddenly, Nadia looking around the table asked, "Where is Mr. Dieter? "He is usually the first one for meals."

The manager was busy serving eggs and sausages, but no one paid any attention to her. They were all staring at the two empty chairs.

Charlie was about to leave and check on Dave when he burst into the dining room. "Sorry I'm late," he apologized, "I must have overslept. Hope you started without me."

Everyone looked at each other with relief.

Unlike other mornings, there was little conversation. By now they were aware of what had happened to Andre the night before, and by some unspoken agreement chose to ignore it.

Finally, Nadia broke the silence. "Do you think it may have been an accident?" she repeated the question she had asked the night before.

Charlie again considered the possibility, searching for an acceptable answer. He was convinced he knew what had happened. There was no doubt in his mind, but he was not sure how he should respond to Nadia. Finally, he decided candor was necessary if they were to remain safe.

"No, it was no accident. I looked around the floor of the mine near Andre's body, and there were no loose rocks. Even, if it was a falling rock, his helmet would have shielded him from the blow. Someone had to strike him from behind with some form of blunt instrument."

"Would it have required a strong blow…a strong person?" Henry asked.

They were all silent. Finally, Dave answered. "Not necessarily, if a person got close enough with a heavy weapon that could do the job. "

"The miners were all killed by someone sneaking up behind them and using a garrote," Charlie offered. "Perhaps it wasn't the same person that killed Andre. It seems likely though it was someone he recognized, or the person was extremely quiet."

The conversation at the table turned to focus directly on their own situation.

"Who would have done such a thing-----and why?" Nadia asked.

Dave Dieter jumped in. "One thing is sure, it wasn't one of us. We were all together while Andre was in the mine."

Elaina was close to tears. "But....but, who then?" she asked looking around the table.

"I don't know. It is difficult to tell. It would seem likely that it is one or more of the Russian miners," Charlie replied.

Elaina stared at him. "So we are trapped here, and someone wants to kill us...is that what you are saying?"

Charlie shrugged, "that is pretty much the way it looks."

"I wish.... I really wish I could get out of here," Elaina burst out, almost in a moan. Tears filled her eyes.

"I am sure we all do," Nadia reassured her, patting her arm. "But we can't---at least not for awhile."

"I know one thing," Henry told them. They all turned to look at him. "I didn't come this far to die in Kazakhstan. If I had wanted to do that I would have done it a long time ago."

"If we are finished eating lets go to the lounge and decide what to do next," Charlie suggested. It seemed better to carry on the discussion somewhere more private. The kitchen staff appeared to be paying scant attention to them, but it had occurred to him that one of them might be keeping the miners informed on what they were doing.

"Do we continue working on the project?" Dave asked.

"Certainly," Charlie replied. "That has to be the reason someone is trying to do away with us. We can't leave, so we might as well do what they sent us to do."

He had noticed, while they were eating, each of them would occasionally steal a glance toward the empty chair that Andre once occupied. As they left, he turned and removed the chair from the table, and placed it against the wall.

Previously, the lounge served the advisors as a place to relax at the end of the day. This morning, their focus was one of preservation rather than relaxation. They each filed in and found their place among the mismatched furniture.

After they were settled Charlie began, "I would suggest that from now on we work here in the hotel instead of the administration building. Would that be a problem for anyone?"

"Elaina and I have made it a practice to bring our laptops back here each night so we can work here as well as over there," Nadia replied, looking to Elaina for confirmation.

Elaina nodded, still visibly upset.

Dave shrugged his agreement. "No problem for me, I bring my notes back here each day anyway."

"I have all the payroll records in my room, we can start getting those in shape now," Henry offered.

"How are they coming?" Charlie asked.

"Well the mine management kept really poor records. It was obviously not a priority with them. But, from what I can see they could cut their personnel by at least 40% and still run a productive operation."

"I think that is pretty typical from what I have seen in other Russian-run organizations." Charlie told him. "The *nomenklatura* in the Kremlin were principally interested in creating employment. They had no interest in such bourgeoisie considerations as profit, so they never had to worry about such mundane matters like efficiency,"

Dave chimed in, "that may be why the miners don't want to see anyone else take over the mine and upset their applecart."

Elaina looked at him. "Do you think they would kill for that?"

"I think it is damn good possibility," Henry intervened. "Not only does their pay depend on it, but their way of life as well. People have killed for a lot less."

"We can't just sit here and wait for someone to get rid of us." Nadia told them. "We have to do something." It was obvious that none of them could concentrate on the project when their own life was threatened.

Charlie had been thinking about that as well. "There is someone who might be able to throw some light on what is going on here."

"The fellow that gave you the note?" Nadia asked. "I've been wondering why he did that."

"So have I. The problem is how to get him to tell us what he knows."

"Try the old carrot and stick approach," Dave suggested.

Nadia giggled. "The Russians refer to that as the *whip and gingerbread*."

Charlie stood and looked at Nadia and Elaina. "Look ladies I am hesitant to suggest this, but you are the only *gingerbread* I can think of that might influence him."

"And the whip?"

"The whip, Nadia, is that unless our runny-eyed friend tells us what is going on, we will inform the mine manager that he was the one who passed us the note. He took great pains to slip it into my pocket without the rest of them seeing him."

"Why would he want to have done that?" Dave asked.

"That's what we will try and find out." Charlie replied.

There seemed to be tacit agreement among them that the approach might work. The remainder of their discussion centered on how to implement it without endangering the women. They all finally agreed they would try to approach the miner in the brewery, and attempt to get him in a private conversation to try and find out what he knew.

Dave would go in first, sit by himself, and hope that as time passed, he would no longer be noticed. Later, Charlie, Nadia, and Elaina would go to the brewery, and position themselves so that Elaina could make eye contact with the miner.

Afterwards, Charlie would leave and the women would remain, trying to charm him into joining them. Dave would also stay behind, at a separate table in order to provide the women with some level of security.

Charlie knew it was a feeble attempt at the *honey trap* approach that was part of spy's tradecraft throughout the centuries. Using a desirable woman to try to seduce a lonely man into divulging information he was keeping to himself had a proven record of success. This seduction, however, would have to be in public, and without benefit of any eventual gratification. There was not much chance for it working, but lacking an acceptable alternative, it seemed worth a try.

The inside of the brewery was eye watering smoky. The odor of stale beer mingled with sweaty men in a smoky atmosphere provided a noxious result. The mine manager and his assistant sat apart from the others. All eyes turned to the newcomers who were presenting a novel and welcome intrusion into the miner's deadly dull daily routine.

Charlie stole a glance at Dave seated in the back of room, concentrating on his beer. Nadia and Elaina found a table where they could look more directly at their target, while Charlie went to the bar.

Returning with their drinks, he positioned himself at their table with his back to the miners.

The women had been nervous about the plan from the beginning, but for lack of anything better were willing to play their roles.

The beer tasted dreadful. The Russians avoided any form of pasteurization in their brewing process, and it resulted in a foul tasting mixture, unlike any other in the world.

Elaina was an accomplished flirt, both by nature and practice. She soon became the focus of the miner's attention. A coy smile drew the gaze of her target, while Charlie reviewed what they hoped to accomplish. It would be up to Nadia and Elaina to lure the man away from his manager.

If they were successful, after the required small talk, the two girls would attempt to direct the conversation toward the death of the five miners. Underlying their conversation would be the veiled promise of further intimacy in return for his information. Also implicit in their conversation would be the threat of revealing what he had previously given them that led to the location of the bodies. Elaina was to be the gingerbread and the threat was to be the whip.

"I really don't like doing this," Elaina whispered.

"Neither do I," Nadia agreed.

"I don't either," Charlie added, "but I can't figure out any other way of finding out why he passed me the diagram. But, I don't blame you. If you really want to leave, we can leave right now."

Elaina shrugged, again glancing at the miner and smiling.

"OK then, I'm going to finish my beer and check out of here," Charlie told them. "Dave will keep an eye out for you, and intervene if it becomes necessary."

He quickly emptied his glass, and left.

In the hotel lounge, Charlie and Henry reviewed where they were on the project but, try as they might, neither of them could focus on what they were doing. Time passed slowly as they waited for the two interpreters to return. Finally, Henry stretched out on the sofa, and fell asleep.

"Well that didn't work," Nadia exclaimed disgustedly from the top of the stairs.

Henry jumped up as Nadia, and Elaina burst into the lounge. "Tell us everything that happened."

The two women began talking excitedly to each other in Russian. They stopped when they realized the men couldn't understand them.

"Unfortunately, there is not much to tell," Nadia began. "After Mr. Connelly left it took only a few minutes for---Boris is his name--it took just a few minutes before Boris came to our table. He immediately sat down. We didn't even have to invite him."

Nadia stopped as Dave entered the lounge with a disappointed look on his face.

"Well Boris sat down---he was really interested in Elaina---he sat down and began telling us how important he was."

"He was terribly drunk," Elaina added.

"Well, all Boris could talk about was himself," Nadia continued.

"We finally just asked him about the diagram," Elaina added. "Several times."

"That's right, several times," Nadia confirmed. "But, either he was too drunk to focus on that. Or too smart."

"I really doubt the smart part. Finally, he started to grab my leg under the table," Elaina told them, making a face. So we got up and left. He looked shocked that we would do that. But it---or he—was getting out of hand. We knew Mr. Dieter was there, but we were afraid the other miners might come to help Boris—so--so we just left," she blurted.

"You did exactly right," Charlie told her. "We will have to think of something else."

"What do we do now," Dave wanted to know.

"Lock your doors," Charlie told him brusquely.

Before going to bed, Charlie checked the list of suspects once more. Nothing leapt out at him. As he dropped off to sleep, the hoarse voice of Emmett Valentine ricocheted around his mind. "Remember, in this business *nothing is like it seems.*"

21

A loud banging, punctuated by a woman's piercing scream, reverberated through the deserted hotel hallway. Charlie leapt from his bed, and hit the floor running. Doors swung open behind him as he raced through the corridor. The thumping of his bare feet on the hall floor matched the cadence of the banging on the hotel room door.

Boris turned in bleary-eyed shock at the approaching figure. He was drunkenly unsteady on his feet, but it did not prevent him from taking an arcing swing at the shadowy form suddenly confronting him.

Charlie parried with his forearm, before landing a bone-crunching blow on the intruder's chin. Boris crumpled to the floor, his bleary eyes rolled back into his head.

Henry, Dave, and Nadia immediately joined Charlie. "It's all right Elaina," Nadia yelled through the door. "You can come out now. It's all right dear," she repeated more calmly.

Elaina peeked out, with her door slightly ajar. Seeing Boris' limp figure on the floor she began to withdraw into her room once again. Nadia caught the door before it closed. "That's all right don't worry, he can't hurt you now." Inside the room, Elaina stood shivering in only her bra and panties.

"Here, put on your robe, and tell us what happened." Nadia told her in a soothing voice.

"I was sound asleep, when I heard tapping at my door. I may have heard it at other doors, but it could have been only a dream. I thought it was one of you, so I went to see who it was. There was Boris. I slammed the door, and threw the lock. It only made him angrier, and he began pounding on the door again. That's what you must have heard. I started to scream louder, but he only pounded harder. I was afraid he was going to break the door down. Then what would I do?"

Elaina began to tremble again, and Nadia put her arm around her shoulders to comfort her before leading her back into her room.

The men dragged Boris into the lounge, out of sight of Elaina.

"What do we do with this bastard?" Dave wanted to know.

"I feel terrible about this," Charlie told them. "I got her into this. I thought we had taken enough precautions so the girls would be safe. It never occurred to me that he would come back here."

"Well the plan worked part way," Henry said. "Elaina sure got old bleary-eyed Boris' attention. He must have been thinking about her---could not get her out of his mind, I bet. I imagine he convinced himself that she would want to see him too, if only he could find her and get her alone. His plan didn't work all that well either. Now that we have him we can find out what you wanted to know."

"All right, but how do we make him talk?" Charlie asked as Boris began to stir.

"I know how to do that," Henry replied.

Dave and Charlie both turned and stared with considerable skepticism at the small accountant. "You can?" they chorused in disbelief.

"Listen, I know what you are thinking, but you're wrong. Unfortunately, I have seen enough men broken in my time to fill a damn book. The Russians were expert at it, and I have no bloody reservations about using their own techniques on a drunken Russian miner that was intent on raping Elaina."

Charlie and Dave looked at each other. "OK," Charlie told him. "What do you want to do?"

"Tie his hands, and take off his pants. I don't care which you do first."

"Take off his pants?"

"That's right take off his damn pants. Russians are like anyone else. You put them in their skivvies in front of other men, and more particularly women, they feel humiliated.

"You remember Abu Grebe. The British press was full of it, and I imagine the American papers were as well. Those soldiers really didn't physically harm their prisoners. Just stripped them, and put women's panties on their head for the pictures. Ok—Ok--It was not nice, I grant you that. But you should see what the Russians do. Now take off his pants."

Boris was now awake and struggling with the rope binding his hands that Dave had found in the kitchen. They removed his belt and stripped off his trousers. He wiggled and squirmed, but could do nothing except shout curses at them.

And Boris did just that—loud and long.

Red Jockey shorts! The men snickered, and Boris' face became flushed.

"Dave you were smoking a cigar the other night. Do you have any left?" Henry asked.

Dave nodded, and started down the hall to his room. He soon returned with a wide grin on his face.

"My last one," he told them. I hope it will be used in a good cause."

Henry looked at the band. "Habana Primo?"

"That's right," Dave told him proudly. "It's the best old uncle Fidel has to offer." He lighted the huge cigar with obvious satisfaction, and exhaled a puff of smoke directly in Boris' face.

"Do you still have the diagram of the mine that he gave you?" Henry asked turning to Charlie.

It was now Charlie's turn to trot down the hallway. As he was going out the door he saw Henry approaching Boris with the cigar and slowly circle the lighted tip around his right eye, and then the left eye; while all the time laughing with maniacal glee.

Our little bookkeeper has become a changed man, he thought rummaging in his desk for the diagram.

In the lounge, Boris face was contorted with fear. The bright flush of embarrassment had now turned ashen.

"You've got to make them think you mean business," Henry said, as if he had heard it repeated many times before.

Charlie showed Boris the diagram. Henry blew on the end of the lighted cigar until it glowed a bright red in the dimly lit lounge.

Boris shook his head, and cursed in Russian.

Like hell I am," Henry replied, and placed the burning tip of the cigar on the back of Boris' hand.

He screamed, shaking his head in pain.

"He is not going to tell you anything," Dave said.

Henry drew closer to Boris and slowly advanced the cigar toward his bloodshot eye.

Dave reached out to grab Henry's arm, but withdrew his hand when he saw the expression on his face. He didn't like this, but he knew how important it was to get the miner to talk.

Before Boris could shake his head again, Henry quickly changed the direction of the cigar from targeting the Russian's eyes to pointing it menacingly at the man's crotch. Henry slowly approached closer, a wild look in his eyes and a broad grin on his face.

Boris screamed while trying to squirm away. Then he began spewing long sentences in Russian. It was obvious he wanted no more of this crazy Englishman.

"Now is the time to get Nadia," Henry told them, backing off slightly, and blowing again on the glowing end of the Habana Primo.

Charlie knocked on Elaina's door, "It's Charlie Connelly Nadia. We think Boris has decided to tell us what he knows about the diagram, but we need you to interpret."

Nadia, cracked open the door, and peeked out. She had heard Boris' shouts, and wondered what was happening, but until she heard Charlie's knock she didn't think she should get involved.

Now, Nadia looked in the lounge and was shocked at what she saw. Her mind searched for the proper English adjective. *Bizarre* was the first one that immediately came to mind. Boris was sprawled across the sofa, with his hands tied behind him, and his pants in a heap on the floor. Oh my God she thought, Red shorts, how utterly Russian. To make it even more curious, Henry was standing close-by, blowing huge clouds of smoke in the miners face.

"Maybe you should not be so rough on him. He looks frightened to death," she told them.

Charlie ignored her question. He didn't like doing this, but he looked away.

He had looked away before--several times in fact, during his association with the Agency. Not only in relation to what others had done but, God help him, what he had done himself. Each time it became a little easier than before. Although he was beginning to feel sorry for Boris, this was not the time to reduce the pressure. He had to know if Boris had killed the miners, or if it was someone else. More importantly, he needed to know if the same people who killed the miners had also killed Andre, and might now kill them as well.

No, this was not the time to let up on this miserable Russian.

"Ask him, Nadia," Charlie demanded, "to tell us everything he knows about the dead miners and why he gave us the diagram. Tell him if he doesn't we will start again, and this time it will not be just a threat. He will never be able to be with a woman again." Henry moved closer to make the point. "Also, if he doesn't, you might add, we will tell the other miners where we got the diagram, and let them deal with what is left of him."

Nadia looked curiously at the three consultants. They looked deadly serious, and repeated in Russian what Charlie had told her in English.

Henry moved even closer toward Boris, blowing on the tip of his cigar to emphasize whatever Nadia was saying.

Boris began to talk, with an occasional prompting from Nadia. Finally, she turned to repeat what he had told her. "He had gone to work that day drunk. He says that it was not that unusual. All of the miners would do that. You had to be drunk to be a miner--according to him. That day he had drunk even more than usual. He got sleepy, and wandered off to find a place to lie down. He came across an old pathway and curled up. For just a few minutes, he tells me." Her expression registered disbelief.

"Anyway, a noise woke him, and he saw a figure he did not recognize rounding a corner. He looked like a miner, but not one he knew. Well, Boris stayed quiet until the other man was out of sight before trying to find what he was doing there."

"Can he tell us what the man looked like?" Charlie interrupted.

Nadia repeated his question in Russian, and then shook her head negatively. "He says it was too dark to tell. He never got a good look at his face, and he still may have been a little drunk."

Nadia apparently was having difficulty believing all that she was hearing, and evidenced her skepticism in the tone of her voice.

"OK, sorry I interrupted," Charlie apologized.

Boris now needed less prompting from Nadia. It was as if he had become anxious to tell his story.

"He says," Nadia continued her translation, "that after he was sure the other person was gone he got up to see where he had come from. He was afraid of what he might find. In recent weeks miners had turned up missing, and no one knew where they had gone. Sometimes they were missing at work, and others were missing from town.

"It had gotten so bad that most of the men refused to go to the mine any longer. They thought it was haunted. Just a few would still go to work each day."

The miner began to talk again, barely waiting for Nadia to finish her translation.

"He tells me that after going around the corner and squeezing through a crevice he found five bodies. The ones you found he says. They had been dead for some time. He didn't know what to do. All he knew was that he wanted to get out of there, as fast and as far away as possible."

When he finished, Boris lapsed into a moody silence, seemingly unwilling to continue. After an unexpectedly harsh verbal nudge from Nadia, he began talking again.

"At home that night he thought about it. He couldn't sleep," she translated. "The vodka was no help. He did not know who he could tell. What if he told the mine manager and he was involved in the killing in order to get the mine to close."

Everyone was now sitting down, fascinated with what they were hearing. All of them focused on Nadia, and her translation of Boris' story.

"The next day was the meeting with you people," Nadia continued. "He decided to draw up a map and try and find a way to give it to you so that you would find the bodies. He knew that you could not be involved in the killing since you had just come to Tekeli, and had no reason to kill the men."

Nadia turned to Charlie. "That's all he knows, he says. Now untie him and give him his pants back—he says."

"In a minute," Charlie told her. "Ask him to tell us who he thinks killed Andre?"

Nadia repeated the question to Boris. He shrugged his shoulders as best he could with his arms tied.

"He says he has no idea," Nadia told them. He doesn't think that it was one of the miners. They all appeared to him to be very saddened by the deaths of the men you found.

"Thank you Nadia. Do you think we should ask him why he was pounding on Elaina's door?"

"That is pretty obvious, but anyway he has said that he thought she wanted him to come and see her. He thought she would be easy."

Nadia returned to Elaina's room to tell her what had happened, while the men untied Boris and tossed him his trousers. He put them on, and slunk down the stairs, muttering Russian obscenities the entire way.

Back in his room, Charlie studied the list of possible suspects he had prepared earlier, then crumpled it in disgust and tossed it into the wastebasket. He turned and gazed out his window. A bright moon cast shadows over the sleeping village. He could see that it had been snowing again. The paths to the brewery, that the miners cleared earlier, were drifting in again.

After a moment of reflection, he returned to his desk and removed the chair. Making certain it could still support his weight; he retrieved the gun he had hidden on top of the armoire. He twirled the cylinder a couple of times to make sure that it was working properly, and then slid it under his pillow feeling stupid he had not thought of it before. Finally he dropped off to sleep.

22

Breakfast was a curious meal. The prevailing mood was one of melancholy, seasoned with a considerable dash of angst. Everyone was overly quiet and polite. 'Please pass this,' or 'would you like some of that.' The men looked older than they had the day before, and the women appeared much more vulnerable. Dave silently spooned his coffee with his liver spotted hands. Finally, he stopped and yawned. He had slept poorly, but he was not alone in this.

Each one was attempting to digest what had taken place the night before, and wondering who might be next. They were well aware of the potential danger they were in, made even worse by the inability of any outside help to intervene.

Henry, on the other hand, had a better appetite than usual. He was satisfied with his performance the previous night. He felt he had won back his position with the group.

"Are there any more sausages?" he inquired of the server.

"Do you like our Kazakh sausages," Nadia asked as his plate returned with another helping.

"Yes as I matter of fact I do. In England we call them bangers."

"Really?"

"Yes, they are made with pork. They are really quite tasty," he added approvingly.

Now, all eyes focused on Nadia and Henry, instead of on their plates.

"In Kazakhstan," she smiled sweetly, "we call these sausages *chuchuk*.......they are made of horsemeat. I am surprised you find them so *tasty*."

Everyone stared at Nadia, who was smiling innocently .

Henry choked--his face turning a bright crimson. Stuffing the napkin to his mouth, he rushed from the dining room.

That was the end of breakfast. The mood was broken. Everyone rose and adjourned to the lounge.

Charlie had received a cryptic note from Emmett on his computer. It contained merely the reference Nd60 and a question mark. Retrieving it from his pocket, he handed it to Dave.

"Any Idea what in the hell this means?"

"Where did you get that?" Dave asked. Nearby the women began assembling their work for the day, ignoring the conversation between the men. "You remember that mineral sample Andre collected from the mine? He thought it might be important. You looked at it and were unable to classify it with your equipment. I gave it to young Pembroke when he was here, and asked him to send it out to have it analyzed when he returned to Almaty. (Charlie didn't bother to tell Dave exactly where it had been sent for analysis.) "I think this is their answer, but I certainly don't understand it."

Dave looked at the email more closely. "I am not sure, but let me get my mineral handbook from my room. I'll be back in a minute."

While Dave was gone, Charlie watched Nadia and Elaina going about their work. They were hard working young women, and it was unfortunate that they were now in a situation where they were at risk.

Soon Henry came into the lounge, still somewhat pallid from his quick exit from the dining room. "Bloody horsemeat! These people hide it in everything they cook." He sat down next to Elaina, and the two of them began organizing their database for the final report.

Charlie was beginning to feel like the British colonel Nicholson in the *Bridge on the River Kwai,* who aggressively continued to work for his Japanese captors because he felt it was his duty to do so. He hoped that was not the case with him. He was well aware of their situation, but saw no option other than to keep doing what they were sent to do.

His train of thought was broken by Dave's footsteps echoing down the hallway at a parade ground clip. He burst into the room with a broad smile on his face, and thrust his dog-eared minerals handbook at Charlie. "I found your Nd60 here. It is just as I thought. It's one of those rare- earth elements we were talking about yesterday.

"My God was that only yesterday?" he paused before continuing. "Nd is the symbol, and 60 is the atomic number for the rare-earth element neodymium. My book tells all about it. You can read it for yourself. I have to work on finishing my part of the project."

"Ok, alright, I will take a look at your book," Charlie assured him, "but just tell me one thing before you take off. If that stuff is in that black hole out there would it make the mine more valuable to other owners?"

Dave was already halfway out the door. "*Hell yes*—is that clear enough for you non technical person?"

Charlie sat down on the sofa and began thumbing through the thick book. *Neodymium is a soft silvery metal which tarnishes in ordinary air.* He began skipping through the technical description, attempting to find some passages that he understood. *Most of the world's neodymium is mined in China and Mongolia.* That made sense. China was just over the border.

He continued to search through the pages for things that were at least somewhat clear to him. *Neodymium glass solid-state lasers are used in extremely high power (terawatt scale), high energy multiple beam systems for inertial confinement fusion. The current laser at the UK Atomic Weapons Establishment is a 1-terawatt neodymium-glass laser. ....They are also used in computer hard disks and in power versus weight electric motors in hybrid cars, and generators for aircraft and wind turbine electric generators.*

Charlie set aside Dave's reference book and thought about what he had learned. It appears, he decided, that if the mine at Tekeli contained rare-earth elements, in addition to its already valuable lead and zinc deposits, it could provide a valuable acquisition for a variety of countries. Enough to die for, as the phrase goes.

~~~

Charlie was not the only one thinking about the discovery of rare-earth elements at Tekeli. Half a world away, Emmett looked over the results of the analysis from the researchers before condensing it into the short message he had transmitted to Charlie.

Now, he was wondering how the recent discovery of beryllium would affect his project *Silk Road*. He had thought about it for some time, evaluating the alternatives and consequences, but the only thing he was getting was frustrated He decided to give up, and go back to his apartment.

He stuffed the manila folder into his old leather briefcase. It had been around almost as long as he had. The brass clasp was beginning to pull away from its base, but still provided sufficient security if closed properly—and Emmett always made sure that he had closed it properly.

He impatiently buzzed the garage to signal the driver to bring his car around to the entrance. Afterwards he set the locks on his files and turned off his stereo and the lights. In the empty hallway he peered into a small peephole in the center of his closed door. The electrodes scanned his retina, and a faint click indicated the lock was set for the night.

The express elevator sped past the intervening floors and deposited him at the Agency's marble-lined lobby. Striding
~~~

across the reception area, he waved to the guard and glanced, as he always did, at the memorial to fallen CIA officers with its row of stars without names, He wondered if Barry Durand's star was included yet, but decided he would check on that tomorrow---or possibly the next day.

He nodded briefly to the statue of William J. Donovan on his right as he approached the entranceway. His glance veered from the statute to the inscription on the wall above it. The words had been taken from John 8.23. The biblical reference was transferred from the original Agency headquarters to where they were now in the lobby of the new building.

Ye shall know the truth and the truth shall make you free.

It's just that sometimes it takes longer than others, Emmet decided, and it often needs a lot of help.

By the time he reached the revolving door, his car was already parked at the curb, its super charged fuel injected engine idling noiselessly. It was a large black nondescript Buick Park Avenue, heavily armored, with deeply tinted windows. Emmett climbed into the backseat, and immediately disappeared as the car pulled from the curb, headed toward the gate.

Several years before, a radical had assassinated a member of the Agency's staff while he was waiting to clear security. This resulted in even tighter measures at the entrance. However, the procedures were slightly less onerous to leave the premises than to enter. The marine on duty quickly waved them through. Once clear of the gate, the driver accelerated on to Dolly Madison Drive.

At first, Emmett had resisted using the special limo service, but he finally decided that the convenience it offered made up for whatever reasons he harbored about using it. He was particularly grateful for it this night.

The weather had turned cold. Not as cold as Kazakhstan he guessed, still thinking about the project, but damn cold never the less. To make it more miserable it was raining steadily. It was the kind of downpour that challenges the wiper blades and finds them wanting. This kind of rain could easily turn to snow. Soon it did.

The driver did not speak to Emmett during the ride, or Emmett to him. Both driver and rider were schooled in the demands of a secret life, and conversation was unnecessary—and undesirable. The driver knew the destination without asking. It was a small apartment hotel in the center of McLean, Virginia, only a few minutes from the headquarters building at Langley.

For several years, when his wife was still alive, they had lived together in Georgetown. After the cancer took her, the house was too large—too lonely and too close to the wrangling and political machinations of Washington, so he moved.

Inside his apartment, Emmett put a tape in the cassette player and a packaged dinner in the microwave. Tonight he was having veal scaloppini and Chianti.

Before eating, he turned to the picture of his wife on the mantel, taken years before, and raised his glass in a silent salute. She had been gone for many years, but she was always there.

After dinner—it had not taken him long to finish--he removed the file from his briefcase, and paged through it more carefully than he had in the office.

He had to admit he had seldom heard of rare-earth, but now it was of considerable interest to him. The presence of the unique mineral element could explain why there was the sudden interest in the Tekeli mine, and why the project might be in jeopardy.

He was well aware that the U.S. military had become extremely concerned that some minerals such as cobalt, lead, and zinc, that had at one time been abundant, might suddenly become scarce. Because of their alarm, they were stockpiling these materials, along with lithium and some rare-earth elements they might need in the future. He understood all of that, but the immediate question was not what, but who else would be interested enough in the mine to kill for it.

He wondered if it was too late to call Vienna. He decided to try anyway, and set the scrambler before dialing Vincent St. Claire's home number.

"Damn it Emmett don't you ever call anyone during working hours?" The voice leapt out of the speaker phone loud and clear--and very angry.

"Seldom Vincent. I work during working hours and talk at night. How are you old friend?"

Vincent relented, he felt sorry for Emmett. He realized that he was a lonely man with a great deal of responsibility. He could understand that very well---very well indeed. "So what is on your mind tonight Emmett?"

"It looks like the mine at Tekeli could contain the rare-earth element neodymium, in addition to the lead and zinc we already knew was there.

"And you know that how?" Vincent inquired, surprised at the new development.

Emmett gave Vincent a quick briefing on how Charlie Connelly had samples taken from the mine, and had given them to Roger Pembroke when he visited Tekeli. After Roger returned to Almaty, he had the samples flown out in carrier pouch to Washington. The Agency's experts analyzed them, and determined that it was the rare-earth element neodymium.

"So now Vincent," Emmett inquired with superficial detachment, "tell me what you know about rare-earth and who would be interested in controlling the Tekeli mine for it."

Vincent paused briefly before replying, "I know enough about it to know that if there is neodymium there, it could explain why people may not want to see the project completed on time. By the way, can you turn down that damn music? It is hard to hear what you are saying. What is it any way?"

Vincent's criticism of his musical selection hurt Emmett. "It's a tape of Andre' Rieu's orchestra playing Viennese waltzes. I put it on especially for you."

"I hate Strauss," Vincent replied. The two men had worked together for a long time, and it was late. Late enough to be cranky.

"Tape did you say tape? Are you still playing cassette tapes Emmett?" Vincent chided him. "You are not exactly at the cutting edge of technology old man. What you need is an IPod."

Emmett turned down the volume, and hastened to change the subject. "The reason I called was I would like your opinion regarding who might be trying to sabotage the Tekeli mine, and your project there. I have my own opinion, but I wanted to hear your thoughts as well."

Vincent felt flattered that Emmett sought his opinion. It was not a frequent occurrence. He must be more worried than he let on.

"Well old friend I was wondering about that myself. It is obvious someone wants that mine taken out of the hands of the Kazakhstan Government. I know you always suspect the Russians, but consider this. We know that China is buying up mineral resources all over the world, using income from U.S. debt to make their purchases. They are particularly interested in building strategic reserves in metals, particularly rare-earth metals, in order to give Beijing increased ability to influence global prices in a commodity sector it already dominates."

"How do you know all of this Vincent?"

"Details of their stockpiling plans haven't been made public. But, the Global Bank pays close attention to things going on in China, just as the CIA does in the Mideast. For us, that is where the action is right now.

"We believe China may be playing rare-earth roulette with the capitalist countries. Our representatives in Beijing tell us that the outlines of their effort are apparent in recent statements from Chinese government agencies, and the state controlled companies, as well as reports that we monitor daily in their government run media.

"So what does this all mean to us?" Emmett asked, thinking over what he had just learned.

"If by *us* you mean the western powers; it means that China can better control the price of the rare-earth elements making them more valuable while, at the same time, making them more expensive for other countries to obtain for their own industries"

"Such as?" Emmett asked.

"Such as oil refining, cell phones, and high technology batteries for military applications. That could be why, old boy, that the glorious Peoples Republic might like to see the project at Tekeli fail to be completed until they have a better opportunity to get their hands on the mine."

Emmett was impressed by Vincent's information, but felt he had to criticize him for something. "You seem only concerned with the project, rather than worrying about the people you have sent there."

"Come on—come on Emmett. Don't play choir boy with me. We both have put men in jeopardy in the past. It comes with the territory."

Vincent concluded the conversation with, "by the way, did you know that Connelly and the rest of them are snowed-in up there, and we couldn't get help to them if we wanted to?"

The line went dead, and Emmett shut-off the scrambler. Vincent had certainly won that conversation he conceded. Up to now, he had focused all of his attention on Russia, believing that all things evil emanated from FSB Headquarters at Lubyanka Square. Now he was having difficulty realigning his thinking toward China. He consoled himself that the country was currently more communistic in its political hierarchy than

Russia. They don't call them the People's Republic for nothing he decided.

Tomorrow, he would have to think how he might get Charlie out of there if it became necessary, Vincent's project be damned.

23

The mood around the dinner table had not improved during the day. Each of them was still concerned over what had occurred at the mine, and how it might affect them.

They were all experienced professionals, having worked on these types of projects before, and were comfortable working under pressure to complete their work on schedule. This was the first time, however, any of them had worked under conditions where their lives were at risk.

Charlie shared their concern. He had never felt so isolated. In the past, if it became necessary, he was always able to maintain contact with Langley, and if that became difficult, he could at least meet with the local CIA Station Chief. Here, at Tekeli, the snowstorm had made that impossible.

Charlie had unlocked Andre's empty room and retrieved the last bottles of wine, but it was having little effect on the diners. Occasionally there were attempts at conversation, but once attempted they quickly failed. The hotel manager and her staff, ignoring the mood of her customers, busied themselves with their own responsibilities.

After his experience at breakfast, Henry was more cautious what he ate, concentrating exclusively on the bread, which was always excellent, washed-down with water glasses filled with Sauvignon Blanc.

Charlie tried to get their minds off their situation by attempting to focus their attention on the project. Clearing his throat to attract attention, he began with "so Henry, how close to completion of your assignment are you?" It seemed to work as everyone's attention was diverted from their plates to the accountant. Even Dave looked up and stared at him, interested to hear his reply.

Henry seemed pleased to be the center of attention. "I have pretty much gone as far as I can with the data I have. I can only do so much with them so I guess my analysis is complete. Now, I am preparing my recommendations and after that I will work on the presentation with Elaina."

Elaina agreed with what Henry said. "I'm already beginning to prepare the charts for the presentation. It won't take much longer."

"What about you Dave?" Charlie asked, munching on an apple for his dessert.

"Apples are originally from Kazakhstan you know," Dave mimicked Sammie Wang. Then, he added more seriously, "pretty much the same as Henry. There is really not much more I can do, other than round off the rough edges."

Nadia nodded in agreement. "I already have part of his charts done, and have started putting your information together as well Mr. Connelly. Both Elaina and I have the Russian versions done, and will begin concentrating on the English ones now, but that will take more time.

Charlie rose from the table. "It looks like we are pretty close to being on schedule then. Now if we could just get out of here without anyone more being killed we will be in great shape."

As they headed down the hallway, Charlie added as an afterthought, "be sure and lock your doors."

Back in his room, Charlie noticed frost had coated his window, so that he was looking at the outside world through an icy prism with wildly distorted refracted images. He shuddered. The room felt unusually cold.

His thoughts turned home, and his wife Beth. They had been apart for long periods before, but this time it felt very different. Not only did Kazakhstan seem to be located at the end of world, but the mine was even more isolated because of the weather conditions.

Fear had also been his traveling companion during his previous associations with the CIA. This time he was unsure of the enemy and their motives remained unclear.

The difficulty in communicating with Beth also provided and added element of distress and distraction. He was never sure that his emails were getting through. The few messages he had received from her were incomplete and disjointed, seemingly unrelated to any he had sent. This made him uncertain if the majority of his emails ever survived their transmission.

He decided to try again to reach Trevor and provide a status report. The first time he tried, he heard only a crackling on the line. He repeated the attempt with similar results. The third attempt connected him to Trevor's recorder.

He left his message, and began reviewing his own recommendations to the Kazakh Government regarding the viability of the Tekeli mine. Perhaps work was the best answer to his problems. While it might not solve them, it might at least provide a reasonable distraction.

He quickly became tired, his eyes burned from reading under the room's poor light, and he decided to go to bed. He checked the Beretta to make sure that it was still under his pillow, and soon fell asleep.

Morning came sooner than it should. Rays of light penetrated the thickening frost on his window. He looked outside and was not surprised to see that it was snowing again. More lightly than before, but still more than they needed.

The walkway to the brewery had filled in overnight. At least it gave the miners something to do. He thought he could see an outline of footprints leading to the hotel, but was not sure. Anyway, it would probably be someone on the staff, or the miners attempting to clear another path.

The pushups came easier this morning. He must be getting back in shape. He had halfway expected a call from Trevor this morning, acknowledging his message of the night before. None had come by the time he had showered and shaved and left the room for breakfast.

On the way to the dining room, he decided that he would lay off the sausages, himself. They hadn't hurt him when he wasn't aware that they contained horsemeat. Now it was different. What was that old adage about what you don't know can't hurt you. He had never believed that, and he decided this was not a good time to change his opinion.

Passing Henry's room, Charlie noticed that the door was slightly ajar. He thought that unusual. All the people had been locking their doors, even if they were in the rooms, or when they were to be gone for only a few minutes. He peered in and saw Henry still in bed, the sheet drawn up around his chin. Apparently, the wine had proved an effective sedative.

Only a faint light filtered through the window. Drawing closer to wake him, Charlie noticed a red strain trickling from each ear and running down the side of Henry's mouth. Then he was shocked to see that Henry's eyes bulged open, staring sightlessly at the ceiling. Charlie's stomach churned.

"Oh my God--poor Henry! "

Bending over to close his friend's eyelids, he noticed a slender leather cord embedded in his neck. What he found revolted him. What kind of a demented bastard would find it necessary to murder a nearsighted accountant?

He felt terribly sad for Henry. He had a difficult life, only to return to meet his death in the country he had escaped as a child. What a terrible way to go. How ironic for the circle of life to close in such a bizarre fashion.

As he gently pulled the edge of the sheet over the lifeless body of his friend, the realization flooded over him that if someone would kill this type of man, for whatever obscure motive they might have, none of them would be safe.

Charlie locked the door securely behind him, and walked slowly toward the dining room. An almost tangible pall hung over the room as the rest of the group sat apprehensively around the table waiting for their missing members.

They all turned to watch as Charlie, at a loss for words, silently removed Henry's chair from the table, placing it against the wall next to Andre's. The realization of what his action implied came suddenly and powerfully to them all.

Dave was the first to speak, "Oh my God, what has happened to Henry? Did he die in his sleep?"

Both Nadia, and Elaina sat silently, too shocked to speak. Tears flooded Elaina's dark eyes, and she buried her head in her hands. She and Henry and made an odd pair of opposites, but they had grown close as they worked together.

Finally, Nadia spoke in an uncommonly shrill voice, "tell us what has happened to him Mr. Connelly?"

Charlie coughed. He was still having difficulty finding his voice. He paused to better collect his thoughts, then briefly told them how he found the body before describing in considerable detail the shocking manner in which Henry had died. He felt it increasingly important they fully realize the danger each of them faced.

Following Andre's death, they had all begun to suspect that they were in danger, but each had chosen to believe all the deaths related only to the mine, and might not place them at risk. Now that illusion was over, and a more distinct reality set in for them all .

"Who do you think will be next?" Dave asked, not expecting an answer.

"How do we protect ourselves now?" Nadia asked. "We already stay close together in the hotel in the daytime, and lock our doors at night."

Elaina had stopped crying. She dabbed her eyes with her handkerchief. "Why didn't Henry lock his door? He was always so careful about everything."

It was a good question. Charlie had wondered about that himself. The door was certainly unlocked when he went in. There were no signs of break-in, or he would have noticed it when he entered and when he left. Henry must have forgotten to lock it when he returned from dinner. It was the only explanation.

"He shrugged, "it was not locked when I entered," was all he could say.

The group had lost their appetite, and decided to meet in the lounge in an hour. If anyone had any ideas, they would discuss them then.

Charlie rushed down the hallway. Once inside the room he took the phone and dialed Trevor Gunn. The line sounded dead. He hung up and tried again. He could hear it ringing. Thank God. On the third ring a female voice replied. "Mr. Trevor Gunn's office, Lorisa Grankovskayo speaking."

Charlie hesitated a moment, taken aback by the secretary's name. "This is Charlie Connelly. I need to speak to him immediately."

"I am sorry Mr. Gunn is in a meeting. He will have to call you back."

"No, no, I need to speak to him now," Charlie shouted. "I mean right *now!"* he tried to be as emphatic as possible without sounding rude. He recalled Trevor's description of his well-built secretary being dumb as a rock, and she sounded as if she had no idea who he was.

"He told me he didn't want to be disturbed, Mr. Connelly. I am sure he will get back to you soon," she told him, her voice seeping with indolence.

To hell with not being rude he decided, ready to abandon any semblance of civility. "Listen woman, you had better get off your ass and get him on the phone immediately, or your days at Global Bank are definitely numbered."

"Well it better be important," she conceded placing him on hold. This only made Charlie angrier.

"What is it Charlie? I have been trying to call you, but couldn't get through," Trevor's voice came over the line.

"I found Henry's body this morning, He had been murdered in his sleep," Charlie blurted, still infuriated from his conversation with the secretary.

The bluntness of Charlie's answer got Trevor's attention. "MY God old man, tell me all about it."

And Charlie did, uninterrupted for the next several minutes. He described in considerable detail how Henry died and the seeming connection to the dead miners. He also described how Andre died, and the presumed linkage to all of the deaths.

"There is someone here who doesn't want the mine to be taken over right now," he told Trevor. "I have no idea who, or exactly why, but there is a definite connection to these deaths and our project. We need to get out of here as soon as possible or your damn project will be washed up, and incidentally your hired consultants as well." As his words rushed out, they helped to clarify his own thinking.

Trevor listened sympathetically, his normal British resolve fading with each sentence. "I understand old man, and fully agree with you, but do you have any suggestions. I know you are snowed in up there. I don't think the Land Rovers can navigate the roads. I have been trying to figure out how to get you out, but nothing comes immediately to mind."

Charlie couldn't fault him. He had to admit he had been thinking about this as well, and had been unable to come-up with a workable solution.

"Look Trevor, you know Roger Pembroke. Call him. Maybe the yanks can come up with something. They have better resources here in Kazakhstan than the Bank. See what they can do and get back to me."

He knew, but did not say, that the CIA had planned and executed extractions from more hazardous and remote locations than Tekeli. When he was in Ukraine and the KGB was hunting him the local agency people helped him secretly get out of Kiev.

After his conversation finished, Charlie took out the one-time pad Roger gave him, and encoded a message to Emmett. When in doubt stir the pot. That had always been his motto, and it could not hurt here.

24

Almaty

At the American Embassy in Almaty, there was an air of anticipation rippling through the many offices assigned to the staff. A group of traveling congressional representatives was coming to visit. The U.S. Congress was in recess. During such periods, many government officials consider it their responsibility—even their duty--to travel to distant lands in order to acquaint themselves with the prevailing conditions of the area. They believe that only in this manner would they be able to adequately represent their constituents in Idaho, Nebraska or Florida for example. In order to do this, it is often necessary for them to have their wives accompany them to obtain, according to theory, a woman's insight into the cultural aspects of the country.

Such junkets were not common in Almaty. Most congressmen have little idea where the country is located—if indeed they know such a country even exists. Typically, these information gathering excursions prefer to center their investigations on more desirable locations such as Paris, Vienna, or Hong Kong where the shopping and accommodations are superior.

Occasionally, however, some of the more adventuresome, and perhaps dedicated representatives, venture to lesser-known locals, such as Kazakhstan, for legitimate fact-finding missions.

The purpose of this particular visit, as they had stated to the Congressional Budget Office, was to acquaint themselves with the new petro-power that was rising from the ashes of the former Soviet Empire. Their hope was to cement their country's relations with influential representatives of the Kazakh government and, as a result, promote the efforts of American oil companies operating in the area.

The American Ambassador in Almaty was looking forward to the visit with considerable relish, hopeful that it would provide an opportunity to thrust his name in front of some the more influential members of the Foreign Relations Caucus. As a result, he had directed *all hands on deck* at the Embassy; particularly within the offices of the Cultural Attaché Michael Pearlman.

Unlike the ambassador, Michael viewed the upcoming visit as a major pain in the ass, and a consummate distraction from his more important responsibilities as CIA Station Chief; such as gathering confidential information and running *Joes.*

He had called Roger Pembroke to his office in order to make sure that his new assistant was picking up his cultural duties. The two of them were going over the points of interest in Almaty that the congressmen, and their wives, might like to visit, and the arrangements required to transport them to the Caspian Basin in the manner they had come to expect.

The congressional representatives had expressed an interest in viewing the expanding activity taking place in the Tengiz oil fields that was driving the economic metamorphosis of this emerging country. Afterwards, they planned to meet with Kazakh officials and possibly persuade them to ease up on the pressure they had been placing on American business interests.

Pearlman already had a discussion with the embassy's military advisor regarding the logistics of transporting the delegation across country.

Kazakhstan is roughly four times the size of Texas, and local air transportation is as slim as the country is wide. A local commercial airline would be unable to provide the necessary security for such an important delegation. On the other hand, the specially equipped C-130 the group employed to travel to the country was, because of its huge size, not able to land anywhere near the oil fields.

Between the two men, it was decided that the only plausible solution was to cajole or coerce the use of a couple of military helicopters to ferry the congressmen across country. Unfortunately, the nearest ones that might be available were stationed at the Manas Air Base outside of Bishkek, Kyrgyzstan. While the two of them had agreed on the solution neither had come up with a workable plan to obtain the necessary aircraft.

The Manas base is an important transportation hub for the United States. It provides for the supply of much of the manpower and materials needed for deployment to Afghanistan. As a result, the base is extremely critical to the successful conduct of the war. It is also increasingly sensitive since the Kyrgyz Government was overthrown in the recent *tulip revolution*.

The new administration was proving less receptive to the previous lease agreement. Russia had rushed to establish a better relationship with the new government than the Americans had, and appeared to be working behind the scenes to get the Americans expelled.

In spite of this, considerable strings were being pulled in Washington, in the proper place with the proper people, to persuade the American military to provide local transportation for the congressional delegation in Kazakhstan.

Once Pearlman was satisfied they were assured of the cooperation of the Air Force at Manus, he was willing to discuss the more mundane plans for the visiting dignitaries.

Roger had prepared a brochure containing a list of economic statistics and demographic facts he copied from an online CIA directory of the country. He handed it to his boss to review.

The station chief briefly glanced at the brochure before yawning, and handing it back. Roger had just got to the points of local cultural interest when Mei Lyn interrupted.

"Sorry to bother you, but there is a call from Mr. Gunn at GBC who wants to speak with Mr. Pembroke. He says it's important."

Pearlman nodded his agreement, and Roger told her to "put him through please." He winked at her as he picked up the line. She smiled in return, and closed the door behind her.

Pearlman pretended that he had not noticed the exchange between the two. Their association had become the gossip of the Embassy, but he had been young once himself and she was one damn good looking woman.

Trevor began talking immediately, once he knew that Roger was on the line. "I just got a call from Charlie Connelly up at Tekeli. One of our consultants there—an Englishman named Henry Butt--was murdered in his sleep last night. That now makes two of our people, in addition to the five Russians that were found in the mine."

The usually unflappable Brit was obviously excited, and very concerned over his conversation with Connelly. "Charlie thinks that whoever is doing the killing might very likely strike again, and wants to be taken out of there before that happens."

"So why don't you have them drive out. Surely finishing the project is not as important as their lives," Roger told him.

"I entirely agree with you old man about the project, but they are snowed in. We can't get up there, and they can't get out."

"How many are there?"

"Left you mean? Two American advisors and two Kazakh interpreters."

"So..." Roger replied hesitantly, not sure exactly why they were calling him.

"So," Trevor picked up the thread. "Charlie thought that you people at the Embassy might have some means of extracting them that we do not."

Roger had been holding the receiver so Michael could hear the conversation, and his boss shrugged a maybe.

"Let me see what we can do. If we figure out something I will get back to you," Roger assured him.

Trevor would have preferred a more definite reply, but decided, under the circumstances, it was probably the best he could expect.

After the conversation ended, both Roger and his boss looked blankly at each other, each one expecting the other to say something.

After a long pause, Pearlman said. "I may have an idea. Let's see if we can get hold of the Old Man."

The American Embassy in Almaty, like many around the world is equipped with a highly classified and secure communications room. It was there that Michael Pearlman took Roger Pembroke. Crossing the hall, he unlocked the door to a small closet filled with brooms, pails, and assorted housekeeping equipment.

"You also do clean-up?" Roger asked.

"I guess you could say that," Michael replied, jerking on a dangling light cord above their heads. He paused briefly before giving the cord two more quick jerks. The back wall of the closet slid open and almost immediately began to close again.

Pearlman quickly wedged his body between the wall and the silently sliding door to allow Roger to slip past him into the darkened room.

"This is our DOS—Dome of Silence," Michael said proudly. "I bet you thought they only existed in the Maxwell Smart movies."

Once inside, Pearlman quickly flipped a concealed light switch before sliding a plastic card through a small reader on the wall next to him. "I had just 20 seconds to do that before an alarm goes off and the damned broom closet fills up with Marines.

"After we moved into the embassy we brought over a bunch of Navy Seabees under the cover of being a college glee club from the University of Iowa. We told everyone on the outside they were on a cultural exchange program. Some of them would tour the area while the others worked to set this place up so that we could communicate without being overheard by some creep like WikiLeaks.

"Fortunately, no one ever asked any of them to sing, or I don't know what they would have done. After a month, they went back to their regular duty with the fleet."

Pearlman sat in a chair in the center of the tiny room, beside a large communications switchboard. Motioning Roger to sit in the only other chair, he flipped a switch on the console and checked his watch.

Roger looked around him. The walls were constructed of heavy steel sheeting, and were painted a dull battleship gray. Suddenly, he looked down as he felt jets of air going up his pants leg.

"Oxygen," Pearlman explained as a large transparent plastic dome slowly descended from the ceiling covering the two men. "All of our equipment is cushioned and covered to mute any noise that might emanate from them. The geeks refer to it as a *white sound system* because it masks both the outgoing and incoming voices."

A muffled ring startled both men. "It's only our call coming through, Pearlman explained. He quickly flipped another switch on the softly glowing console. Almost immediately, Roger heard the familiar voice of his mentor above the barely perceptible purr of the ubiquitous scrambler.

"Ah Roger how do you like Central Asia?" Emmett asked.

"He likes it fine," Pearlman replied, but we seem to be having a little problem here that you might be able to help us with."

"All right let's hear it, and I will see what I can do."

The sounds of Emmett Valentine's ever present music floated over the air, muffling some of his words.

"What is that music we hear Mr. Valentine?" Roger asked gently, hoping to get him to turn down the volume. He sometimes wondered if the old spymaster's hearing might be failing him.

"Do you like my selection? I didn't think that you could hear it. Perhaps I should lower the volume a bit. It is Shostakovich's Symphony No.5. He is one of my favorite composers. Partly because old Joe Stalin hated him. Anyone that Stalin disliked has to be good. Pravda described the Symphony as sly decadence," he chuckled, turning the dial.

Pearlman spoke quickly while he had the opportunity. "We just got a call from Trevor Gunn over at GBC. He just heard from Charlie Connelly up at Tekeli. Connelly told him that someone murdered the second one of the consultants up there in his sleep. I think Henry Butts was his name. Whoever did it used a garrote to strangle him."

"Yes I know," Emmett broke in. "Charlie sent me a brief message about the death. It seems they are having an epidemic of killings at Tekeli. Who do you think is the perpetrator?"

"Connelly doesn't know," Roger answered, "but he thinks that it is someone who wants to stop their project and get control of the mine."

"Apparently, it appears there may be rare-earth up there," Emmett offered. "Our experts analyzed the sample Roger sent out, and they believe that chances are very good it is beryllium. Do you know any other place in Kazakhstan that has beryllium?"

"I looked into that," Roger answered quickly. "There is only one place that I was able to find. It is the Ulbinskiy operation in Oskemen. The place is a joint stock company. Major stockholders include the Kazakh firm KATER, which is an umbrella organization for this country's nuclear industries, and the Russian financial group TVEL."

Pearlman glanced in astonishment at his new assistant.

"Then it must be the Russians," Emmett exclaimed. "They don't want any competition they don't control."

"Yeah maybe," the station chief replied. "On the other hand China is on our Eastern border and they already control 40% of the world's lead and zinc production. Everyone knows they are anxious to control the international supply of rare-earth. I think they could be a good bet."

"Perhaps," Emmett replied unconvinced. "Anyway what can I do to help?"

"Connelly wants to get out of there before anyone else gets killed," Pearlman replied. "You can't blame him. The roads are closed because of snow. There is no way they can drive out, and no way someone can drive there to extract them."

"I also want him out. We owe him that. He has always played square with us, and if he wants to get out of there, then I *want* him out of there."

"Alright," Pearlman agreed, "I have a plan, but we need some people in Washington to go along with it. We are going to lose the satellite any minute, so I'll send you a message with more of the details, along with the names of people we would like you to see. OK Emmett?"

Emmett had been wondering how to get Connelly extracted after his discussion with Vincent. Now he was pleased to hear that someone had a plan.

"All right I will do whatever I can," Emmett's voice was already fading.

Pearlman closed the circuit and turned to Roger. "That was damned impressive what you told the old man. How did you know all that crap about beryllium?"

"It was on that fact sheet I gave you to review." Roger answered, as he helped to close down the DOS and turn off the lights.

25

Tekeli

Charlie tried vainly to concentrate on finalizing the recommendations that would complete his part of the project. It was becoming increasingly difficult to focus on the job at hand. His mind kept reviewing, and re-reviewing, the circumstances that led up to the danger they were now facing. Even the lounge, with its garish yellow sofa, and red plush overstuffed chairs seemed to be threatening, and the walls more confining than they ever seemed in the past.

Dave had taken to walking up and down the hallway, attempting to relax. Charlie could hear him padding towards them in his stocking feet. Charlie rose, stretched, and waved to him as he passed.

He decided to go into Henry's room, and remove the personal items from the body. He should have done it earlier, but the shock was too great then. He and Dave had talked about moving Henry's remains to the ice house when they could, but he knew Trevor would want to send anything of value back to whatever dependents he could locate.

Charlie had kept the room key, and he put it into the lock. It turned easily. There was only a faint light coming through the open window curtains, and the body covered with the white sheet presented a ghostly image. He felt his stomach turn once again recalling Henry's face and bulging eyes he had witnessed the night before.

He turned on the lamp, and went through the papers on the desk, trying to put-off checking for the poor man's valuables as long as he could.

"Can I help?" Dave asked coming into the room.

"I think we are going to have to move old Henry to the ice house and put him with Andre," Charlie replied. "We can't leave him here indefinitely."

He threw back the sheet and was repulsed once more by what he saw. Henry's perpetually pale complexion was now turning a ghastly blue. He braced himself before reaching down and removing Henry's watch.

His trousers where hung on a peg on the door, and Charlie removed the wallet. There was nothing inside except a little cash and a few credit cards, along with a faded photo of a man and wife that Charlie guessed was more than twenty years old.

He handed the wallet to Dave before making sure there was nothing on the bed that might provide a clue to who had taken Henry's life. There was nothing. The bed and the room seemed completely undisturbed. There apparently had been little resistance, and Charlie wondered if Henry had even seen his attacker.

Charlie went over to the door and examined the lock. There was no sign of a break-in or scratches on the door that might indicate the lock was forced.

"Shall we do it now?" Dave asked, looking out the window. It has stopped snowing, and he thought that it might be as good a time as any."

The two men went back to their rooms for their coats.

Before leaving his room, Charlie locked Henry's meager belongings in his carry-on bag. He then tried to call Trevor to see if he had heard anything from the embassy about getting them out.

Nothing. Just what was now becoming a too familiar crackling on the line. He tried once again. Still nothing. He swore, and left his room making sure to lock the door.

Dave was already in Henry's room staring at the body. "He was a good man. What a shame to go that way. Particularly after the hard life he lived. Do you have any idea, Charlie, who the hell might be doing this?"

"None. Absolutely none. I keep turning it over in my mind but nothing results. I believe it must be someone who wants to prevent us from reporting on what we have found here. Who that might be completely escapes me."

The two of them carefully wrapped Henry's body in the sheet. The blood was dry but the sheet remained stained around his head. When they lifted the body, they both noticed that blood had seeped through and stained the bedding beneath. Charlie wondered if they should try and remove the leather thong around his neck, but decided against it.

Henry's body was heavier than both of them had thought, and it was difficult maneuvering him down the narrow stair well. Elaina and Nadia looked on silently from the hallway. Neither asked where they were taking Henry. They both knew. "Nadia finally asked, "Is there anything I can do to help?"

There was no response from the men, who had reached the bottom of the stairs. They set the body on the floor in order to catch their breath. Once they got outside, they knew they would be unable to put him down until they reached the icehouse. While they were resting, Charlie tried the door to the empty room. It was locked securily.

"Ready?" Dave asked. Charlie nodded and together they both stooped and lifted the lifeless form of their friend.

Outside, it was a pewter colored sky, and the promise of more snow was heavy in the air. They trudged through the drifts, which were up to the knees of both men.

Charlie noticed a small group of miners on their way to the brewery pause and watch the strange procession. He was sure they were wondering who or what was inside the blood stained sheet.

None of them offered to help, and neither of the consultants expected them to. The Russians had remained belligerent during the entire time of their visit to Tekeli, obviously viewing them as the enemy. Even considering this relationship, Charlie found it difficult to believe they were the ones who had killed Andre and Henry.

By the time the two men finally reached the icehouse, Dave was breathing heavily, and his usual ruddy complexion had turned a bright crimson.

Charlie was glad that he had taken Andre's coat, but he was still cold.

The two of them lifted Henry and placed him on a slab of ice next to Andre. Stretched out side by side the two dead consultants made a tragically odd pair. One covered with a dirty trench coat and the other by a bloody sheet.

"We will have to figure out how we can get them back to their families, but right now I don't' know how," Charlie said.

"Maybe we should have a Viking funeral for them, if we can't figure out anything else," Dave told him.

"What----what?" Charlie asked perplexed.

"Set a fire, and burn down the ice house," Dave replied.

"It's too damn cold to get a fire going, hopefully we can think of something else. Let's get out of here before we freeze to death," Charlie told him, heading out the door.

Dinner that night was a sad event, each one wondering what would happen next.

After they finished, Charlie stayed behind toying with his coffee, and watching the manager and her helper clean off the table. He had never paid much attention to the women on the staff before. They were just there, cooking, cleaning, and otherwise out of the way.

"Can I get you anything else Mr. Connelly?" The manager was a tall woman with dark hair, dark eyes and an olive complexion. Probably in her late fifties he thought. She may have been attractive when she was younger, but now her face bore the faint creases associated with a troubled life.

"No, no Madam Manager—"

"Call me Riana," she offered.

"All right Riana. You do a fine job, particularly under the circumstances. I was just wondering where you live? I never see you or your helpers coming and going, but you are always here."

"We have small rooms behind the kitchen where we stay when the hotel is open."

"And when it is not, do you live in town with the others?"

"No Mr. Connelly we do not. We are not really Russian, we are Kazakhs, and we live in the hills close to town. Why do you ask?"

Charlie ignored the question. "Is there possibly a separate entranceway to the hotel behind your rooms?

"No there is not. Would you like to see for yourself?"

"As a matter of fact I would," he told her rising from the table. "I am sure you realize that someone is trying to kill us, and assuming it is not you, I wonder how they are getting in without our knowing it."

The manager led him behind the kitchen where there was small dormitory type room with two bunk beds, and a closet. Charlie looked around the room before cautiously opening the closet door. Inside was only women's clothing, hung neatly in rows.

"You can see there is no doorway here," Riana told him impatiently.

"I can see that," he replied, shoving the clothes aside to examine the back of the closet.

"Is there a duplicate set of keys to our rooms?" Charlie asked unwilling to give up.

"No there is not." She replied, in a tone leaving little room for uncertainty. "Duplicate anything is for the more expensive hotels. Not here," she told him emphatically. "I do have a master key," she said pulling a small key on a large ring from a pocket in her skirt. "I keep this on me at all times, except when one of the girls needs it to clean the rooms."

"I know why you are questioning me. I don't blame you. I have been wondering about it myself. We all have. My girls and I are just as terrified as you are, but there is nothing we can do."

Charlie had nowhere else to go with the question, so he thanked her, and returned to his room.

Walking down the hallway, he made a point to check that all the other doors were tightly closed. A sliver of light was apparent under Dave's doorway, but the girls' were dark. They had apparently already gone to bed.

If any of them had been lax before he was sure they were more careful tonight. It was obvious at dinner that Henry's death was on everyone's mind, and they were all concerned what might happen next.

Once inside his own room he was careful to lock his door. It was too early to go to bed, and he was too exhausted to work.

He turned on the short wave on his nightstand, and found the BBC. The sound of Big Ben announced that the news from London was just starting. He decided to lie down and listen to what was going on in the outside world, hoping it would take his mind off what was happening at Tekeli.

It didn't work.

Two Muslim men were arrested taking pictures outside of a *nuclear facility in New Brighton.*

He recalled the phrase "walking back the cat," he once heard Emmett Valentine use to describe a thought process starting at the end, and working back to the beginning. The most recent event was the murder of Henry Butts. The chain of events, Charlie decided, leading up to his death seemed to start with the miner's note slipped into his pocket at the presentation, but he was having difficulty forming a nexus between the death and the note.

There were riots in London in response to cuts in social welfare

As he played and replayed the film of events in his mind, things seemed to become more clear, or at least less cluttered. He was better able to determine the pieces that were missing, by focusing on those he had. Tomorrow, he decided, he would have to talk once again with Riana. She had not told him all she knew. He was certain of that, and he thought he now knew why.

There were heavy rains in the northern part of Great Britain, and moving over the Channel.

Charlie Connelly no longer cared about the weather over the Channel, or any of the rest of the news from the BBC, because he didn't hear it. He had fallen asleep, leaving the London reporter to continue without his distant listener.

26

Charlie wasn't quite awake, but he wasn't fully asleep either. He sensed, more than saw, someone in the room standing beside his bed, with his back to the shadows.

Charlie opened his eyes to see a figure bending over him, and immediately felt a cord tightening around his throat. He tried to yell out, but could not as the cord grew tighter and tighter.

He fought the air, knocking the radio from the nightstand. It landed with a resounding thud. The BBC was reporting on a falling Euro, but Charlie didn't hear. He was fully awake now and consumed with fear. As the cord tightened, he could feel his breath rushing from his lungs and blood rushing to his face. He desperately wanted to cough, but could not.

Suddenly Charlie saw the outline of a man, clothed entirely in black, standing over him. At the same time, his hand landed on the man's head and grasped onto an ear. He could feel it through the heavy woolen hood covering the man's head. He hung on tightly, and twisted it with all the strength he had remaining. He heard a curse in an unintelligible language, accompanied by a slight loosening of the cord around his neck. It was just enough to allow Charlie to twist to one side and get his legs positioned between himself and the body of his attacker. He shoved with all of his might, and the black-clad body staggered a few steps backward.

Charlie leapt from the bed, landing off balance. The man butted him in the midsection. And he landed back on the bed, his breath escaping in a mighty puff of air. The man hesitated, fumbling for a knife tucked in his belt.

The hesitation gave Charlie a chance to find the gun underneath his pillow. As the man advanced, wildly swinging his knife, Charlie got off a shot at close range. The man dropped back clutching his cheek, and bolted from the room.

The two of them raced through the darkened hallway, and down the stairs. On the bottom floor, Charlie noticed the door to the room Roger had occupied was slightly ajar.

The man fled out into the night, Charlie following close behind. The night air was frigid, but the moon shone brightly outlining the two figures plowing through the deep snow. Behind them, the hotel lights were flicking on in all the rooms; their occupants trying vainly to identify the figures running across the snow.

The two men blundered through the woods, cracking branches and scattering snow with each heavy step. Charlie considered taking another shot, but decided that it would be futile. He didn't want to stop for fear the man might duck through the trees and get away. He was heading for the mine, and if he got there he would lose himself forever.

Charlie didn't want that to happen, and he kept up his pace. He still felt short of breath. His throat still raw from having been strangled. The cold air seared his lungs like a hot knife. He felt himself fading, but he could not let the black clad figure escape in the dense woods.

Charlie's feet felt like blocks of wood, and the muscles in his legs were screaming for relief. The snow was slippery underfoot, and the man in front would zig then zag to prevent a second shot.

A cloud cover moving-in hid the few remaining stars, and made the running figure more difficult to distinguish from his surroundings.

"Stop!" Charlie shouted, "you son-of-a-bitch," he added under his breath. The man didn't answer, but darted into a thick stand of birch. His black figure was starkly outlined against the white bark. The trees low hanging branches poured snow over his disappearing shoulders giving him a ghostly appearance s he ran.

If the man was who Charlie thought he was he was far more familiar with the terrain. But Charlie was mad—damn mad, and even though his breath was coming in short painful bursts his fury drove him forward.

Charlie could feel himself fading, and he desperately squeezed-off another shot. The Beretta barked in the night, its echo resounding through the forest. The bullet missed its mark, kicking up a scattering of snow to the right of the fleeing figure. Startled, the man leapt to his left, losing his balance, but caught himself with one hand, preventing a fall. By the time he straightened, he was only a short distance ahead.

Charlie shouted "**Sammie!**" guessing it to be him. "Stop I am taking you back." Startled by the mentioning of the name, the man paused and began to advance slashing the long-bladed knife in front of him like the grim reaper brandishing his scythe. The blade glistened ominously as he ploughed forward through the deep snow.

"**Stop!**" Charlie shouted once more. The man did not. Charlie raised the gun, cradling the butt of the small Beretta in the palm of his shivering hand.

"You're afraid to shoot," the man shouted mockingly, beginning to duck and weave his way closer toward Charlie, slicing the air with each forward step.

The small .22 caliber roared like a cannon in the cold night air. The man clutched his chest before crumpling to his knees. Charlie paused before firing a second time at the kneeling figure. The second shot caused the man to topple face-forward in the snow. The blood drained from his chest, and formed a crimson rivulet on the white ground.

Charlie walked cautiously toward him, prepared to shoot again at the slightest movement. There was none. He stared down at the black-clad body outlined like a menacing scarecrow in the snow. An outstretched hand still clutched the knife. Charlie's hands trembled, and his body shook from the freezing cold, intensified by his fear.

Bending over the body, he turned the man on his back, and tugged the black balaclava over his head. It was sticky with blood from the first shot in the hotel room. It finally came off, and Charlie felt an enormous pang of remorse when he confirmed that he had indeed killed Sammie Wang. The amusing Sammie of the drive over the Silk Road to Tekeli. The friendly helpful gopher, obtaining records from the miners and their clerks the project required, but found difficult to obtain.

A moral revulsion flooded over him, but rapidly subsided when he realized that it was also the same Sammie Wang who had killed five miners, and his two friends Andre and Henry. To say nothing of the Sammie who had just tried his best to strangle the life out of him with a leather cord.

Charlie kicked the knife from the outstretched hand, and turned to leave. He stopped abruptly, returning to find it buried in the snow. The knife had a highly ornamented curved blade with a patterned bone handle. Perhaps it would somehow provide a clue to why Sammie had resorted to such lengths to close the mine and stop the project.

A thread of light creased the eastern sky as Charlie stumbled toward the breaking dawn, and the warming shelter of the hotel.

Once inside, he leaned against the wall trying to catch his breath. Feeling better, he kicked the spare room door fully open. He hesitated, scanning the inside with his pistol pointed forward. He was unsure what or whom he might find.

The room was empty, the floor littered with piles of discarded clothes, and stacks of dirty dishes. Sammie had eaten well while he was in hiding, and someone had taken very good care of him.

Nadia and Elaina were waiting for him at the top of the stairs, shocked by the long knife he clutched in one hand and the gun in the other.

"What happened?" Nadia asked. "What was all the shooting about? Are you—are you all right?" she added hesitatingly, shocked by the grim look on Charlie's face.

"Later, now go into the dining room," he replied.

Reaching the top of the stairs he had to pause once more to catch his breath. The chase through the woods, and the fight had taken its toll on him. He was exhausted, but he knew there was still much to be done.

Dave Dieter sat at the table, idly stirring his coffee. He had been sound asleep when he heard a gunshot, followed by the sound of men racing down the hallway. It took him a few minutes to get some clothes on before seeing if it was safe to leave his room. In the hall, he could see Charlie's door standing wide open so he knew that he was involved, but had no idea where he might have gone. He found Nadia and Elaina huddled together in Nadia's room, staring out the window, and decided to join them.

Dave had originally thought about running outside, but always the cautious man, he did not. He didn't know where to run. Obviously, someone had a gun, and he did not. Dave decided that prudence was the best part of valor, and had waited to see what might develop.

Riana and her helper were setting the table. The smell of burnt toast came from the kitchen. They had forgotten about it, wondering what was going on outside. When Charlie entered the dining room, they stopped what they were doing and stared at him. His expression was uncharacteristically grim.

"Do you recognize this?" he asked, tossing the knife on the table. It slid across the polished wood surface towards Riana. She immediately recognized the ornamental blade, and muffled a deeply evolving guttural scream, covering her mouth with both hands. She began to shake, her legs became weak, and she started to collapse.

Dave leapt from his chair in time to catch the crumpling figure, before guiding her, ironically enough, to Henry's vacant chair.

"Whose knife is this Riana?" Charlie demanded.

Nadia and Elaina looked at him appalled by his coldness.

"Charlie don't," Nadia told him. "Not so harsh. Look at her. She's frightened to death."

He ignored her. "Tell us Riana, if you would be so kind," he demanded mockingly. "Please tell us who owns such a fancy knife?"

"Sammie Wang" she shouted angrily. "He is my nephew. Where is he? You have to tell me what has happened to him."

Everyone, except Charlie, was shocked by her answer. Even he, however, was surprised at the relationship between Riana and Sammie.

"He is in the woods, laying face down in the snow where I shot him. He was the one that killed the miners, as well as Andre and Henry. You knew that damn you. Now I want you to tell us why he was doing it, and who was working with him. I can't imagine that one day he just woke up and decided he would start killing people."

"I am not going to tell you," she screamed beginning to sob once again. "You can't make me."

"Perhaps not," Charlie replied coolly. "However, if I can't, I am sure the miners over in the brewery will be able to find a way--probably one at a time on top of the table. They will not be too happy when I tell them that it was you and Sammy that killed their friends. Either you talk to us, or you talk to them. Make your choice and it had better be pretty damn fast."

"If I tell you, will you help me?"

"I can't promise you anything if you do, but I sure as hell can promise you what will happen if you don't."

Riana rose to her feet, and paced back and forth before facing the group. "All right where do you want me to start?"

"Start with Sammie," Charlie directed. "What in the hell was he doing. What caused him to attack us?"

Riana hesitated; a nervous tick had taken command of her right eye. "It's hard to explain to people like you coming from rich powerful countries, but I will try. Sammie is—was a Uighur," she cleared her throat before resuming her explanation.

Dave interrupted. "Uighur--Uighur—what in the hell is a Uighur?" He had been riding in the second car and missed Sammie's explanation during the trip to Tekeli.

Charlie shook his head trying to get Dave to shut up, but he knew it was too late. "We pronounce it—or it sounds like Wegers. I'll tell you about it later. In the meantime think Gitmo and Bermuda."

A glimmer of recognition crossed Dave's face, but now Riana was badly confused.

"Anyway," she began again, ignoring the interruption. "Our heritage has become terribly muddled over the ages. I am Kazakh and Chinese, and raised under Russian rule. My husband, when he was alive, was a Turkic Muslim-a Uighur. Sammie was his brother's only son (she had now unconsciously adapted the past tense when referring to her nephew) -- and raised a Uighur. He grew up in the city of Urumqi. It's the capital of Xinjiang Province. "Over there," she pointed, "on the other side of the mountains.

"Being Muslims in a Han Chinese province, they were always under the heel of the dragon. The area is rich in mineral resources. China's other Tibet it is sometimes called."

At first Riana's words had come haltingly, but as her story progressed she became almost defiant.

"This allows China to rule the Muslim Province with an iron hand. They refer to it as *the peaceful liberation*. The Hans impose all kinds of oppressive taxes and regulations. At the same time they are stealing the output from the factories and controlling the production from the mines.

"The Chinese keep flooding the area with people from other provinces, who are impregnating the Uighur women in order to dilute the race and abolish their religion.

The Uighurs have been trying to resist. As the Hans grew more oppressive the Uighurs have become more aggressive."

Charlie could tell that Riana was striking a responsive chord with Elaina and Nadia, who were listening sympathetically. Even he was becoming receptive to her story, but caught himself by recalling Henry's bloated face.

"Since the Russians were forced by the Taliban to withdraw from Afghanistan, and the Central Asian Republics won their independence from them, the Uighurs decided to increase their own resistance to the Chinese. When they acted before, it was mostly in the western areas close to the Kazakhstan border, but lately they have been attacking even in Beijing.

"Ok--Ok," Charlie interrupted. "We get the picture, but what about Sammie?"

"Ah yes, poor little Sammie. He was everyone's friend growing up. But, he was a small boy who grew into a little man. Everyone picked on him. When he went to college, he fell in with a group of revolutionaries who were intent on fighting China, and establish an independent Muslim state. Most of them were all talk, like college boys are, but there were some who were very hard-core revolutionaries."

Dave rose to his feet, and went to the kitchen, retuning with a pot of coffee. He filled everyone's cup. When he came back a second time he placed a cup in front of Riana. She smiled appreciatively, and took a sip before resuming her story.

"A small group of them somehow made contact, through the Muslim world, with al Qaeda. They traveled to Tangiers and from there to Damascus. From there they were smuggled into Afghanistan, and eventually to a training camp hidden away in the mountain area of Waziristan.

"They learned to kill with their hands—Sammie was particularly good at that, he was so small. They also trained them to shoot and plant explosives, anyway they could kill without the use of large weapons. They pledged a fealty to Osama bin Laden before they left, and they eventually got back to Urumqi dedicated to fighting their Chinese oppressors."

The kitchen helper began serving plates of eggs to those assembled around the table. She had difficulty understanding English, and was in a hurry to finish up and go to her room.

"But how did he end up here?" Elaina asked. She was beginning to lose sympathy with Riana after learning Sammie's association with al Qaeda.

"I am getting to that," Riana told her. She paused, took a sip of her coffee and resumed her story. It was important for the foreigners to know what it is like in Central Asia and what motivated her nephew to take the action that he did.

"Sammie finally got a job with Global Bank. He needed money. His English was good, and he was very helpful to them. They started sending him up here to collect information for a project they had with the Kazakh Government. That was how he learned about the mine—what it produced—and how important its production was.

"Later he learned, from his people in Urumqi, that the Chinese wanted to get control of Tekeli for its deposits in order to keep their own mineral prices high. The Uighurs set out to keep the mine out of the hands of the Chinese to defy them. They thought, for awhile, that somehow they might get control, but later they didn't care who had it, as long as it wasn't the Hans."

"So Sammie started killing the miners to keep the local people from operating the mine until someone other than the

Chinese was able to get control," Charlie asked incredulously. "That's not rational."

"At those al Qaeda training camps you are trained to hate and kill, not to think and evaluate," Riana replied bitterly.

"At first I didn't know that was what he was doing," Riana continued. "Then I came to realize that each time he visited here another miner would disappear. I told him I knew, and asked him to stop. It just wasn't right, I told him." Tears began to well-up in her eyes. "He said he would. He promised he would—but he never did."

"Alright," Dave interrupted, "granted he wanted to do away with the miners to close the pit down—it seems like pretty distorted thinking—but given that, why kill poor old Andre then Henry? Why in the name of God would he do that?"

"He knew that you people would find that the mine could be worked profitably, and would recommend that the Government either work it or sell it. He was afraid that the Chinese would get a chance buy it. He knew they were buying up mineral resources all around the world. He wanted to prevent that from happening to Tekeli."

"Did he say anything to you about rare-earth?" Charlie asked.

"There were some Uighur miners that worked part time at the mine. Sammie told me once they thought there was something in there that was more valuable than just lead and zinc. I didn't understand what he was talking about. And I really didn't care. I just wanted the killing to stop."

Charlie was about to ask Riana if she felt like that, why she continued to hide him. Before he got a chance to ask her, Dave broke in.

"How in the hell did you ever figure out that it was Sammie?" he asked staring at Charlie.

"Yes Mr. Connelly," Nadia chimed-in. "We all thought that Sammie had left Tekeli a week ago."

The interruption irritated Charlie. He had wanted Riana to continue, but he felt that he needed to explain.

"I didn't really *know,*" he began as he rose from the table and stretched. He was still cold and wanted to take a hot shower, but he felt obligated to explain.

"I drew up a flow chart of events, like we would do in a corporation. Then I made a list of all the possible people that could be involved. I compared the list to the flowchart and began eliminating those that I believed would have been unable to commit the killings. This time when I finished, I had eliminated all of them except Sammie. I decided that wasn't possible, so I threw the damn thing away.

"Yesterday I tried doing it again," he continued, walking into the kitchen for another cup of coffee. There was a tray of burnt toast on the shelf, and he picked up a piece and ate it. He coughed, but struggled to continue.

"As I said, yesterday I tried it again, with the same results. Before I fell asleep, I decided it must be our old friend Sammie. When I chased him down the stairs and out in the night, I noticed the door to the room at the bottom of the stairs was partly open and the light was on. I decided that Sammie must have sneaked back and had been hiding there all along.

"Isn't that right Riana? Isn't that what you did for your nephew?"

"Yes," she sobbed. "He hid there, and I took care of him. He *was* my relation after all, and he was doing it for the Uighurs. After he left, his people sneaked him back in here. They have learned to live in the night, and this is a familiar area to them. They come and go as they please.

"Now what are you going to do with me?"

Charlie and Dave, Nadia and Elaina looked at each other. None of them had the answer. Suddenly they heard a sound in the distance that distracted their attention.

27

Whop-whop-whop-whop-whop- The sound grew louder and louder until it was shaking the rafters of the old hotel. The light fixture over the table began to sway back and forth, and the dishes rattled in the kitchen sink. None of the others recognized the sound. Charlie did. It had been many years before, but it was a sound he would never forget. He leapt to his feet, heading for the stairs.

Half way down he turned to shout back at the others, "pack your things, and gather your papers, we are getting the hell out of here." They all stared at each other in amazement. He bolted down the remaining stairs and out into the still bitter air.

A large helicopter, with long slender skids, hovered over the clearing below the hotel. He watched it settle slowly to the ground. A door on the side slid open, and Roger Pembroke leaped out.

"I'm damn glad to see you," Charlie greeted him. "I was afraid no one would come."

"It wasn't easy. It's on loan, so to speak, and I have to get it back before anyone knows it's gone. Hurry-up and get your group on board. Quick! Quick! Quick!" he shouted, above the sound of the engines.

"But, but how?" Charlie stammered.

"Not now. Later, we can talk later. Get your people, and let's get out of here."

Families were coming out of their houses, staring in amazement at the thrashing chopper. Even the miners, that spent their days in the brewery, left their tables to see what was causing the commotion.

Charlie turned and headed back to the hotel. Dave stood, bag in hand, at the top of the stairs, Nadia and Elaina were coming out of their rooms, not sure what was happening. "Pembroke is outside," he shouted. "He will tell you what to do. We're going back to Almaty. Make sure you have all of your files and laptops."

Halfway down the hallway he heard Nadia shouting to him. "What are you going to do about Riana?"

"F…forget her. We don't have time for that now. Get your things and get on the helicopter," he shouted ducking into his room.

He paused unsure where to begin. After a moment, he began tossing things randomly into his travel bags. When he finished packing he unplugged the laptop, and checked the desk drawers, throwing any remaining papers in his bags.

He grabbed Andre's coat from the closet, and threw it over his shoulders. He had almost forgotten his gun. He had stuffed it in the coat after shooting Sammie. He removed it from the pocket, and looked about the room. His first thought was to hide it somewhere, but was afraid that it would soon be found. Instead, he wrapped the Beretta in a hand towel, and put it back in his coat.

He hurried out of the room. Once in the hall he hesitated and returned. He had forgotten his shortwave radio. It was still on the floor. He picked it up, stuck it in his bag and bolted down the hallway.

On his way out of the hotel, he stopped in the dining room. Riana was sitting at the table, frozen in position, staring transfixed at Sammie's knife still on the table in front of her. Charlie snatched the knife from her, and put it underneath his arm before heading toward the stairs.

"What's going to happen to me now?" Riana screamed. There was no answer. "He was my only nephew," she shrieked at the man disappearing out of the hotel doorway.

The rest of them were already in the helicopter. A tall marine, dressed in fatigues, had helped them abroad, and guided them to their seats. He was now helping them buckle-in as Charlie dashed from the hotel.

Roger stood in the helicopter's open doorway, franticly motioning him to hurry-up. Charlie tossed him the knife, and threw his belongings on the metal deck. The chopper was already beginning to hover when he got fully aboard.

The blades sliced the thin air, as the helicopter rose above the small town, circled and then headed south. Charlie glanced out the window, and watched Tekeli disappear behind him. Looking back, it appeared to be a serene mountain village covered with a protective blanket of clean white snow. Sometimes, you leave a place with regret, he thought, but he was leaving Tekeli with the utmost sense of relief.

Roger steered him toward the back, both of them steadying themselves on the seatbacks as they went. Half way down the aisle, Liana reached out and brushed Roger's sleeve. "You never called," she smiled coquettishly.

"I really tried, but I could never get through, we'll have to do lunch sometime, when we get back to Almaty." He turned toward Charlie and winked, leading him toward the rear of the plane.

"This is a pretty plush bird," Charlie observed, glancing around the inside of the helicopter, still trying to catch his breath. It had been a tough night and a difficult morning, but he was greatly relieved to be finally out of Tekeli. "How did you manage this?"

"It wasn't easy" Roger grinned, "we borrowed it from a visiting congressional delegation. I have to get it back before they know it's gone or my career as a Cultural Attaché is over, at least according to my boss Roger Pearlman. After you called

Gunn, he called us and said you needed out. He told us that a couple of your people were dead, and you were afraid the same thing would happen to the rest of you."

"I guess that pretty well sums it up," Charlie told him. The chopper, by now, was operating at full speed. The vibrations and the sound of the rapidly rotating blades made it difficult to talk. They had to shout at each other.

"I told you," Roger continued, "that my boss is the CIA Station Chief. Being a cultural attaché is only a cover. Well sometimes, it comes in handy. We were making arrangements to entertain some VIPs from Washington, and we needed a helicopter to ferry them out to the Caspian oil fields. Pearlman thought it was a big pain in the ass, but it turned out to be a heaven sent gift. All we had to do was borrow it for a few hours to whip up to Tekeli, and get you people out. Pearlman called Mr. Valentine, and then sent him an outline of what he wanted to do. The old man thought it was a fine idea, even turned down the volume on his CD player to listen," Roger grinned.

"But you must have had to get permission from the Air Force before you could borrow their bird. I have heard they don't take lightly to the idea of someone wandering off the beaten path with millions of dollars worth of fighting equipment."

"That is where Mr. Valentine came in. He told us he got you into this, and he would see what he could do to get you out."

"That was big of him," Charlie commented wryly. He had always marveled at the breadth of Emmett's contacts. This was not the first time they had come in handy. He was grateful at the thought that the old man wanted to help.

He stared out the window at the ground below. They were speeding over the same section of the old Silk Road that had taken hours to drive a few weeks before. The snow gradually disappeared, and he looked down at the barren steppes he thought so boring coming to Tekeli. Boring is good he decided. He would never knock boring again.

As he looked out, he saw they were passing over a small community of yurts that the nomad tribesman lived in as they moved from location to location. Some of them came out, and looked up in the sky as the helicopter passed.

Several horses, tethered in a makeshift corral beside the tightly clustered dwellings, reared at the unusual sight and loud noise. As the chopper sped towards Almaty, the nomads and their lifestyle were quickly left behind.

"So what has happened to you, since I left?" Roger asked

Charlie turned away from the window, wondering where to begin. It was difficult to talk over the engine noise, and he attempted to keep it as brief as possible. There would be plenty of time for a full debriefing after they got on the ground, but Roger certainly deserved an explanation. He began by telling him how he had found Andre in a mine shaft with the back of his head bashed in, and Henry strangled with a leather cord. The next night when he had gone to sleep, a man dressed completely in black came into his room and tried to strangle him.

Roger leaned closer as they talked, not wanting to miss anything. "I broke away from him," Charlie continued, "and he ran out of the room. I fumbled under my pillow and found the gun I had hidden there."

"You had a gun?" Roger asked surprised. "You got a gun into Kazakhstan. That was pretty ballsy."

"As a matter of fact I did," Charlie told him, reaching into his coat pocket. "I'm glad you asked. I had almost forgotten about it." He pulled-out the small Beretta wrapped in a towel, and handed it to Roger. "Do me a favor. Have Pearlman give it to your *housekeeping* people they will know how to clean it up, and make it disappear."

Roger took it, and stuffed it into his coat pocket. "So some guy comes into your room and tries to strangle you, then what did you do?"

"I shot him, but the bullet only grazed him. I was never a very good shot with one of these things, particularly lying on my back, but it must have scared him. He ran down the hallway with me running after him. We got to the bottom of the stairs, and I noticed that the doorway to the room you stayed in was partially open. Then I knew, or at least I was pretty sure that I knew, who I was after."

"Who the hell was it?" Roger asked leaning still closer.

Charlie ignored the question. "Once we got outside he took off for the woods. You remember the large grove of birch trees down the hill from the hotel?"

Roger nodded, and Charlie continued. "It was cold as hell, and I had left my coat in my room. There wasn't time to get dressed. Anyway, I was damn sure I was not going to let this bastard get away. He had killed five miners, Andre, Henry, and had tried to kill me. I was going to chase him into hell if I had to. I was beginning to shake so hard from the cold, I was afraid I would collapse. I squeezed off another shot. It missed, but came close enough to scare him, and he stumbled. By the time he righted himself I was pretty close. He pulled out this knife." Charlie pulled out the long bladed knife he had brought on board. Look at the design on the blade; I think it's a Uighur knife.

"What kind of knife?" Roger asked staring with renewed respect at the retired corporate guy sitting beside him.

"Put it with my gun and show it to Pearlman. He can figure out where it came from. It will give him something to do," Charlie grinned. "He started toward me swinging this blade. I told him to stop, but he just kept coming. So I shot him. He fell down on his knees, and I shot him again."

"Who was it? Who did you shoot?" Roger yelled, his voice rising above the sound of the rotors.

"It was Sammie—Sammie Wang."

"Sammie Wang? The funny little fellow I rode up to Tekeli with. My God I can't believe it."

The chopper was approaching the outskirts of Almati. Soon it was over the American Embassy. As it slowly descended, Michael Pearlman waited impatiently on the roof, tightly clutching a large umbrella. A marine, in dress uniform, stood beside him.

When the helicopter settled on the concrete deck the crew hurriedly opened the door, and rushed their passengers out.

The blades kept spinning. The pilot never considered shutting down the engine. He was already behind schedule, and was in a rush to get back in the air and on to his next destination. Dave led the way, bending double to avoid the props. Following closely behind were Nadia, Elaina, Roger, and finally Charlie.

Once out of the protection of the plane, a raw blast of wind driven rain lashed the departing passengers. They huddled together, cold and unsure what to do next. As soon as everyone cleared the wash from the blades, the marine pushed past them striding toward the helicopter where a member of the crew pulled him aboard.

Roger paused long enough to introduce Charlie to his boss, and hand him the package that he had given him. "Needs to go to housekeeping," he shouted over the noise. He quickly turned and ran back, leaping through the helicopter's doorway as it took off.

"He has to shepherd the congressmen," Pearlman laughed, extending his umbrella over the girls, and herding them toward the stairs.

Trevor Gunn was nervously pacing back and forth in the empty lobby. His smiled when he saw Charlie and the others emerging from the elevator. "Jolly glad to see you," he told them, shaking the men's hands and hugging the girls. "We have to be on our way. I tried to get the Kazakhs to extend the schedule, but they would not hear of it. It's still on for first thing tomorrow, and we have a lot to do before that."

Trevor led them toward the Land Rovers that were waiting in the driveway. He paused long enough to thank Michael Pearlman for what he had done getting the people out of Tekeli. "I owe you a dinner," he yelled to him climbing into the driver's seat.

"Two of them," Pearlman shouted back,

Afterward, he pulled Charlie aside as he was getting into the car and told him, "we'll get together as soon as you finish the presentation. If I don't let you go now, old Trevor will have a nervous breakdown. Sounds like you had a lot of fun up there in the mountains, and I want to hear all about it." He patted Charlie on the back

"Thank the maestro for me," Charlie yelled back to the station chief as he followed Trevor to the cars.

Trevor motioned for Charlie and Dave to join him in his car. Nadia and Elaina rode in the second Rover, with Trevor's secretary behind the wheel. The two women were still trying to adjust to what had happened to them since Charlie had come into the dining room, early that morning. They had been rushing ever since, and were exhausted. They welcomed the opportunity to relax in their seats.

Trevor's secretary swore as she ground the gears, and jerked the car from the curb.

28

Almaty

It was late in the afternoon. The streets of the city were almost empty. The few people they saw were hurrying to their next destination to escape the driving rain. Dave nudged Charlie pointing out the window to an old woman walking nonchalantly along the sidewalk, her head sticking defiantly from the top of green plastic garbage bag that protected her clothes.

"That's real technological innovation" Dave commented with a grin. "I'll have to remember that."

Watching the old woman, Charlie glanced in the car's side mirror, and was surprised to see the trailing Rover pull to the curb. The door opened and Nadia got out and began running down the street clutching her coat tightly around her. Trevor apparently had not noticed, and continued on his way.

Inside their building, his secretary informed them that Nadia left to check on her cats, and would join them shortly. He shook his head in disbelief, before herding the group hurriedly up the stairs.

The offices were empty. Everyone had already left for the day. An old babushka busied herself emptying ashtrays, and dusting the tops of a long row of filing cabinets, totally unconcerned with the new arrivals.

They all followed Trevor into the conference room where they had first assembled. It seemed to them that it had been months before, but in reality it was only a matter of weeks.

As soon as Roger called to say they had developed a few ideas on how to get Connelly and the crew out of snow-bound Tekeli, Trevor began preparing for their arrival. He had the utmost confidence in the resources available to the Americans, and if Roger believed he could get them out, he was confident they soon would be back.

He also knew the time would be short between their arrival and the meeting, so he began assembling the supplies they would need. There was a stack of large tablets for making flip charts, numerous boxes of marking pens of assorted colors, a large Russian-English Dictionary, a case of bottled water, and two pots of almost fresh coffee brewing on the burners.

"Anything else that you need, just let me know," Trevor told them. "I have alerted a Chinese restaurant down the street, and as soon as I give them a call, they will bring in your dinner. Tomorrow, after the meeting, we will all go out for a celebratory meal. You certainly deserve it."

They all looked at each other. "We sure as hell do," Dave replied caustically.

Trevor motioned for Charlie to follow him into his office. On the way they passed his secretary who was putting on her coat to leave. "Before you duck-out, please call the Lotus Petal and tell them to bring the dinner I ordered.

She wouldn't be much help here," he whispered to Charlie. "Her talents are elsewhere."

Nadia came up the stairs, her face flushed from hurrying. "How are the cats?" Charlie grinned and pointed toward the conference room.

"Oh my—they really missed me," she smiled, heading in with the others.

"She does good work," Charlie told Trevor, taking a chair beside his desk.

"That's good to know. Now tell me what in the bloody hell was going on up there. I knew there would be problems. There always are, but not the kind you encountered. Start from the beginning."

Charlie did what Trevor asked, as completely as he could. He began with finding the note in his shirt pocket and going on from there. His story included the death of Andre, and Henry, and the attempt by Sammie to strangle him. From there he went on to tell Trevor how he chased after him, and finally described to Trevor how Sammie had come at him with the knife, and ultimately how he was forced to shoot the little man before leaving him face down in a snowdrift.

He ended his story with the final comment, "he had the blade, but I had the edge."

As the two men sat looking at each other, Charlie suddenly recalled the iconic line from the movie "The Untouchables" where Elliott Ness is advised, by Shawn Connery playing Malone, on how to get Capone,

You wanna know how to get Capone? They pull a knife – you pull a gun. They send one of yours to the hospital you send one of theirs to the morgue. That's the Chicago way.

He chuckled to himself. Perhaps the city had unconsciously become more ingrained in his character than he realized.

The voice of Trevor Gunn brought him back from his reflections. "My God Sammie! I just can't believe it. He was always so friendly and accommodating. I will never again trust anyone who is not an Englishman."

Immediately recognizing what he had just said he quickly added with considerable embarrassment, "And you Yanks too of course."

Rapidly changing the subject he stammered, "But--but--why did he do all this? I just don't understand."

Charlie went into considerable detail describing his conversation with Riana. When he finished Trevor merely looked at him with astonishment. "I am shocked. Completely shocked! I think we had better talk to my boss in Vienna. He has to be aware of all this," he said, grabbing the phone.

When Vincent St. Claire's voice came over the speakerphone, it eerily reminded Charlie of listening to Emmett Valentine. The husky timbre was somehow similar—perhaps a characteristic of age he thought. There also seemed to be a familiar distinguishing pronunciation. It felt reassuring to him to be dealing with someone who had been through similar situations before.

This time Trevor did the talking, occasionally looking toward Charlie for a nod of corroboration. It was best this way. The Englishman was able to relate the facts with a detachment that Charlie did not—could not share.

Listening to Trevor describe the events to Vincent, they were recalled graphically by Charlie, as if he were viewing an ancient black and white film. When it came to the part where he and Sammie confronted each other, the mental movie began to run in slow motion. The shot that dropped Sammie to his knees echoed like clap of thunder in his head. The second shot was less loud, but still caused the kneeling body to fall slowly—ever so slowly face forward in the stark white snow.

Had he actually killed a man, he wondered, or was it just a very bad dream?

......"so I would strongly advise" the ever rational voice of Vincent St. Claire brought Charlie back to the reality of Trevor's office, and everything compressed into sharp focus.

The subject they now had to discuss was how much to tell the Kazakh Government officials about the deaths, and the attempt by the Uighurs to scuttle the project. There was general agreement among the three of them the less said the better.

The Kazakh Government was becoming a considerable source of potential revenue for the Global Bank. The country's revenue from oil and minerals was continuing to increase, and their influence in the region would surely follow.

There is always a fear among consultants that problems occurring on a project will be viewed by government officials as the result of the personnel, rather than the circumstances. If that occurs, it will usually lead to the consulting agency finding themselves no longer in demand. The tendency then is to downplay the negative aspects of the project and the findings.

After considerable discussion, between Trevor and Vincent, they concluded the presentation should stick exclusively to the mine and its management, avoiding any discussion relating to the deaths of the miners, and the advisors.

"Just the facts mam" Trevor offered, before explaining to Vincent it was a quote from the tele he had seen some time ago.

A hell of a long time ago, Charlie thought, but said nothing.

As the conversation was ending, Vincent St. Clair had one more thing to add. "I think you people know a Michael Pearlman at the American Embassy."

Trevor asserted they did. "Good man—been a lot of help."

"All right," Vincent concluded. "I believe after the presentation is over Charlie should sit with him, and fill him in completely on what has occurred."

After the phone conversation with Vienna was over, Charlie turned back to Trevor as he was leaving. "You understand that you will have to retrieve the bodies of Andre and Henry and return them to their family." Trevor was surprised. He had not really thought of that. "I have what little personal effects I could find. Remind me to give you them tomorrow."

"Where are the bodies now?" Trevor asked, not sure how he was going to do that.

"In the ice house, up at Tekeli," Charlie replied leaving the office.

In the conference room, everyone sat around the long table eating Chinese. There were several empty cartons already deposited in the wastebaskets. The room had taken on the distinct odor of sesame oil and ginger. It had been a long time since they had eaten, and the food from the Lotus Petal rapidly disappeared.

Once they finished the food, and the empty cartons were disposed of in the overflowing baskets, everyone returned to the task at hand.

Nadia and Elaina concentrated on preparing the flipcharts and separating each page with a heavy line running from top to bottom. The words appearing on the left side were in Russian, and the corresponding information appearing on the right was in English. How appropriate Charlie thought.

While they worked, the flickering tubes in the overhead lights cast everything and everybody in a pallor that transformed the room's occupants into a jaundiced looking group of tired workers.

The glare seemed to accentuate Elaina's olive complexion, and to drain the color from Nadia's already pale face. The men's features bore the strain of their fatigue written in the deepening lines crisscrossing their faces and foreheads.

The two men finished first, and their facts and conclusions now flowed into recommendations carefully transferred by the two women to the large white pages.

Dave dozed fitfully, and Charlie leaned back in his chair, extending his long legs and feet to the seat of another. It was only a few weeks earlier, in this same room, that the group originally became acquainted. So much had transpired since then. The number of people was now considerably smaller than it was originally. Andre, Henry, and Sammie were gone, and the remaining people were forever changed.

As Charlie watched the work on the flipcharts continue, his thoughts returned once more to Tekeli. It bothered him that he felt so little regret over killing a man—any man.

He believed he had no other alternative. The little man certainly deserved killing, after doing away with so many people in such a questionable cause. Nevertheless, it worried Charlie that he might be becoming callous. Could it be he was engaging in a wishful blindness? Perhaps it was. It *was* the second time he had taken a life-- once in Ukraine, and now Kazakhstan. Was it becoming easier, or perhaps since he believed he was left with no alternative, the end actually *did* justify the means.

"We are done!" Nadia announced closing the cover on the charts. "Finally!" Elaina emphasized, collapsing in the chair next to Nadia.

"Let's get the hell out of here," Dave said waking, and standing to stretch. "It's two in the damn morning," he grumbled looking at his watch.

Charlie left the conference room, heading for Trevor's office. He found him, sleeping soundly on his leather couch.

Nadia wanted to go home, and Elaina wanted to call her boyfriend, but they had to be at the meeting early the next morning and Trevor did not intend to give any of them a chance to oversleep. They piled into the Rover, and left for the hotel where he had made reservations.

Darkness had engulfed the city in a heavy cape. The downpour that drenched them earlier had cleansed the air, and now the night was dark but clear. The streetlights cast shadows across the deserted sidewalks, and an occasional solitary light revealed the contents of a passing store window. The street vendors had boarded-up and abandoned their food stalls earlier in the evening. Stray dogs searched for the remnants of food left behind on the soiled sidewalks. A discarded page from yesterday's' newspaper blew across the street, threatening to cover the Rover's wet windshield. Trevor swerved sharply to avoid it.

The bright lights in the hotel driveway were a welcome sight to the tired travelers. They quickly piled out of the car, eager to claim their rooms and get some sleep.

The lobby was empty except for a lone night clerk, dozing behind the reception desk. Trevor stayed behind to leave an early morning wake-up call with the night clerk, while the others headed for the elevators.

Once in his room, Charlie placed a call to Beth. The call finally went through, and Charlie spoke into the echo chamber of a bad long distance line.

"Hi Hon, how are things in Chicago?" He related a sanitized version of his experience, skimming the surface of events—he always did—careful not to reveal the depths of his concerns. There would be ample time to fill in the details once he was home.

My God, he thought after completing the call, will I be glad to get home. What in the hell was happening to him. This was not at all what he envisioned retirement to be.

In spite of his concerns, he eventually fell into a profound sleep. He awoke early the next morning oddly refreshed.

29

Trevor waited impatiently in the Rover for his group to appear. He looked at his watch. It was still early, but he wanted to get to the meeting-room to make sure that everything was set-up correctly. Earlier, he had an opportunity to scan the list of prospective attendees, and was impressed with the number and level of people that would be listening to the presentation. He found their names where he had put it in his briefcase, and checked it again while he waited.

First Deputy Minister of the Economy

Deputy Minister of Industry and Trade

Deputy Minister of Labor

Deputy Chairman of the Committee for the Utilization of Foreign Capital

Deputy Minister of Finance

Deputy Director of Ferrous Metallurgy

Deputy Chairman, State Committee on State Property Management.

Glancing up from the list, he saw his people straggling though the revolving doorway. They didn't look good. The hotel's continental breakfast had failed to banish their fatigue and, as they climbed into the Rover. It was hard to ignore the dark rings under everyone's eyes. Even the young women looked tired. The last few days at Tekeli had taken its toll, and the late night preparation for the meeting had not helped. Trevor put the list back in his briefcase, and pulled away from the hotel.

Almaty had yet to achieve its morning pace, and the busses and trams held only a scattering of riders. An occasional van, making its deliveries before the business day began could be seen curbed in front of a store. Trevor's passengers were not sufficiently awake to notice.

The government's Administration Building was not far from the hotel. It had been strategically positioned in the center of the city. Its imposing size dwarfed the other structures around it. Armed guards, in faded green uniforms, surrounded the building's perimeter. The two at the door looked closely at everyone's credentials.

The recent revolt in neighboring Kyrgyzstan had caused considerable dismay among the government officials in Kazakhstan, and they had doubled their efforts to maintain their security. This was starkly evident at the Administration Building.

The lobby floor was made of expensive Italian marble, and the women's heels clipped a brisk rhythm as they approached the elevator. It was still early for the majority of workers to arrive, and most of the offices remained empty. The elevator went directly to the fifth floor without having to stop. Trevor wanted to get there early and make sure that everything was set-up satisfactorily. He had built his career at the Bank through attention to detail, and he did not intend to leave anything to chance.

Opening the wide double doors to the conference room, he immediately saw that the floor was polished to such a high gloss it reflected the light from the bright balloon shaped ceiling lights. The night crew had arranged the tables in an extended rectangle, and placed pads of paper and bottles of mineral water at each place. Trevor scanned the room. "Perfect," he told Charlie much relieved.

Nadia and Elaina immediately began setting up the large charts they had finished the night before. They were both dressed in the best clothes they could find in their travel bags, and looked particularly efficient.

The conference room began to fill. Each of the arrivals seemed to be instinctively aware of their individual place at the table. The Kazakh agency heads took the most prominent positions, and their Russian subordinates found seats at the far end of the tables. Before independence, their positions had been the opposite.

For generations, the Russians led and administered the country, while Kazakh officials filled subordinate positions. After the country broke free of the Soviet Union, it was difficult for the inexperienced administrators to grasp the reins of power. Now the government was running more smoothly, and the ministers and deputy ministers were becoming more confident in their roles.

Trevor greeted all of them affably at the door. Once everyone found his place, he strode to the front of the room and began his welcoming comments. The men decided the night before that Dave would follow Trevor and would describe the capacity and potential of the mine. Elaina would be his interpreter.

Charlie was to follow them with the financials. Elaina had picked up the thread left dangling by Henry's death, and competently wove it into logical conclusions. When Charlie suggested that she give that portion of the presentation herself she declined, intimidated by the thought of speaking to a large group of officials. As a result, it fell to Charlie to include the payroll data and receivables in his presentation.

As Dave began, Charlie leaned against a wall in the rear of the room. He was reluctant to show any signs of fatigue and took shelter behind a thin smile as he strained to focus his attention on Dave's talk.

"Enough lead and zinc for the next 25 years." Dave emphasized his finding with his pointer, first on the English line, and then moving across the page to the Russian translation.

This potential capacity of the mine got the audiences' attention. It had been widely believed that the existing vein would be running-out soon. Dave had planned his talk to attract their interest at the beginning so they would be more attentive to the routine bits of information that would follow. Everyone had done a good job wringing the emotions out of the past weeks work, leaving only the remaining facts relating to the operation of the mine.

Elaina seemed to be handling her part well. A few of the men appeared to be more interested in the interpreter than they were in Dave's data points. One of the Russians poked the man sitting beside him and winked suggestively.

It was difficult for Charlie to maintain his concentration on the familiar information Dave was describing. Instead, he watched as a waiter, wearing a starched white jacket, entered the room and began setting up huge urns of coffee on a table by the door. Another man carrying a basket of rolls quickly joined him. They proceeded to quietly serve the men assembled around the table.

The conference room was gradually filling with cigarette smoke. They apparently had never heard, or if they had didn't care, that smoking can be injurious to your health. It reminded Charlie of the similar rooms he had sat in twenty or thirty years ago in the United States.

Try as he might, he was unable to prevent the week's events from shuttering, like a photo slide show, through his thoughts. Watching the disjointed and disconnected scenes emerge and dissolve, he became increasingly convinced that what he had done was the right thing to do. Looking around the room at Nadia, Elaina, and Dave, he realized that if he had failed to kill Sammie none of them would be there.

Studying the men at the table, he wondered if any of them knew more of what was going on at Tekeli than he did. It was not unheard of in the newly independent states for nepotism and dishonesty to trump effective government. It could be entirely possible for some of the local officials in Almaty to enrich themselves by working with other countries against their own national interest.

Dave was coming to the end of his presentation. Almost in passing he added "...and a preliminary analysis of deposits has indicated traces of rare-earth."

Only a few of the people around the table seemed to catch what he said. There was a flicker of understanding in the eyes of one or two of them. Trevor had planned it that way the night before. Later, he would fill in the details in private meetings with the major officials. He didn't want the possibility of rare-earth to obscure the basic elements of the presentation, but they could not avoid mentioning its presence as a possibility.

Dave finished, and laid his pointer on the table.

Trevor had told the audience in his opening remarks that questions should wait until the presentation was over.

Charlie picked up the stick, while Nadia cleared her throat and took her place on the other side of the charts.

As Charlie began to speak, he recalled the initial presentation to the miners at Tekeli. This audience appeared less hostile, and more interested in the information he was presenting than the managers at the mine did.

The global financial crisis sweeping the world economies had yet to reach the borders of Kazakhstan. There was considerable concern, however, that if the meltdown persisted it might impact the demand for Kazakh oil. If that were to happen, it would place greater importance on the country's ability to exploit their mineral resources.

The audience appeared pleased with what they were hearing regarding a source of revenue they had previously discounted, which might prove to be more valuable than they thought initially.

He began to summarize the projects findings

-- Present level of staffing is far too high

-- Consolidate operating departments

-- Restructure production-planning department to make it more efficient

Charlie scanned the men sitting at the table. He had their attention. He continued after Nadia completed interpreting.

-- Modernize management information system

-- Divest non-core assets

-- Establish a more competitive pricing formula

He finished by telling them they owned a valuable asset at Tekeli, and they should consider providing a new management structure that would enable them to maximize the mine's profit potential.

Whenever it is necessary to wait for an interpreter, it lengthens the time involved in the presentation. In order to maintain the men's attention Charlie kept it as brief as possible, telling them that the printed report would soon be available from Trevor Gunn at the Global Bank.

"Why won't the miners work the mine?" It was the first question asked, coming from one of the Kazakh officials at the head of the table.

"Mining is a dangerous job, under the best of circumstances," Charlie answered. "There have been a number of unexplained deaths before the study group arrived at Tekeli. That is behind us now. And there should be no problem. If the current management should refuse to go back in the pit, fire them and put in new ones."

It was the critical question. Charlie wondered, once more, if some of the men seated around the table might have a greater involvement than he knew. It would be possible with Kazakhstan's proximity to China and Russia, that some men in the audience might prefer a different outcome in the fate of Tekeli than the ones he had described.

There were other questions, from the audience regarding the findings, and finally Trevor rose to conclude the meeting. He promised the officials at the table he would soon be providing them with a document containing complete details of the conclusions and recommendations.

The audience rose to leave. Charlie turned over the last page of the charts and felt a wave of relief that his job was finished. The presentation had never been a problem. He had made many of them, but now he could look forward to catching a flight out of Almaty and home.

Trevor was delighted with the results of the meeting and congratulated everyone as they got off the elevator. He planned to take them all back to the hotel to rest before their going away party that evening.

As they piled into the Rover a black sedan slid up behind them, driven by a young marine in dress uniform. "Mr. Connelly," the marine called out, "Michael Pearlman at the Embassy sent me to get you."

Charlie shrugged, and climbed into the car. He recalled the station chief had told him they would talk after the meeting, but he didn't imagine it would be this abrupt.

He waved to Trevor as the sedan pulled from the curb, and squeezed into the heavy lunchtime traffic. Charlie was unaware that a second black sedan, carrying two of the Kazakh officials from the meeting followed closely behind them.

30

The marine guided his car through the traffic, and eventually pulled into the American Embassy at 99 Furmanov St. on Almaty's embassy row. There was only one slot remaining in the reserved parking section. The young man slipped the sedan into it, then motioned to Charlie to get out and follow him.

Once they were inside, the marine nodded to the grizzled desk. He then led Charlie at a rapid clip down a long hallway.

The office doors were open on each side of the aisle. Charlie peered in at the workers busily engaged at whatever people in American Embassies do. Occasionally one of them would glance-up from their work, and immediately look away. It was not their business to be concerned with visitors—unless of course they were important government officials.

Charlie and his guide soon came to the end of the hallway, and paused in front of a closed door with a sign indicating that the **Cultural Attaché** occupied this office. Inside an attractive Asian woman glanced up at the marine.

"Mr. Connelly for Mr. Pearlman," the young man announced with as much authority as he could muster.

"Mr. Pearlman is expecting you," she smiled, opening the thick office door. The marine turned on his heel, leaving Charlie to enter the large office by himself.

"Hi Charlie, good to see you again, thanks for coming."

"I didn't know I had a choice," Charlie replied. "Your young friend didn't act as though there was an alternative."

Pearlman ignored the response. "As you know, I am the CIA Station Chief here. I 've heard a good deal about you from our mutual friend Emmett Valentine. Please sit down." He motioned to a large leather chair in front of his desk. "We are the ones who arranged to get you out of your igloo up at the mine."

"I thank you for that," Charlie replied, unsure of what might be coming next. He couldn't keep from looking at the deep scar on Pearlman's face. The man might have been reasonably good-looking if it was not for that distraction.

"Young Pembroke filled me in last night. After he dropped off the congressmen over at Tengiz, he was able to get a secure line set up on the chopper. However, I wanted to hear about it personally from you. It sounds like you had one hell of a time up there at Tekeli.

"Before you begin, I have asked a couple of associates of mine from the security branch of the Kazakh Government, to join us. You may have seen them at your meeting this morning.

"Mei Lyn," he shouted through the partially closed door, "I believe there are two men waiting in the lobby for me. Can you retrieve them please?"

While they waited, the station chief told Charlie how he had known Emmett Valentine during the darkest days of the Cold War. Even though Pearlman was younger than Emmett was, he had great admiration for him. He assured Charlie if the old man had confidence in him it was certainly good enough for Michael Pearlman.

Mei Lyn retuned, accompanied by two husky men Charlie had noticed seated in the front of the room during the presentation. At the time, he had thought they appeared to have a few more sharp edges about them than the rest of the government officials, but he thought nothing more of it as he concentrated on his presentation.

Charlie was amused as he watched the two men's eyes rivet on Pearlman's assistant as she turned and left the room. Afterward, they grinned at each other, and then at Pearlman.

He couldn't blame them, she was an attractive woman. But, there was something, about her that was hard to place. She seemed strangely familiar--a mental itch he couldn't scratch--but he turned his attention to the two newcomers where it belonged.

Pearlman used no names, which is unusual anywhere in the world, but particularly in Central Asia where people place great importance on national and family heritage. He did explain that both men were with the KISA--the Kazakh Internal Security Agency, and they had worked together with him in the past.

The station chief began by telling his local associates a little bit about Charlie's connection with the Global Bank, which they already knew. But, he also vaguely hinted at a previous association between the American and his own organization.

While Pearlman talked to the security people, Charlie looked around the office. At one side of the room was a tall bookcase filled with leather bound volumes by American authors that some functionary had decided years ago befitted a man of considerable culture.

A large oil painting of a Kazakh horseman with a hunting falcon poised on his arm dominated the opposite wall.

"....and so Mr. Connelly will tell you of the events that occurred while he was at Tekeli."

At the sound of his name, Charlie began thinking about what he would say-and not say. He was unsure exactly how deeply he should go into what happened, but decided that he would concentrate on the deaths, the Uighurs, and the motive. He had told the story before, several times. Now, all he had to do was to hit his mental start button, and the tape would begin to play.

When he got to the part about finding Andre sprawled on the floor of the mine in a puddle of blood it was difficult to continue. He paused momentarily. Then, the recounting of discovering Henry strangled with a leather cord--his face already turning blue--was equally difficult to convert to an unemotional description. He stumbled and paused once again before continuing.

He would never be able to confront violent death with the equanimity that some professionals were capable of displaying. By the time he got to the circumstances surrounding Sammie's death it was easier to describe.

All things considered, Charlie told his story with admirable detachment. The same could not be said for the Kazakh officials. They immediately began to pepper him with questions.

"So why was Sammie doing this?" It was the obvious question asked by the more heavyset of the two intelligence agents.

"Yeah why?" Pearlman asked. "I never did understand that." By now he had risen and was standing behind the two Kazakhs staring directly at Charlie.

"In a word *hatred,*" Charlie replied. "Sammie hated the Chinese, who in his eyes occupied the Uighur territory. He believed the Hans were going to take over the mine to acquire the minerals he knew were there. He had somehow learned something else that was not generally known. This was the added element of rare-earth that might also be present.

"When he learned that, he decided he was going to do everything possible to prevent the damned Chinese from gaining control of the mine. He knew the Middle East has oil, but China has huge supplies of rare-earth, and seems more than willing to put the world over a barrel to advance its competitive position.

"He felt the best way of preventing Tekeli from falling into the hands of the Hans was to scare the miners out of the mine, and do away with the people who were there to advise your government on its true value."

"That was you people? They wanted to do away with you consultants?" the slim Kazakh agent asked.

"Yes, that's right. The Global Bank project people. Us. Sammie realized he couldn't get us out of there, so he decided to kill us instead."

"And the hotel manager helped him?" It was Pearlman's question. He had returned to his desk, and was taking notes.

"The hotel manager," Charlie confirmed. "Sammie was her nephew, and she felt obligated to help him—to hide him at least. And feed him as well," Charlie added as an afterthought.

"Against the interests of the Kazakh Government?"

"Yes, I guess that's correct," Charlie told the heavyset agent. "Against the interests of the Kazakh Government, and sure as hell against the interests of the hotel's guests."

"And her name was?"

"I don't know her full name. I called her Riana."

The Agent wrote it down.

"Anyone else?" he asked looking up from his pad.

"Well I don't know for sure. He was very close," he grinned "to one of the servers. She played the dombra."

"Her name?"

"No idea," Charlie replied, raising his hands to emphasize his lack of any further information.

The men rose to leave.

"Mei Lyn" Pearlman yelled.

The young woman ducked into the office, almost by the time he finished calling her name.

On the way out, the heavy set agent sidled up to Charlie and put his arm around his shoulders. "What was the name of the good looking interpreter the mining expert used?" he asked with a nudge. "She is a real *deesh*.

Charlie paused, "Magda" he replied. Her name is Magda."

There were the obligatory handshakes, and Mai Lyn led the men back to the lobby.

"Her name wasn't really Magda was it?" Pearlman asked.

"Was I that transparent? No her name is Elaina. I should not have done that. I shouldn't have lied to him."

"Don't worry old man. Lies among spies don't count." Michael assured him.

"I'm not a ..." Charlie began, but stopped when he saw Pearlman's tilted stare.

"Your Mai Lyn is a very attractive woman," Charlie said, rapidly changing the subject.

"She is that," Michael agreed. "She and young Pembroke are very close. Very close indeed," he grinned.

During the conversation with the Kazakh agents, he had recalled the meeting he had with Trevor Gunn the first day he arrived in Almaty. Trevor had told him then that Sammie's wife worked for the American Ambassador' wife, and had been very helpful to the Bank.

"How did you find her?"

"I didn't exactly *find* her. She worked for the Ambassador's wife."

Bingo. A light of confirmation went on in Charlie's mind.

"What is her last name?"

"I really never thought about it. Mai Lyn is Mai Lyn."

"I think you had better check on that," Charlie suggested.

Pearlman was already fishing through his desk drawers. "While I look, how about a drink?"

Charlie nodded, and the station agent pulled two soiled glasses from the same drawer. He wiped the inside of one of them with the wide end of his tie, before filling it halfway with scotch and handing it to Charlie. "Chin-Chin."

Pearlman finally found the personnel file he was searching for, and began flipping through it. "Son of a bitch!" "Son-of-a-bitch!" he roared, slamming his fist on the desk. "Her name is Mai Lyn Wang. I never really checked. I just assumed she had been scrubbed by the ambassador's office." His face was turning a deep crimson.

"I thought it might be Sammie's wife," Charlie replied. "And Barry Durand? Did you ever find out who gave up Barry Durand?"

"Son of a bitch," Pearlman exclaimed, more loudly than before. "It has to be her. I had almost given up on that. I was about ready to send Pembroke back there. We have to turn her--or kill her. We can't just let her walk away. By now she must have an encyclopedia of information on what we have done, what we haven't done, and what we want to do."

For his part Charlie was satisfied he had put the final pieces of the puzzle together. It turned out that he was the only one who had them all. Now, he wanted to get the hell out of Almaty. He had done his job for the Bank, and coincidentally for Emmett, he only wanted to go home. He finished his drink and rose to leave.

"Wait a minute—just a minute. You can't leave now," Michael told him. "You have to help."

"Help what—help how? I'm done."

"Look, we have to question her. Have to find out what she knows. Make sure she was the one that turned over Durand. To whom. And Why."

"Of course you have to question her, but you can do that without me. I'm not an interrogator. You do it. Have Roger do it if you don't want to."

"He won't be back until later tonight, and he has been too close to her. Anyway, she knows both of us. Don't look at me that way Connelly. I don't mean that the way you think. Well maybe Roger, but I've never touched her. It's just that we have worked together. I'm compromised, so to speak. You're a stranger to her, and you were up there at Tekeli. Hell, you killed her husband. You can scare the crap out of her with what you know."

Pearlman continued. "If something gets screwed up somehow, I'm not saying it will—but if something happens the Ambassador will be all over me like lice on rice. You, on the other hand, if something bad happens, the worst thing will be that you have to fly home in coach class. You get what I mean?"

Charlie thought about it, and knew the man had made his point.

"Look," Pearlman added, "it's almost quitting time at the Embassy. People will be pouring out of here soon. I'll have housekeeping snatch her, and everyone will just think she has left for the day. These people know what they are doing—they have done things like that before. I'll have them set her up for you. They will take care of everything. It will be easy. All you have to do is do some heavy questioning—scare the hell out of her and see if you can get her to come clean. It's really your duty."

Charlie considered what Pearlman had told him. He had to admit it made sense. He *would* like to know what she had done, and just how deeply she was involved with everything. If he flew out now he would never know, and always wonder. He finally decided he couldn't just walk away and leave the job half done.

"Ok, I'll take a shot at it, but I will need help. Get Nadia for me. She is over at the hotel getting ready for the party. Explain that I need her to work with me a little more in order to tie up some loose ends before I leave."

31

The station chief immediately set the housekeepers in motion, and sent the young marine driver for Nadia. After she returned, Charlie took her aside and explained what had developed, and what he needed her to do. They were going to play the good cop/bad cop routine.

She didn't' have to ask which role she would play "Like the gingerbread and the whip," she offered, to assure him she understood the concept.

The two of them reviewed their parts, as well as what they wanted to accomplish. Charlie was sure Mei Lyn had given up Durand, but he wanted her to confirm it. It was the only way he knew of finding out why she had done it, and who else might be involved.

"I am going to have to scare her Nadia, but I don't intend to physically harm her. You remember Henry telling us about Sammie bonking one of the serving girls just after we got to Tekeli?"

Nadia giggled. "Bonking—bonking. What a funny word. I had never heard that term for it before.

"Neither had I," Charlie admitted. "It must be British, but it seems descriptive enough that anyone can visualize the act without getting overly graphic. I am sure it will come up during our conversation with her. I don't imagine she will be too pleased to hear about the sexual escapades of her husband while she was toiling away in Almaty. It makes her look like a fool, and no woman wants that."

Nadia had watched as Charlie questioned Riana. She had to admit he had got results,. She also remembered Andre and Henry. They were both good men. She recalled her own fear as well. None of them knew who was going to be next. She shuddered at the thought.

Pearlman got the message from housekeeping that everything was ready. They had grabbed Mei Lyn when she was leaving the office for the night, and put her in the secure communications room.

"Let her stew for awhile," Pearlman told them. "She was efficient, but I never got the impression she was very brave."

Charlie wanted to get the questioning underway, and one way or another, finish and get on his way home. He looked at his watch once more. "Let's get this show on the road," he finally announced, rising from his chair. "We have waited long enough."

Pearlman led the two of them down to the communications room. After entering the code, he squeezed them through the door before it closed automatically. He planned to watch from a small slit in the door that had been put there for safety purposes.

Once inside, they both had to pause to get their bearings. It was midnight dark, with a single bright light spotlighting Mei Lyn in the center of the room. She was the star, alone on center stage, but she was a pitiful sight. The housekeepers had stripped off her clothes, leaving only her underwear.

They had also secured her arms to the chair, and her legs were splayed with her ankles manacled to the chair's legs.

The light shining on Mei Lyn's face caused her to squint, as she tried to locate the person or persons she heard coming through the heavy door.

"Who is it? I want to see the ambassador," she demanded.

Nadia stepped forward from the shadows, while Charlie remained cloaked in the dark. "I am sure you do dear," Nadia told her in her sweetest voice. "But you can't do that right now. Maybe later if you answer our questions—but not until then."

"*Our* questions, who else is there?"

Charlie affected his deepest most authoritative voice. "I am here. I am embassy security. We have found out that you have been passing classified information to other people and we want you to tell us what, and to whom."

"You have the wrong person. I signed an agreement when I went to work for the ambassador and I have never broken that agreement."

"You are Sammie Wang's wife. Is that right? "Charlie asked.

"Yes, but there is no crime in that."

"We know he was working for the Uighurs to get the mine at Tekeli shut down so the Chinese couldn't get it."

"No, not my Sammie. He is a good man."

This was Nadia's cue. "I am surprised to hear you speak so highly of him dear. Did you know that one night he was seen having sex with one of the server girls at the hotel?

"Doing what?"Mei Lyn shouted. "No not Sammie. He wouldn't do that."

"I saw him dear," Nadia lied. "Right there on the kitchen table. Everyone at Tekeli knew it. Even his Aunt Riana knew it. She was terribly ashamed of him."

"You know Riana is his aunt? Who are you?"

Tears began to flow from Mei Lyn's eyes, and Charlie knew that she believed them. He let her think about it for a while. Finally, he told her "We want to know why you gave up Barry Durand's name."

She hesitated, and began to squirm. "I did not. I would not. You can't make me. Wait until the ambassador hears about this."

"Oh yes my dear, we can make you talk all right," Charlie told her, standing in the darkened part of the room, attempting to make his voice sound threatening. "You can choose to help us or not. That's up to you, but I would strongly advise you to cooperate. Have you heard of water-boarding? We refer to it euphemistically as *enhanced interrogation*. You will be placed on one those things, and you will end up pleading with us to let you talk.

"And then, of course, there is rendition. You know what rendition is don't you? We can always have you flown out to Saudi Arabia, and let them question you. You know what they do to Asian women don't you? Those A-rabs really like Asian women."

Charlie paused to let her think about what he had told her. "Why did you give up Barry Durand's name?" he asked again.

Mei Lyn motioned with her head for Nadia to come closer.

"Yes my dear, what is it that you want?" Nadia asked, drawing nearer to her.

Mei Lyn whispered something that Charlie couldn't hear.

"She has to go to the toilet," Nadia told him blushing

"As soon as you tell us what we want to know," Charlie assured her. "Then we will take you out of here."

"Sammie---Sammie," Mei Lyn sobbed. "Help me."

"Look, let me make it easier for you," Charlie told her in a softer tone. "We don't want to have you sent to the Arabs. It would take too much time. We know that you and Sammie are Uighurs and that Sammie doesn't' want the Chinese interests to control the mine. We already know that. He was the one that told us you were helping him by stealing information here at the Embassy."

"He told you that?"

"Yes right before he ran away with the serving girl," Charlie lied. "I guess she was a Uighur too. He kind of left you holding the bag didn't he?"

Nadia added, "I think it is terrible how he treated you dear. You did all the work here in Almaty while he was bonking (she was beginning to like using the term) all the women at Tekeli. Even the dombra player we think."

"The dombra player? She is my sister!"Mei Lyn wailed.

That did it Charlie thought. "Now tell us who you told about Barry Durand."

"It was someone at the Russian Embassy. I don't know exactly who. Sammie told me that whenever I found out something interesting about the Americans I should just call a certain number."

"What was the number dear?" Nadia asked kindly.

"I did nothing really. I only passed on gossip," she said ignoring the question. "One day I heard the ambassador tell his wife that one of their people—Barry Durand was going to the oil fields to try and find out what the Russians and Chinese were doing over there."

"What did you say the number was?" Charlie asked. She told him. He knew that Pearlman was listening to everything that was being said and would immediately begin checking it out.

"So you called this number and then….?"

"Well, a nice old woman would answer, and we would chat for awhile. Then I would tell what I really called about. That was all. It was nothing really."

"That was all? You always called that number?" Charlie asked.

"Almost always. Sometimes, if it was too detailed she told me to use a …a...what they called a dead drop,"

"And that was where?"

"The newsstand in front of the Russian Embassy. I would stick it under the counter before it opened, or after it closed."

"Then what would happen?" Charlie asked her.

"Then I would usually get an envelope at my apartment with money in it."

"What did you do with the money after you got it?" Nadia asked.

"I would give it to Sammie."

"You poor thing," Nadia sympathized. "You *were* made a fool."

"Why did the Russians want to know what Durand was doing?" Charlie asked, almost finished.

"Sammie said they didn't want the Americans to get any more control over the drilling than they already had. If we helped them, they would help the Uighur's against the Chinese."

"Can I go to the toilet now?" Mei Lyn implored. "I got to go bad. Now you know I didn't really do anything. Nothing at all. It was all Sammie's fault."

Outside of the interrogation room, Pearlman was waiting for them. "Good job people," he said, clapping them on the back. "Let me make arrangements to take you back to the hotel Nadia. We owe you one, and we will see that you are well compensated for your trouble."

After Nadia left, Charlie asked the station chief what he was going to do with Mei Lyn. He felt badly about how he treated her.

Pearlman assured him that he had done the right thing. "If you had seen the photos that I did of Durand lying in bed with his throat cut, it would resolve any remorse you might be feeling.

"I plan to turn her over to the Kazakhs. They can decide. I am sure they won't be too happy to learn what the Uighur's want to do at the mine. Or for that matter the Russians over in the Basin. I also want to find out what else she may have passed on—and to whom. But, I want her out of here before the ambassador knows she is gone. This place is turning into a bag of snakes."

"What are you going to tell him, when he finally learns she is gone?" Charlie asked.

"Oh I guess something to the effect that she had to return to Urumqi to visit her ailing mother."

"Not bad. I guess that would work, for awhile at least."

"We specialize in dissembling and disinformation. This is merely child's play," Pearlman replied, grinning broadly.

Charlie headed for the door.

The station chief stepped in his way. "Just one more thing, I need to call Emmett to fill him in on what we found out today. He will be pleased to learn that we have the answer to who burned Durand. I want you there to fill in any of the things you know that I don't."

"You can do that without me. I have had a belly full of this foreign intrigue crap, and I want to get it behind me," Charlie told him. "You understand. I'm not one of you guys. I just help out now and then, and right now it's then, and now I'm out of here."

"I understand," Pearlman assured him, standing his ground. "I don't blame you for feeling that way. You have to understand, however, that it is embarrassing for this old pro to be shown up by a damn NOC. Hell you're not even really in the *game.* I should have vetted Mai Lyn. Instead, I assumed the Ambassador had done that. That kind of assumption can get you killed in this business. And, maybe it did for Durand."

Charlie felt sorry for him. "Look," he explained, "I know I am classified by the agency as a person with non-official cover. I know that this can be a problem sometimes, but I have been around enough to understand that you are a NOC as well--as in *no other career.* I realize that may be a bigger problem. You don't have to tell Emmett I had anything to do with discovering your mole. Make it sound like you figured it out. I really don't care. I have already had one career, and one is enough for me. I don't need another."

The station chief looked closely at Charlie. "Come on, it will only take a few minutes more. When we are finished, I'll have an embassy car take you back to the hotel, and then have them pick you up tomorrow. Tomorrow, we will have someone at the airport that can grease your way through Kazakh customs. It will be cool," Pearlman assured him, putting his arm around Charlie's shoulders and leading him back toward the DOS.

By the time Charlie finally got to the hotel, the group was already on dessert. It was *Kulmak,* a kind of thick pancake they had eaten once or twice at Tekeli. Trevor was at the head of the table, waiting for the check. "Please join us," he offered. Charlie shook his head, and picked up an apple instead.

Dave Dieter was already heading back to his room, but paused when he saw Charlie arrive. The two of them shook hands, and wished each other good luck. "Have to keep in touch," they both agreed.

Roger Pembroke had returned from his hosting duties with the congressmen. He sat across from Elaina and Nadia, and was planning to drive the two of them home. Nadia first of course.

Charlie sat down beside Nadia, and whispered, "you really did a good job with the interrogation,. You have a lot on the ball and, in addition, you're a great young woman."

He slipped her Pearlman's card. "You should call him tomorrow. I talked with him, and he has a job opening, and would like you to apply. He will have to check out your credentials, but I assured him there is no problem. He thinks his opening could lead to a whole new career for you."

They all rose from the table together. Roger was eager to leave. Charlie kissed Nadia on the cheek, and told Elaina and young Pembroke good by. He and Trevor shook hands.

Heading toward his room, Charlie turned and hurried to catch up with Nadia. "By the way, it might be best not to mention anything about our little conversation with Mai Lyn to anyone." He paused, and then added as an afterthought, "particularly Pembroke." She understood, and smiled her agreement.

The flight tomorrow would be a long one, and he needed a good night's sleep. The weeks in Kazakhstan were the longest years of his life.

32

Istanbul

The flight from Almaty to Istanbul was overnight, setting down at Ataturk Airport in mid-morning. Charlie managed to catch a few hours sleep, but still felt tired. Clearing customs was easy. Pearlman had given him a diplomatic visa.

The ride to the hotel was uneventful. After he was settled in his room, he headed directly for the rooftop lounge. The only people there were a lone bartender, and a dozing waiter. The startled waiter leapt to his feet, awakened by the footsteps of an unexpected customer.

Charlie gazed out the window of the lounge, slowly sipping a Bombay martini. He had decided to stop over in Turkey on his return from Almaty. It seemed to provide certain symmetry to his journey. Closing the circle perhaps.

His thoughts turned, once again, to the people he had met. The face of his dead friends continued to haunt him—they would be seared in his mind forever. Trevor had assured him that he would make sure that both men's remains would be returned to their families.

He rarely thought about Sammie any longer. Such is the blessing of selective memory. He had noticed, sometimes when he least expected, he would be overtaken by a cold chill, followed by a shiver running down his spine. He attributed it to the bitter cold he experienced chasing Sammie through the snow that dark night in Tekeli.

Outside of the lounge an almost impenetrable fog was beginning to roll in. As he watched, the prow of an ancient freighter slipped out of the advancing bank, followed silently by a rusty bow with undecipherable Chinese figures.

The old vessel was coming into harbor after passing the Golden Horn, and was now bearing relentlessly toward the Bosporus Bridge. The hull moved up the channel, towing the fog bank behind.

It looked to Charlie like a phantom vessel that was arriving from a ghostly port, and reentering the world of commercial reality. Occasionally, the sound of a muffled foghorn would penetrate the thick lounge windows, providing an additional eerie aspect to the scene. It matched Charlie's mood perfectly.

He looked away from the window, and motioned to the waiter for a second martini. God knows he deserved it after what he had been through.

The waiter was deep in thought, rocking heel to toe alongside the empty bar. Charlie snapped his fingers, and held up the empty glass. The bartender saw his only customer demanding attention. He nudged the waiter, and turned back to preparing the martini.

Before the bartender finished mixing the drink a loud jangling of the bar's telephone demanded the waiter's attention. He listened intently, then hung up the receiver and began writing in a hotel notepad. He was finished in seconds, then folded the note in half and laid it carefully on his tray alongside of the sweating cocktail glass.

Charlie heard the telephone, and watched as the waiter approached his table. He took a sip of his drink before picking up the note. He opened it slowly—apprehensively.

Very few people would know how to contact him. One was his wife, and the other was—sure as hell it was Emmet Valentine's number. No note, just a number. He had done it again. He knew the old man wasn't trying to get in touch to congratulate him on the successful completion of his assignment. Not Emmett. He didn't work that way. Charlie decided he was going to have to quit coming to this bar. But then, somehow they always knew how to find him.

He took another swallow of his martini. A longer, deeper one this time.

The harbor was now completely blanketed in fog. The bridge had totally disappeared, and the foghorn was shrieking its warning at more frequent intervals.

Charlie fished the olive from his drink. It was large, dark green, with a small pimento. Very good. He had always heard that Turkish olives were some of the best. He would have to see if any of the stores at home carried them.

He took another sip, and thought about how his life had been affected by Emmett and his nameless, faceless friends. Spooks they were called, and spooks they were. Sometimes he had been touched in a good way. Other times—not often he had to admit-- but sometimes he was affected very badly.

On the other hand, the acquaintanceship had always provided an element of intrigue, and yes a distinct challenge into what might otherwise be a pedantic life as a retired corporate guy. It kept him out of the garden, spending his life aimlessly pruning roses.

He considered signaling the waiter for another drink, but decided against it.

He knew his association with the Agency had occasionally led him into circumstances where he had little control. Not something he was used to, and certainly not something he cared for. This had resulted on one or two occasions where his life was placed in danger.

Like at Tekeli. If he had lost the toss of the dice-- and that was certainly possible--what would happen to Beth? Could she adjust to being alone, with no one to talk to? Probably, he decided, she was resilient and resourceful, but was his exhilaration worth the price of her bereavement. Not even close, he decided. Not at all an even trade.

What would she think if she knew he had killed a man? A second one in fact. Well she would never know. One thing that could be said for the Agency, they knew how to keep a secret.

Charlie reached over to the empty table beside him, and grabbed the package of hotel matches stuck in the ashtray. He fumbled for the discarded toothpick he had put aside when he ate the olive. He skewered Emmett's note with the toothpick before setting it on fire. A slight smile creased his face as he watched it flame, then smolder, and eventually die-out. Charlie shook the ashes into his empty glass, before signing the check. He rose from the table, looked around the empty lounge, smiled, and returned to his room.

Author's Note

Death on the Silk Road is a work of fiction. Its purpose is purely to entertain. The names, characters, and incidents included in this story are made up by the author. Any resemblance to actual persons, living or dead, businesses, companies, or events is entirely unintended and completely coincidental. For example, there is no actual organization known as the Global Bank Corp, but there are many similar organizations whose charter is to advance developing countries and their economies through the provision of financial support and advice.

On the other hand, the relocation of a group of Uighurs from Guantanamo to Bermuda is real, although it might seem unreal to those who may be unfamiliar with the surrounding circumstances.

The locations described in the narrative are also real. In writing about these locations, and the historical events associated with them, they are described as accurately as the author is capable of doing. In some cases, various authorities in various countries may dispute certain aspects of the historical events, but an attempt has been made to portray them in terms that are most generally accepted.

In this context, the author has, on the following pages, included photos of some of the locales visited in gathering background information. They are included to provide the reader with an accurate sense of place, and an added insight to an area of the world that is rarely visited and unfamiliar to many readers.

Photographs

Church in Panfilov Park

War Memorial in Panfilov Park

Kazakh Child on the Silk Road

Silk Road rest stop

Herd of Camels along the Silk Road

Tekeli hotel

Administration Building

Statue of a lead miner

Entrance to lead mine

Dombra players

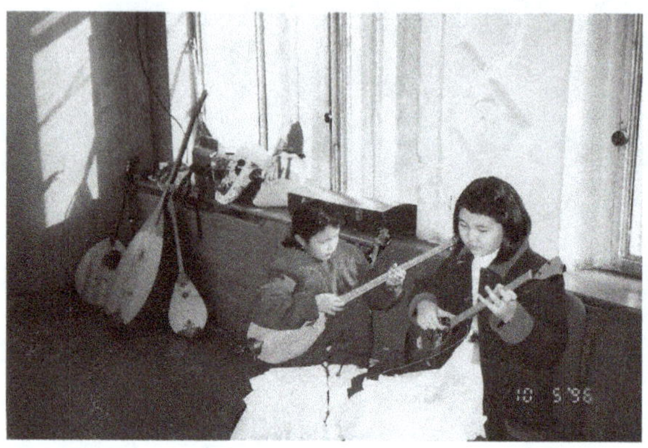

Typical yurt

About the Author

Russ Miller traveled to over 100 countries as a former international marketing executive. Since retiring, as senior vice president, he has served as an advisor on NGO projects for the UNDP, the Vienna based UNIDO, the World Bank, and the IESC, primarily in the post Soviet countries of Eastern Europe and Central Asia. His previous novel, *The Spy with a Clean Face,* also published by BeachHouse Books, won the Silver Quill Award from the American Authors Association. Miller and his wife live in the Chicago suburb of La Grange, Illinois.

Other Books by Russ Miller

AMERICAN AUTHORS ASSOCIATION

Takes Great Pleasure In Presenting The

2009 SILVER QUILL AWARD

(Thriller)

To

Russell R. Miller

in recognition of his book

"The Spy with a Clean Face"

William H. McDonald
Founder

Maria Edwards
President

The Spy with a Clean Face

Russell Miller has adeptly applied fictional flesh to a factual skeleton in a far-ranging tale of deceit and betrayal. The narrative twists and turns through Latin American and Asian locales as the search for a rogue agent ultimately leads to the Chernobyl dead zone; while the newly independent Ukrainian Government teeters precariously between East and West

Charlie Connelly is an average corporate executive, with three children and a home in the suburbs—as well as almost forgotten ties to the Central Intelligence Agency.

He is unexpectedly reminded of this past association when approached by his former recruiter, accompanied by a stunning female agent. Their seemingly innocent request for assistance eventually leads Connelly, Ludlum-like, through the brightly lighted board-rooms and dimly lit backstreets of

Maracaibo, Medellin, Tianjin, and Kiev as he becomes inexorably enmeshed in a murky realm of foreign intrigue.

Eventually betrayed by the political maneuverings of a besieged intelligence agency, and abandoned by his own company, Charlie finds himself working on a NGO project in recently independent Ukraine during the Orange Revolution. Once there, he is again contacted by the Agency, and tasked to locate and eliminate a defecting American spy before he can conclude the sale to Iran of Ukrainian owned missiles.

Journey to a Closed City with the International Executive Service Corps

describes the adventures of a retired executive volunteering with the senior citizens' equivalent of the Peace Corp as he applies his professional skills in a former Iron Curtain city emerging into the dawn of a new economy.

Before this adventure, Russ Miller spent 20 years traveling to over 100 countries as Sr. Vice President of International Development.

Since retiring, he has served as an advisor with the World Bank, United Nations Development Program, and the Vienna-based United Nations Industrial Development Organization, as well as the International Executive Service Corps.

This book is essential reading for anyone approaching retirement who is interested in opportunities to exercise skills to "do good" during expense-paid travel to intriguing locations.

Journey to A Closed City should also appeal to armchair travelers eager to explore far-off corners of the world in our rapidly-evolving global community.

Science & Humanities Press

Publishes fine books under the imprints:

- Science & Humanities Press
- BeachHouse Books
- MacroPrint Books
- Heuristic Books
- Early Editions Books

Educators Discount Policy

To encourage use of our books for education, educators can purchase three or more books (mixed titles) on our standard discount schedule for resellers. See **sciencehumanitiespress.com/educator/educator.html** for more detail or call

Science & Humanities Press,

PO Box 7151,

Chesterfield MO 63006-7151

636-394-4950

Our books are guaranteed:

If a book has a defect, or doesn't hold up under normal use , we are interested to know about it and will replace it and credit reasonable return shipping costs. Products with publisher defects (i.e., books with missing pages, etc.) may be returned at any time without authorization. However, we request that you describe the problem, to help us to continuously improve.

www.ingramcontent.com/pod-product-compliance
Lightning Source LLC
Chambersburg PA
CBHW052005020726
47501CB00004B/1021

* 9 7 8 1 5 9 6 3 0 0 7 4 3 *